The
Trouble
Was a
Girl

TONY MARTIN

ISBN 979-8-9916945-1-3 (Print book)
ISBN 979-8-9916945-0-6 (E-books)

Library of Congress Control Number— 2024920992

This is a work of fiction. Names, characters, places, and incidents are the products of the author's imagination or are used fictitiously. Any resemblance to actual persons, living or dead, events, or locales is entirely coincidental.

Published by J A Martin Publishing Company
jamartinpublishing@gmail.com

Cover Design and Interior Formatting by 100Covers.

Dedication

To my wife Sherry, for her patience, endurance, and encouragement. And for reading, and re-reading, and all her helpful suggestions. And, to my granddaughter, Naomi, whose dedication to writing encouraged me to finish this. Also, to my daughter Katie, for her help in editing my last "final draft", which proved to be invaluable.

Contents

Prologue vii

Chapter One 1

Chapter Two 19

Chapter Three 27

Chapter Four 37

Chapter Five 47

Chapter Six 55

Chapter Seven 65

Chapter Eight 73

Chapter Nine 83

Chapter Ten 95

Chapter Eleven 109

Chapter Twelve 121

Chapter Thirteen 127

Chapter Fourteen 133

Chapter Fifteen 143

Chapter Sixteen 149

Chapter Seventeen 157

Chapter Eighteen 163

Chapter Nineteen 169

Chapter Twenty 177

Chapter Twenty-One 187

Chapter Twenty-Two 195

Chapter Twenty-Three 207

Chapter Twenty-Four 213

Chapter Twenty-Five 221

Chapter Twenty-Six 225

Chapter Twenty-Seven 231

Chapter Twenty-Eight 241

Chapter Twenty-Nine 251

Chapter Thirty 259

Chapter Thirty-One 267

Chapter Thirty-Two 277

Epilogue 281

Prologue

Founders Day, Hope Springs, Oregon 1980

No one could ever seem to find the documents which could say, for a fact, just when our town had been built. There was a fire which destroyed a lot of the papers back around the turn of the century, and much of the town's history had been lost.

It was common knowledge that the town had been incorporated not long after statehood came in 1859—but it had been there for some time before that ever happened. Just how long was anybody's guess.

Someone came up with the idea to celebrate the beginnings of the place, and so, in need of a point of reference, the Chamber of Commerce had chosen 1855 to be the official year of its founding. The month and the day were anyone's guess, and so, with a stab in the dark, the third Saturday in May was picked.

I suspect that was mostly a matter of convenience, as there were those on the Chamber's council who had vacation plans during the summer months, which left May and September as the two best remaining candidates.

At a meeting of the council in late January, a coin was tossed in the air and heads said the founding of the town was in May, 1855, making this its 125th year.

They had decided there was going to be a parade and a small carnival with rides for the kids—and later on there would be some speeches made. In the evening, there were supposed to be fireworks and a reunion of sorts for those of us who had lived here before—back in another time.

I'd walked in from the old place that morning with my granddaughter and grandsons in tow so they could have some fun on the rides—and get out from under their grandmother's feet.

It wasn't as if it was their first time being here. We visited often and brought the grandkids with us whenever we could. We felt it was important for them to understand where their heritage lay—and mostly, it lay in this town: Hope Springs, Oregon.

It had turned out to be one of those fine mornings, late in the springtime, when some of the fruit trees are still in bloom. The birds were out, singing their melodies as they went about their busy daily work. Bees were busy also, quietly moving from blossom to blossom.

Sunshine fell upon our shoulders as we walked along—a respite from the cold and rain of the months just past—and yet only a mere suggestion of the scorching heat that the days ahead would bring.

I found a seat on a park bench close to the tiny town square, near enough so I could keep an eye on the kids, yet still far enough away to enjoy the morning without the irritation of a noisy carnival.

Just as I was thinking the day was about perfect, a young man walked up and asked, "Do you mind if I sit down a minute?"

I turned to look at him. He had a little notebook and a pencil, looking as though he was prepared to write down the scoop of the century. A reporter. Huh!

Then that young fellow turned toward me and, with great audacity, said, "You live around here long, old timer?"

I swallowed so that I just about choked. I started coughing and my eyes began to water. Old timer! Hmph! I wasn't even sixty yet!

Now don't get me wrong—it's not that he was being overly rude; but it always irks me a little when young men and women don't show the proper respect to their elders—and I was his elder.

In my day, a courteous young man would have said, "Do you mind if I sit down, sir?" I know I'm old-fashioned, and I have to bite my tongue a lot. The wife tells me I need to give them a break—that they don't really mean anything by it—that it's just a sign of the times.

Then, using a reporter's trained insight, the young man said, "Are you all right, sir? Can I get you a glass of water or something?"

Finally, a little respect.

"No," I said when I'd gotten my voice back. "I'm alright, thanks."

"Could I?" he asked, after I said nothing further.

"Could you what?"

"Could I ask a few questions…. sir."

He seemed to be perceptive, I'll give him that. I'd only had to choke once for him to pick up on the lack of respect thing.

My dignity somewhat soothed, I shrugged and said, "Fire away, young fellow."

"Do you live around here?" he repeated.

"No, can't say as I do."

The reporter began putting away his pencil and notebook. He looked a little disappointed.

"But I grew up here—a long time ago." I could see his interest was rekindled.

"I'll tell you the truth, mister—I'm the new guy at the paper, and all I get are stories like this— 'Founder's Day'!" He said it like a kid might say "parsnips!" after seeing them on his plate for the third day in a row.

"It's like trying to write a story about Arbor Day—or Groundhog Day. I want something I can sink my teeth into. I want a real story!" He said the word "story" with great dramatic flair. I could tell that he would go far in his journalistic endeavors.

I looked over to where the kids were about to get on the small Ferris wheel. It appeared they were still finding enough to entertain themselves. I thought to myself, *I wonder if I ought to?* And then, *Oh, why not?*

"Alright," I finally said. "I'll give you a story—if you've got the time."

"Anytime you're ready, mister."

Chapter
One

It appeared to me he was wanting to know about our town; yet wanting to see it from a different viewpoint than what could be seen just sitting on a park bench next to a carnival.

It seemed to me he must have been wanting the perspective of an "old timer"; and so, I decided to tell him how it was in our town way back when...

Well, if you look around at the town today, you see nice paved streets, houses with fresh paint, and lawns that are well groomed. Do you know what you don't find? What you won't find is the little town I grew up in.

Most of the streets were graveled when I was growing up around here; and while it's true, we had sidewalks that ran up and down both sides of Main Street, they were made of rough-sawn lumber—not like the nice cement sidewalks which are here today.

Back in those days, the town wasn't much to look at. It was small, and a little worn around the edges. The years of the Depression had taken the starch out of Hope Springs, and left it a little shabby and threadbare.

The people still took pride in their town; it's just that their situations didn't allow that pride to make their town sparkle like it does today. The houses were old looking—rundown. Most were in need of new paint—among other things—and "lawn" wasn't a word which was much in use.

Sure, everybody had a front yard, but grooming it wasn't a priority. We would try to keep the grass and briars cut down, but the city council wasn't handing out awards for the most beautiful landscaping in our community.

In the past half century, things have changed considerably here. I suppose things have also changed elsewhere, but—well—I can only speak for where I was raised; and in Hope Springs, things are different now than they were then.

Oh, some things have stayed the same—the store over yonder—and the tavern across Main from it; but I suppose that it's just the way of man to not let things remain the same for too long.

In the years since, I've learned better—but I was just a skinny kid in the 1930s looking at life in the only way I could. In 1936, I was just a twelve-year-old boy, needing to look out for myself.

Daddy wasn't around anymore; and Momma had the consumption and was wasting away in another place. All of which left me to be raised by my momma's daddy, Granddaddy Morgan.

Granddaddy was a good man—and dependable enough, I suppose; but it was easy to see that when momma took sick, he had not been prepared for the responsibility of looking after a child on his own.

During the week, he was living out in the logging camps; in places where it would be hard to raise a boy. And so, during those times, I was pretty much on my own. When he came back into town, he spent a lot of time in the local tavern, seeming to leave much of our livelihood there.

I suppose all men have their reasons for such things—and Granddaddy did as well. He was always worried in those days. Worried about his daughter dying of consumption in a sanatorium. Worried about how to get by in a world that was in financial ruin.

Worried about failing his only grandson, as he had failed his only daughter.

Even at that, he was a sight better than a lot of kids had—and I had no complaints.

The result of all of this was that I found myself with a lot of free time on my hands and very little supervision. It's not that I was a troublemaker, it's just that, left to their own devices, twelve-year-old boys don't always use the best judgment.

It wasn't all bad, though; the upside of being on your own at that age is that you get to make your own choices—and there are fewer boundaries placed upon you.

People just don't seem to expect as much out of a child as they do a grown man—and are usually more kindly disposed to them.

I went to school most of the time, because—well—living where we did, here in the northwest, meant that fall, winter, and spring were often going to be wet and cold.

So, there being nothing better to do, and no place better to do it—and the fact the school house was where the other kids were—I had no problem being there as well.

Granddaddy always kept a room for us, paid for in advance, at the rooms above the feed store. Whether he was there, or off on some job, it was up to me to scratch out enough food to fill my stomach.

This might have been more difficult had I been a grown man; but as I said before, being a young boy on my own eased some of the acceptable limits of society.

For one thing, I found the grocery store owner, Tom Girvan, would look the other way as I came through his store—as long as I didn't get too greedy—or go too often.

Maggie, who ran the diner, had a heart almost as big and sweet as the slice of apple pie she always seemed to have ready for me. None of these people ever made me feel I was poor or needy, or someone of a lower class. But then, in 1936, we were all lower class.

Even with the generosity of others, it was often difficult to find enough sustenance to get by on. You might recall I mentioned I was a *skinny* twelve-year-old boy.

On top of all that, I had my paper route. This would begin at the back of Jim Clancy's Come On In Tavern—where the papers were dropped off at 4:15 sharp each morning. It would be a rather winding route through the south side of town, and then on out to the few small places which were on the fringes of our community as well.

When I say "fringes", I mean anything within a mile or so. Lyle Fletcher had the north side of town and the outlying places on that side as well. It was always a race to see who could finish his route first.

The daily paper cost its customers three cents a day in 1935, when I began delivering it. Out of that, I kept a penny. In the good times, I had between 20 and 25 customers on my route—which put around a quarter in my pocket each day. In a month's time, I could make about six dollars, or a little more sometimes.

Just after I turned my route over to Lyle's younger brother, Bobby, they raised the price of the paper to a nickel, out of which the carrier kept two cents. Bobby thought he'd hit the jackpot—until he saw that half of his customers had to give up their subscription. The price was just too high.

I told him that if he would give them back a half-cent out of his own pocket, then they would likely keep subscribing—and he would still make a half-cent more than I had been. But Bobby never was too bright, at least not where finances are concerned—which is unfortunate, as he went into banking later in life.

The memories I have of those rides are of crisp, clear mornings with stars sparkling high above; the sounds being only the squeak of the seat on my bike—and the noise of the chain as it moved around the sprocket.

Besides the occasional bark of a watchful dog, the town lay quiet and still sleeping as I rode through the streets delivering the thinly rolled paper which made up the news in our county.

By the time I reached the outskirts of town, there would be lamps beginning to burn in the kitchens, and a man here and there carrying a lantern to light the way to an outhouse.

The cows would be lowing in the pastures by then, calling out to the farmers—telling them to hurry to the barn—that their bags were full, and they were in need of being milked.

I loved the stillness and the quiet of those early mornings; of knowing I was seeing the things in the world I lived, before anyone else was given that opportunity. It seemed to me that I alone was being given a preview of the coming day.

I remember how it felt, still to this day—that each morning gave itself to me—that I had been chosen to experience the breaking of each new day; chosen out of all the other people in the world.

Lord knows there was little enough during the depression years to make a person feel special. We took it where we could find it, I suppose. Be that as it may, to this day, I still enjoy rising early and watching the sun come up in the eastern sky.

There were other mornings though—mornings when I'd return to the room above the feed store cold and wet; soaked to the bone by cold winter rains.

Those mornings I'd climb the stairs to our room shivering from the cold and quickly change out of wet, soggy clothes, into dry ones—all the time trying to rub some warmth back into my thin body.

I know there were as many, or more, of those mornings; but in my mind, all these years later—I guess I just choose to hold on to the memories of those other mornings—times of wonder and contentment.

The town was like any of a hundred others a person might pass through in this part of the country during those years. Times had been difficult for quite a while—but not as bad as in other parts of the country, I suppose. There were jobs to be had for a man who would work long hours in the woods or in the mills.

It seemed that every other canyon had a logging camp set up with a small sawmill and a boarding house for the men, which was little more than a long narrow room with cots set up for sleeping, and a pot-bellied stove to keep them warm at night. It wasn't much, but it was work—and it was a sight better than most of the rest of the country had been getting.

The town lay at the end of a long, wide valley, which was prime farmland—surrounded by small mountains—the beginnings of the foothills of the Cascades.

Through these years, the farmers had been fighting their own battles to survive. Over time, some had moved on, forced to sell because of lean years, while others bent their backs—and their wills—literally forcing themselves to hang on.

We were still seeing the effects of the "Great Depression", as it would later be referred to in the textbooks in the schools; but we knew it wasn't going to last, because we saw signs all around us that things were beginning to get better. Mostly, you could see it in the people themselves. They weren't desperate anymore—not like they had been.

Hope—just as desperation—is a thing that is easily seen, and quite noticeable, even to a young boy. The women were more pleasant than they had been for a long time—stopping occasionally to visit with one another on the street.

The men didn't shuffle along with their heads hanging down—as men do when they have too many needs and not enough answers. Folks had begun to walk with a stride of confidence; with their heads held high and a good word for those they would meet.

To the casual observer, our town may have appeared to be just like any other small town in the Northwest. In many ways, I suppose it was—as I've mentioned before. But towns are made up of people, and in that sense Hope Springs was unlike any other town anywhere.

We had good hard-working men and women in our town, as well as our share of lay-abouts. We had people who believed there was nothing they couldn't accomplish—as well as those who were just as certain they would fail at whatever they tried.

"Hold on, mister," the young reporter held up both his hands to stop me, like he was trying to push back a door to keep an unwelcome guest at bay.

"You don't understand," he continued. "I'm looking for a big story... not some small-town recollections of years gone by. I know there had to have been something that happened in this town that's worth writing about; some problem or difficulty that stirred up something. Surely there has to have been some trouble of note."

"Well," I said, "If I were to be completely honest, there was. The fact was, the trouble was a girl."

"Now, that sounds more interesting." The young reporter had lowered his hands and picked up his notepad once more. "Let's hear about that."

"Alright, but you'll need to let me tell it the way it needs to be told. You may have thought I was going to just tell you about the way things were way back when. Well, I suppose I will... some.

"But, as I was saying earlier—our town was comprised of good, hard-working people—mostly. You may have thought I was going to tell you about what it was like to live back in those days—in a little run-down town like this; but this town is more than lumber and bricks, and streets and sidewalks—even more than schools and churches and businesses.

"This town is really about all these good people who have come out to celebrate its birthday today. And it is about all of those people who are no longer here today to join in.

"This story I'm going to tell you is Homer Long's story, as well as Maggie Davis', Frank Kimble's, Etta Prince's, and a dozen more. Among them is Harley Matthews"

The reporter looked up from what he'd just been busy scribbling. "Harley Matthews?" he asked.

"Maybe I should begin with Harley."

The reporter made a move as if he were about to interrupt again, but I cast a glare at him. It was a look I had practiced for decades and had used effectively on both my children and grandchildren. Although it had never worked on my wife, the reporter bit his tongue and settled back in his seat.

I sat back and began to talk once more...

In 1935, Harley Matthews came to our town. Like most of us, Harley was from somewhere else, and so it was easy to accept him with open arms.

In those days, you liked a person until he showed himself to be unlikable, and you trusted a man until he proved he couldn't be trusted—and Harley was a likable man with few vices.

In many ways, the things which were good and true and right about Harley were the same sort of things that were good and true and right about our town when I was growing up here.

I imagine all towns have their strengths, as well as their weaknesses. When a town is getting started—and as it grows—you'll sometimes see a lack of confidence; a need for direction.

If the town is to survive and prosper, it is only because it grows beyond those imperfections and learns to rely upon its strengths.

This town has been around for a long time now—and that's a testament to the fact that it long ago became what it was always meant to be.

Oh, it may be pretty small potatoes as far as cities go—and it is hard to look around here and point out something a person could mark down in the annals of history that will amount to anything important to mankind.

But for as long as it has been here, it's been making a difference in the lives of the people around here—and after all, how much more can you ask than that?

You see, I've always thought that Harley Mathews is like this town. I mean, if you were to hold him up to compare with other great men and women—the ones who litter the pages of history books—and thwart the minds of boys and girls in the high-school, he would seem fairly insignificant.

To the casual observer, there is little to set Harley Matthews apart from the rest of humanity—and I suppose that's as it ought to be.

But then, I have always felt that the history books are filled with pages and pages, celebrating people for singular acts of greatness.

The Harley Matthews's, the Maggie Davis', and the Paul Anders's are the real people of note in this world. They are known for their daily lives and how their lives affect those of us who live in their world.

Harley was a man with both strengths and weaknesses. However, there was a time in his life when his confidence failed him—a time when he was only going through the motions—not getting anywhere. There was a time he didn't know where to go.

If he could only find that direction—discover that purpose—we all knew there wasn't a thing that would keep him from growing into the man we all suspected he could be, and hoped he would become.

———————

I believe heroes can come in different ways. Some are created. They are promoted as heroes long enough, and often enough until everyone accepts them as such—even though they couldn't explain why if they were pressed to. Such people may, or may not, deserve that praise at all.

Others truly are heroes. They have done some great thing which is measured by bravery or accomplishment, so that people everywhere recognize them for their deeds.

But then there are those who are heroes only in the eyes and imaginations of little boys. Of such was the dubious state of heroism to which Harley Matthews belonged. To a twelve-year-old boy in a small town in the Northwest in the 1930s, Harley Matthews was as close to a hero as I had ever been.

He was a tall, lanky man, a little shy of thirty years of age in 1936. He had sandy colored hair that was seldom combed—though I believe it was a different story while his mother was still alive. I know it was in the years that were to follow—but not because Harley ever cared much about such things.

He had what could be called "regular" features, if one was to give a generous assessment. I don't suppose that he ever cared much about that, either. His arms were long, and he had big, bony hands—hands that seemed to have been made for things other than what our town had to offer.

He would sit sometimes on the bench outside the feed store on Main Street, whittling with his folding knife. If a crowd of boys gathered around him—as was more often than not—he would tell them stories which set their minds racing away from the poor, hardscrabble lives which were their own, and into a world which they could only imagine.

He loved to talk about baseball. As a young man in the 20s, he had played professionally in the minor leagues back in the south and the east.

"Why, I can remember it as if it were just yesterday," he would say. "I struck out Dickie McFarland with three fastballs—and did it four times in one game," he would add.

And then he would give us the kicker. "When Dickie got called up in '27, he hit two doubles and a four bagger off of George. At least that's what I heard."

The boys would whistle at that. After all, everyone knew it was George Herman, the "Babe" Ruth that he was talking about. Everybody knew about the Babe. Even girls could tell you that Babe Ruth was the best hitter in the game. In 1927, though, Babe Ruth was one of the best pitchers in baseball too.

Anyone who could out pitch the Babe must have had something on the ball.

He'd tell stories about traveling from town to town, playing in the bush leagues, waiting for his turn to be called up to the majors. His turn never came, though. He told us about it once.

"I was covering home plate after my catcher let a pitch go by," he explained to us.

"We were all tied up in the bottom of the ninth, with a man on third. When the catcher lost the ball, it was up to me to keep him from scoring. That runner on third came toward home like a locomotive.

"I blocked home plate with my body; and when he hit me, I thought that old man Pederson's prize bull back home had just run over the top of me. I felt my right leg snap like a piece of kindling wood."

We all sucked in our breath, and screwed up our faces when he said that.

Little Bobby Fletcher, Lyle's younger brother, cleared his throat and said, "Did you tag him out, Mr. Matthews?" (In those times, children were polite and respectful toward their elders.)

Harley chuckled at that. "Of course, I tagged him out!" he said. "What kind of ballplayer do you think I was?"

We all snickered and shook our heads at Bobby. Everybody knew that no one who was worth their beans would let someone slide home just because of a little thing like a broken leg.

Then he picked up the flute he had been whittling on and handed it over to Bobby. With a quick wink at Bobby, he took that old Barlow knife and stuck it in the calf of his right leg where it just stood there quivering.

We all sucked in our breath again—even deeper than before. That was the first time we heard that particular story—not long after Harley came to Hope Springs—but he would always end it the same way—until somebody brought to his attention that he was putting too many holes in his trousers.

That was before we had learned that Harley's right leg was missing from the knee down; and that what he had stuck his Barlow knife in was his wooden prosthesis.

Years later, I learned the true story. Harley was a promising young pitcher in the minor leagues—but he only got the chance to play a part of one season—1927.

Away from home for the first time in his life, easily influenced, and lacking knowledge of the world and its dangers, Harley had spent a night of fun—drinking and gambling—during a time when such activities were prohibited and ill-advised.

The car he was in missed a curve, rolled over, and ended up on top of Harley, who had been thrown out in the crash. His right leg was crushed so badly there was nothing to be done for it according to the doctor who was called in to treat him.

The diagnosis was both swift and severe. "That leg has to come off," was what he told Harley. The only question seemed to be about how much should they take? After some fast calculating, it was determined to take it off at the knee and hope for the best.

Although that was the "best" they could hope for, it was difficult for Harley to recognize that fact. One night of foolishness had brought to an end the baseball career of Harley Matthews, one of the most promising pitchers of the 1920s.

But it also put into motion a life which would touch others in a way which Harley Matthews could never have imagined then.

I remember my granddaddy, in one of his more insightful moments, telling me once, "All men, everywhere, find themselves on the cusp of greatness sometime in their lives.

"Most folks don't even know they are there. It's sort of like when Captain Clark stood there looking at the Pacific Ocean for the first time, and turned and said, 'Boys, I sure hope that aint just another big lake.'"

Granddaddy had a way of twisting history sometimes, when he was trying to make a point. He and I both knew that Captain William Clark had never said such a thing; and if he had, Granddaddy wasn't there to hear him. But he'd made his point: when we look at our life, we may not necessarily see it for what it is.

He continued. "A person will teeter there as a circumstance, or a situation, tries to pull him, or push him one way or another—with him all the time not knowing that the decision he makes might change the rest of his life."

With the imagination of a 12-year-old boy, I could picture a person on the edge of some precipice; with evil trying to pull him over the edge, while good was trying to pull him back. I had no way of knowing then how prophetic that thought would be.

"Sometimes—more often than not," Granddaddy continued, "a person will allow the circumstances in his life to pull him back into the easy path. That's the life which is ordinary.

"For others though, as they stand at the brink, there will be something which will almost literally push them on into a life that is remarkable. What they do—which direction they turn—is entirely up to them.

"Now Will, being ordinary is nothing to be ashamed of. Most people shoot for ordinary lives and hit pretty close to the mark. But boy, why would anyone want ordinary when they could have extraordinary?"

I couldn't answer that, but it raised an obvious question to me. Just how do you know when you're at one of those times? It seemed to me that if it was a life altering moment, it might be nice if it came with a warning—so that I might not miss out.

I was thinking about the last day of school when the teacher brought home-made ice cream, and me and Del Pruitt had skipped school and didn't get any of it. It sure would have been nice to have known ahead of time that was going to happen.

"Well, that's just the point, son," Granddaddy replied. "You never know which situation is going to be the one which might change the rest of your life.

"That's why a person needs to always be careful of each decision they make in this life. Each choice might just turn out to be the difference between ordinary and extraordinary."

Truth be told, the rain which fell into Harley's life came from a cloud that was silver lined—although I'm sure that it was hard for Harley to see it.

He went back home to Indiana to recover and get used to the changes in his life—from hometown baseball star to hometown cripple. And so, time went on for Harley and his family there in Indiana until his father passed away, leaving Harley to care for his mother.

Feeling it was necessary for them to leave old memories and disappointments behind, he and his mother packed up their modest belongings and caught a train bound for the west coast.

We may never know just what led them to the small town in the valley. I suspect they were drawn to the mountains because it was so different from where they had come, but then settled in the valley when they found that difference too great. But I don't know.

With the money they received from the sale of property in Indiana, he and his mother bought an old rundown farmhouse on the south edge of town.

Though it was old and needed much work, Mrs. Matthews was quite content with her new home. Harley spent his time making sure his mother was comfortable—fixing the things which were in disrepair—cleaning and painting until the old place sparkled.

Life went on pleasantly for some time, with Mrs. Matthews as the driving force behind Harley. He got a job as night watchman at the sawmill on the south end of town and could therefore join the ranks of the employed—which is always necessary for a man to maintain his self-respect in this life.

As always, though, life has a habit of never staying the same for very long; and so it was, that after a short time, Harley found himself on his own when his mother passed away.

It's not that Harley's life changed dramatically, it's just that he no longer had a force driving him—nor did he have the responsibility of caring for another.

Harley began to realize that, although he had self-respect, he had no purpose in his life. He understood that a person who did not have both self-respect and purpose was only partly alive.

And so, this is where Harley's life really began.

Chapter Two

On the north side of Main Street was Hope Spring's only restaurant, with a filling station attached.

Although Carl Davis' name was painted on the sign above the door of the filling station, his claim of ownership had ceased a few years earlier, when he got the notion he could make his fortune in timber.

Unfortunately for Carl, what he knew about falling timber was far less than what his wife knew about fixing cars; and Maggie Davis' knowledge of the intricacies of a combustion engine would fit in a thimble.

Less than a month after finding a man to run the filling station for him, Carl was hit by a limb—a "widow maker"—while attempting to fall a tree.

The old timers had tried to give him all the good advice they could, and had drilled him with, "You need to always watch for any dead limbs that might fall. They come down and hit you, we'll be burying you the next day".

They built the box later that afternoon, and by ten o'clock the next morning, they planted Carl Davis in the ground—a victim of his own foolishness and unreasonable ambitions of prosperity—not to mention a rotten limb the size of a man's arm.

Now, although Carl's name was on the sign that spanned both the filling station and the diner next door, Carl had never tried to lay claim to anything but the filling station. Carl's wife, Maggie, ran the diner.

"What about the girl? You promised me there would be "trouble!"," the reporter broke in, suddenly. I could tell he was getting anxious by the annoyed tone of his voice.

"I'm getting there. Be patient," I assured him. "Now, where was I?" After giving the young reporter a look of reproval, I picked up where I had left off.

———————

The 2:10 bus came rolling over Johnson Hill at about a quarter to three in the afternoon. Like the town, Johnson Hill wasn't that much to look at either—a gentle rise just south of town, high enough though to give a person a good look at the hamlet below.

Maybe it wasn't much, but as the bus cleared the top of the hill on an August afternoon and looked down on the valley spreading below it, the tired little town looked as fresh and bright as a newly laundered shirt on a Sunday morning. At least it did to one young woman.

The bus rolled on over the top of the hill and into the small town below, stopping at Carl Davis' filling station and diner, which served as the bus stop in the small town.

The afternoon was cool and cloudy—unseasonably so for the middle of August—with the sun just beginning to poke its head through the clouds.

It was warming up a little, and the young man at the filling station was sitting in an old straight-backed chair, leaned back on two legs against the wall just outside the door of the garage.

He appeared to be in the middle of taking a mid-afternoon nap. He was dreaming of adventure on the high seas.

Having been the mechanic and pump jockey since Carl's unexpected demise, of late he had been feeling that maybe his purpose in life should be more than just pouring petrol into cars, and fixing old, worn-out tires.

The only thing keeping him at it this long was that jobs like this didn't just grow on trees—and what had happened to Carl, of course. He certainly didn't want to make the same mistake.

As the bus pulled up outside, he leaned a little forward so the chair came back down onto its four legs again, and called out in a loud voice, "Bus is here, Maggie! Looks like you're going to have customers!"

A young woman stepped down off the bus, which had rolled to a stop outside the filing station. As she did, she stretched her arms in front of her, trying to relieve the stiffness which had set in during the hours spent in a cramped position on a thinly padded seat, riding on a bus in need of a new set of springs.

She was a small woman, but she had a determined look about her. A child got off behind her—a girl of about ten or twelve years old. She looked anything but determined. She looked exactly like what she was, tired and hungry.

Maggie looked out through the window as the bus pulled away, and seeing there was a child to tend to, went briskly to the door. With a smile that transformed her otherwise unremarkable face into one of warmth and beauty, she briskly ushered the two of them into the diner, resembling a mother hen gathering her chicks.

As they crossed into the small dining room, she said, "You young folks just put your things down over there by the door and come on over here to the table so I can get a better look at you."

They shed their coats and set their two small suitcases down. Maggie bent down to look more closely at the child. "My, but aren't you the cutest little thing!" she exclaimed. She couldn't help but notice how the girl's eyes strayed to the counter, lingering on a plate with a part of a pie.

"You're hungry, aren't you?! I've seen few young ones who aren't! And, unless I miss my guess," and her eyes went to the young woman, "she isn't the only one who could do with a bite to eat. When was the last time you folks had a good meal?"

"It's been…" She stopped, taken a little off guard for the moment, and then regained her composure. "It hasn't been that long," she finished.

"I'll bet it's been longer than it needs to be," Maggie said, with a knowing nod of the head. "You folks just sit down and let me put something together for you. It'll only take a minute."

"No!" The young woman spoke, more sharply than she had intended. Then, a little embarrassed, and with more composure, she said, "I mean no thank you. It really isn't necessary."

"I won't take 'no' for an answer," said Maggie, as she turned toward the kitchen. "Now you folks just sit down and relax for a minute."

The young woman rushed to catch up with her. "You don't understand," she said in a quiet voice. "I can't afford to pay for any food. I-I don't have any money."

Her voice trembled as she said this last part, and for the first time she appeared to be not so much determined as she was vulnerable.

"Honey," said Maggie, "Of course I understand. I've been watching people get off that bus for years. Don't you think I can tell who has any money, and who doesn't? I can't tell you how many times I would have been cooking for freeloaders if I couldn't. Not that I'm saying that you and your little girl are 'freeloaders', of course."

"She's not..." She stopped herself, and then looked at her hostess and smiled. "I guess we are a little hungry at that".

"I'm glad that's settled," said Maggie. "Now," she said, turning to the little girl, "who's hungry enough to eat one of 'Aunt' Maggie's hamburgers?"

After the midday rush—which was comprised of the town constable, Homer Long, and the young man who helped over in the filling station—Maggie poured a cup of coffee and sat down for a minute at the young woman's table. The child was wrapped cozily in the warmth of a satisfying dinner and pie, her eyes drooping with drowsiness.

"Now honey, tell me how I can help," said Maggie, as she brushed back a graying strand of hair that had fallen down over her eyes. "You don't have to tell me the entire story—just whatever you want to—but the more I know, the more I can help."

"I guess I owe you some sort of explanation," the young woman sighed. Her shoulders fell, as though the weight she was carrying had begun to take its toll. In truth, it had done just that.

She was a young woman—in her mid to late twenties—small and delicately featured. Although Maggie could see evidence of an inner strength as she looked in the young woman's eyes. However, she also knew that all people have their limit—and it was plain to Maggie this woman was close to hers.

"My name is Etta—Etta Prince. Her name is Lucy," she said, motioning to the little girl who had now laid her head on the table. "Where are we, exactly?" she asked.

"You're in the best diner in the grand metropolis of Hope Springs, Oregon. Just where were you headed?"

Etta smiled weakly. "I guess that this will have to do. We were going as far as our money would get us, and this is where it ran out. I guess you could say this place is our last 'hope'." She laughed a little at her joke.

Maggie smiled back, thinking to herself, you can't imagine how many times we've heard that.

"What brings you this way? If you don't mind me saying so, it's a bit unusual for a woman to buy a one-way ticket for her and her kid to go someplace they've never even heard of."

Etta looked out through the diner's window for a long minute before she answered. As she did, she shifted her gaze to the sleeping child.

"Her father died of a sudden illness a couple of weeks ago. I… I guess I just couldn't bear the thought of being around all the things which reminded me of him any longer, and so I sold what we had left after paying the doctor bills, and bought tickets to as far away as I could get. I just want us to have a fresh start—to forget about all the bad."

"Well, you can't live without money," Maggie said. "We'll have to find you a job and a place to live. What can you do?"

"I used to be a schoolteacher in California," the young woman replied. "I guess there isn't much demand for teachers in a town this small, is there?"

"Probably not," said Maggie. "We don't have a lot of turnover right now."

It was ironic, and serendipitous, that although neither of them knew it then, the need for a job was being taken care of as they spoke.

———————

Chapter
Three

Francis Kimble was a tall, thin man who dressed neatly each day in a threadbare suit, and went off to his job as a 5th and 6th grade schoolteacher—as he had for the last year.

He didn't go out and about much during the summer months. When he did, he was dressed in the same manner—looking as though he was preparing for a classroom.

His teaching abilities were far above the standard, and the district was overjoyed that he chose their small town to live in, providing them with the opportunity to hire such an esteemed educator.

He lived next door to Granddaddy and me, in a room above the feed store, which I could not appreciate much. Having my teacher living so near seemed a little too close for comfort.

It was like having to sit in a front row desk at school—or the front pew during Sunday morning services. Although it really wasn't the case, it always felt like he was watching me—and that I couldn't do anything without him knowing it.

He was pleasant enough, though he was quiet and kept to himself. I know that most of the kids at school thought of him as stern and severe—even harsh. It always seemed to me, though, that he was a little sad too.

I had lived with my granddaddy long enough to know that sometimes grown-ups are prone to moods which children cannot explain. To me, things were good, or they were bad. In my twelve-year-old mind, they were never anywhere in between—and they were never good nor bad for long at a time.

Looking back, I suppose that was just a child's way of seeing it. I didn't understand the concept of depression yet—though living with my granddaddy I had seen plenty of it.

It was the policy of the school board, in those days, to periodically check up on all the teachers in the district—especially in the weeks just prior to the start of a new school year. It wasn't that hard to do, as there were only a handful of teachers in our small school.

The school board made a habit of calling on each teacher at unscheduled times—perhaps hoping to catch him, or her in an awkward situation—doing something that might require explanation.

In those days, people in the teaching profession were expected to have exemplary character and were held to a higher standard even than the men who hired them.

The two members of the school board climbed the steps to the second floor over the feed store, and walked down the dark, narrow hallway until they came to Mr. Kimble's door.

They knocked, and when the door opened there stood before them a man with red, watery eyes, who was trying to stand straight—with little success. A bottle was hanging by the neck in his left hand.

He was unshaven, unwashed, and unkempt—and by the vacant look in his eyes it appeared obvious to them that Mr. Kimble was inebriated.

The board members looked at Mr. Kimble—and then at each other; and then turned around and walked back down the narrow, dark hallway, leaving Mr. Kimble holding the door open, watching them leave.

Whatever the demons were that Mr. Kimble had to deal with—or however he had been dealing with them—they had never seemed to affect his abilities to teach. And this was still in the summer vacation months, when school was not even in session.

Still, the school board decided they had no choice but to let him go. None of them wanted to, but they felt they had no other option. Mr. Kimble was a liability which the school district could not afford.

Everyone in the town was surprised to see him go. Well, I suppose Jim Clancy might not have been too surprised, as he was the one who had kept Mr. Kimble well supplied with his liquor.

Being naturally discrete—and knowing a good and steady customer whenever he saw one—Clancy had made sure that Mr. Kimble's deliveries were always on the quiet.

Out of respect for Mr. Kimble, the school board had kept the reason for his dismissal to themselves, and had let him leave quietly. I knew about it because—well—I lived just next door. I decided I would let him go quietly, too.

Following the surprise visit from the school board, Francis Kimble sat down on one of the two straight-backed chairs which comprised his household furniture and waited for his head to clear.

After a long while, he pulled out two very old, much worn traveling bags and began packing up what few belongings he owned. Even in the fog that still clouded his mind, he knew with certainty that his tenure at this school was over.

He had been through this before—at other schools, in other towns—so he knew the drill. After he had packed his bags, he sat down again for a little while to allow the cobwebs in his mind to clear.

Then, he arose on shaky legs and walked to the small sink in his room. He washed his face, combed his hair, and shaved; and then dressed to go out.

Leaving the bags in his room, he went to purchase a ticket to the next little town—wherever that might be. He had been doing this for almost twenty years and it hadn't gotten any easier.

Once, years ago, after I'd returned from the army following the war, I sat down with my former teacher to talk about shared experiences.

As a young, well-educated man from the east, he had left a prestigious position at a well-known college to find adventure in Europe—in France. Doing so had seemed gallant and exciting in the beginning.

It had seemed so clear to him at the time. Funny how it all had seemed so different when viewing it from his home in Massachusetts.

However, when he was in France, he learned there was no gallantry in war. If being terrified for days on end—surviving in the trenches—was considered exciting, then he supposed he had experienced at least that.

In the end, though, Francis Kimble came home again—wounded and sick; a pitiable shadow of a man. He tried to pick up the pieces of his life; but that wasn't possible—at least not there.

Too much had happened in the short time he had spent away from his friends and his family—too much seen that could not be easily forgotten.

He had been able to cope with the actual fighting in the trenches. He had quickly understood that each day, some would live and some would die. What happened in the moment—fighting the enemy and staying alive—became his focus.

It was afterwards, when he had come home again and had time to contemplate what had been done, that the struggle began. He had been able to fight the war—and survive. It was the horrors of war he found impossible to battle, and although his friends and his family loved him, they didn't understand him.

For that matter, he didn't fully understand himself. What he did understand, however, was that in the one place in this world he had always thought he could find refuge, he no longer belonged.

And so, he left his home and began what would become a twenty-year journey from one coast to another, eventually bringing him to the town of Hope Springs.

There had been a lot of towns in between, but for some reason, he had thought that perhaps this might just be the one. He was just on the north side of forty-five years old and was tired of traveling from town to town looking for a fresh start.

He liked it here, too—liked the people—and liked the job. And he even didn't mind all the rain. He'd talked himself into the idea he was going to stay here—finally put down some roots.

But it seemed he had been wrong about that—as he had been wrong about most things in his life. Chief among his mistakes was his belief that he could continue on and live a normal, successful life. Once again, he had proven just how mistaken he had been.

He made his way down Main to Maggie's Diner, to the bus stop there. Maggie was the person one talked to when they wanted to leave town. It was about four o'clock in the afternoon when Kimble walked in and sat down at the table in the farthest corner of the empty diner.

Maggie came over with a menu and a coffee pot and spoke to him. "Well, hi Mr. Kimble, glad to see you. As you can see, you're a little ahead of the dinner rush," she smiled.

The sharp-eyed Maggie easily noticed the somewhat vacant look in his eyes—residual signs of what the school board had witnessed earlier.

"What is it, Francis? If you don't mind me saying so, you look as though you're not feeling too well."

The concern showing on her face was genuine as she spoke. His unusually absent stare—and lack of steadiness—caused her to suspect that the man suffered from something other than an illness.

Kimble took the cup of coffee with hands that shook—spilling a little of the coffee on the front of his shirt. He put the cup to his lips and, taking small sips, drank it without answering her.

After this, he looked up, and his eyes were a little clearer—his mind was not in such a fog. His hands weren't trembling anymore, either.

"I've come to purchase a ticket on the bus," he said, sitting up straighter. It was as though he was trying to force himself to overcome his present condition.

Maggie had returned to her work after he had failed to respond to her earlier. Turning back to him again, she asked, "Are you going on a little end of summer vacation before school resumes?"

"Something like that," he replied. Then he sighed, and let his shoulders fall. "I might as well tell you—it doesn't make any difference now anyway," he said. "People are going to find out sometime."

"Find out what? What are you talking about, Mr. Kimble?" She walked back to where he sat, coffee pot still in her hand.

"I've been let go from my teaching position, Mrs. Davis; I've been sacked." He responded.

With surprise and concern on her face, Maggie sat down across the table from him. "Oh! Francis! I'm so sorry! But why would they do such a thing?"

And then, with his eyes downcast, and his hands wringing — for maybe the first time—Francis Kimble told the story of his life to someone. All of it. Not just the good parts—as he did when he interviewed for a teaching job—he told her everything.

Every so often he would look up to see what the reaction was—expecting to see condemnation in Maggie's eyes. He saw that look every day—looking back at him from his mirror.

But what he saw before him, in the woman's face, was pain; not her own though—no, she was hurting for him. For the first time, he realized he might have hope instead of shame.

When he had finished, he sat there quietly, rubbing his hands together. Maggie sat and looked at him for a minute before she spoke. "Do you really want to leave our town, Mr. Kimble?" she asked.

"I must confess, Mrs. Davis, I do not," he replied without looking up. "But this is my lot, I fear. What other choice do I have?"

Earlier that day, a young woman and her daughter had come into the diner, stranded and in need of a job—and now, it would seem that someone had made a job available.

And, not long before Mr. Kimble had arrived, the young man who lived over the garage, and took care of the filling station, had come in to say that he was leaving to go to Seattle. He was hoping to join the Merchant Marines, he had told her.

Well, she mused to herself, this has been a most interesting day.

It had been an interesting day indeed. "Mr. Kimble," she said, "what do you know about running a filling station?"

As for a place for Etta and Lucy Prince to live, that was another matter altogether. This was an immediate need that didn't seem to have an immediate solution. Maggie had thought long and hard that afternoon and still she had found no answer.

The hotel above the feed store would have a vacancy in a few days, but that wasn't soon enough—and besides, the hotel would ask for cash in advance. Etta had already said that she didn't have any money.

There were no extra rooms anywhere—at least none that a respectable woman with a child could take advantage of. There were several confirmed bachelors in town who lived by themselves, but that wouldn't be fitting.

And then Maggie remembered something. "It just might work," she said to herself, "At least for a little while."

And a little while might just be long enough.

When she told Etta about her plan, the young woman was at first reluctant—and then resigned herself to the idea. Finally, she accepted it with firm determination. She would do it.

Etta was not used to taking handouts, and this was, at best, a gift. At worst, it was stealing—but backed into a corner, a person can get used to almost anything.

Maggie explained that there was an old farmhouse on the south edge of town. Now, although it was occupied....

Chapter
Four

I'd been keeping my eye on the grandkids as I'd been talking, and now stopped, and looked over at the young reporter, to see if he was writing any of this down. I didn't want to waste my breath on a good story if he wasn't interested in what I was saying.

He was scribbling something down on a yellow legal pad right about then, and so I took a deep breath and readied myself to launch off into my narrative once more. This was more fun than I had thought it would be.

It appeared his interest had been rekindled, but about then the fellow stopped writing and tapped his chin with his pencil. "I wonder," he began, "if you might give me a little clearer picture of what the town was like back then. Not just the people—but the town itself."

Well, his interest in the humdrum parts of the story surprised me—especially as I thought I'd already done that, so I just stared at him with a confused look on my face.

I suppose he must have noticed, because he quickly explained what he wanted and why he thought he needed it.

"I need you to give me just a basic layout of what was here back then—so the reader can see the story through your eyes. Has it changed? Is it different now? It would be really helpful. Don't get too detailed," he said. "Just a picture is all that I'm wanting. Talk about it as if you thought I didn't already know anything."

Considering his age and profession, I didn't think that would be all that hard to do—but I figured it was his dime, so if he wanted to listen to me, I guessed I could oblige.

He wanted a "picture" of the old town—well, I'd see what I could do. I thought about it for a minute. Then, closing my eyes, I began to see the town as it was back then.

"Well," I started, "If you think it would help…"

The town was a typical small town in the Northwest—no different, really, than any other in this part of the country back then—and not a lot different from how it is now, I suppose.

As you can see, we have a Main Street which starts at the highway which was, and still is, the hub of the business, religious, and educational needs in the community.

The diner sat on the corner of Highway 99 and Main, where the bus would stop. We had businesses up and down Main Street. Just like every other town, we had a bank, a post office, shops and stores.

There was a barber shop just next-door to the tavern. The barber—Bob Dooley—was fond of stepping next door more and more as the day progressed; his hands becoming less and less steady. It was easy to tell a morning haircut from those in the afternoon. There were few who would risk an afternoon shave.

On to the west, a little further, was the post office; little more than a tiny room with a series of post office boxes on a short wall, with a small window at the end. Behind the window would be the Post Master, Harvey Linders.

Linders rode his bicycle to the post office six days a week—rain or shine—for all the years I lived in Hope Springs. In the winter, he would get wet and cold, and would swear that before the next winter came, he would buy "one of them new auto-cars" and be warm and dry.

In the spring and summer, he would enjoy the peace and quiet of his bike ride and shake his fist at the dust and the racket created by the passing of traffic. By the time the fall rains began, he would swear up and down that he would never own "one of them noisy buckets of rust".

Across Main Street from the diner was the bank. Jason Paulson was the man who people went to when they needed a loan. Paulson was a fair man, but never a foolish one with a dollar.

He was prudent in his decisions, which left more than one man feeling he had been unfairly turned down for a loan. Be that as it may, Paulson kept his bank solvent—even through the lean years—and the town was the better because of it.

Next door to the bank, and across Main from the tavern, was Tom Girvan's Grocery Store. Tom and his wife lived above the store with their daughter.

Because it was the only store in town, it not only carried groceries but also dry goods. When a woman could afford to buy enough material to make a dress or a shirt, Tom's store would either have what they wanted in stock or he would get it from somewhere.

Through those years, Tom Girvan sold little along those lines. Most of the women who sewed in our town back then either altered old garments or used material already available to them.

Many were the children who wore clothing made from used flour sacks. Tom was careful when it came to his money, but he was also fair-minded and generous.

He allowed more than just a few of the needy families in our town to keep a running tab at his store. Tom was a man with good Christian values, and he figured people were generally honest and worth the risk, and that given time, they would pay their bills.

Most did, but there were quite a few of the poor and elderly who went to the grave owing Tom more than just a little money. Tom just wrote it down as 'paid in full', and went to the funeral to mourn the loss of a friend.

Avery Fletcher's Butcher Shop was just to the west of the post office. Avery was Lyle and Bobby Fletcher's dad. Although Lyle and Bobby had no more than the rest of us, they always had meat on the table. It was a treat each time I'd get invited to eat dinner at their house.

Alongside the butcher shop were the smokehouses, which Avery Fletcher used to smoke bacon and hams and sausages. It was Lyle's job to tend the fires that smoked the meats.

I'd help him sometimes, and to this day I can still remember the way the smoke and the meat smelled, hanging from one of the smokehouse rafters as it cured; and it takes me back to another time in the blink of an eye. One of the best aromas in the world is found inside a smokehouse.

Just across 1st street from the smokehouses was the old feed store. It had once been a livery and blacksmith shop, but the need for such a business had all but disappeared long ago.

Even though people weren't driving buggies or riding horseback anymore, the farmers still had crops to raise and livestock to feed, and so it had been converted into a store that mostly sold feed and seed.

What had once been used for a hayloft and storage had been remodeled into a series of small, dingy apartments. It was in one of these that my granddaddy and I lived.

The Palace Theater was across the street from the feed store. It had lasted for only a few years, though. Its owner and proprietor, Ben Foggerty, had been ordering Tom Mix westerns for some time, and had been receiving Shirley Temple musicals instead.

Each time this happened, Ben's irritation rose to a new high. Not that Ben disliked cute kids; he just was partial to Tom Mix.

They had made the mistake—if it was a mistake—once too often, and in a poorly thought-out act of rebellion against the moving picture industry, he burned the movie reel in a garbage can which sat in the alley behind the theater.

Wanting to take full advantage of his act of rebellion, he wadded up the movie's handbills to use for tinder. After liberally dousing everything with kerosene, he lit a match, stood back with a satisfied smile, and watched it burn.

We were all fortunate that this took place late at night, after the theater had closed; because, unfortunately for Ben, he did not take the proper care to make sure his arsonist endeavor was well contained.

Burning far better than he had expected, large pieces of fiery paper and celluloid began to float away. Some drifted up onto the roof, which, because of the dryness of the summer, was like a tinderbox. Before he could do more than grab the till, his business and our only movie theater was gone.

To add insult to injury, the movie people believed their reels had been inadvertently lost in what surely was an accident; and, therefore, his attempt at rebellion went unnoticed. Ben, though, was sent a bill for cost for the lost reels.

Ben Foggerty was a man who allowed anger to settle on him like a fever. He was also a man who could bear a grudge. I don't mean to sound judgmental when I say this. It's just a fact.

Some men allow their temper to rise far past the occasion until it causes them to do foolish things. It's been the ultimate downfall of many men. Regrettably, it took our movie house with it.

The further up Main Street you went, the fewer businesses you'd find. There, it was schools and churches and houses. Most of these houses were older ones—many beginning to show signs of neglect through the Depression years.

These had been hard times which found most people straining to scrape enough together to feed their families one good meal a day—and sometimes not even that.

Frivolous spending on the upkeep of a house just didn't occur to most people. Many a house had tar paper siding—and many a roof was spotted with old coffee cans which had been flattened and nailed on as patches to keep the rain from pouring in.

Main Street just kept on going to the west, and in a short time you'd find yourself on the outskirts of town, with just a few small houses scattered here and there. Eventually this turned into the county road, snaking around a few rolling hills and continuing on into the outlying areas—with farms and ranches and timber.

Timber and farming were, and still are, the primary sources of income here—though the farms are smaller than they once were; and the logging industry has seen better days; but when I was growing up, these were booming businesses. Well… for the depression, at least.

The loggers and mill workers would come in from the logging camps and sawmills late on Saturday morning—catching rides on flatbed trucks which would come in from the camps to haul weekly provisions. They could ride back when the flatbed went back in the late evening—or they could find their own ride back the next day.

Like most towns, I suppose, Saturday was set aside for social activities. After a week's work in the woods—or the mills—men would find their way into town in the early afternoon, and Main Street would become a place of meeting; with hardworking men swapping stories of what had happened over the past week.

Men would greet each other with handshakes and words of welcome—though a fistfight or two was not entirely uncommon. However, Saturday afternoon and evening, on the streets of our town, was generally a friendly and often entertaining time.

The farmers gathered too, of course; but while the loggers and mill workers would mostly collect in front of the taverns on the east end of Main, the farmers invariably met at the feed store.

During the spring and summer months, they would usually gather in an area on the side of the feed store that was in the shade of a huge broadleaf maple tree.

In the old days, this area had been used for blacksmithing, and that tree had been keeping the sun off the backs of smithies as far back as when this town had been built. There was an old forge and anvil, and just inside the big doorway which opened into a storage area, there still hung the blacksmith's tools and apron.

It was a little like stepping into that old poem by Longfellow. All that was needed was a "spreading chestnut tree"—and a "village smithy" with arms "strong as iron bands".

Those days may have been long gone, but occasionally, the forge was put back into use, and the tools came out of retirement, serving as a reminder that although our world had come far over the years—largely because of Henry Ford and the "great war" that had been fought in Europe a few years before—change didn't come easy to some—and for others, not at all.

In the fall and winter months, the farmers would sit around the pot-bellied stove that heated a back room of the store. The room was used for bookkeeping duties during the week, but on Saturday evenings it would be filled with men in old bib overalls—and with the smells of cigars, pipe smoke, and musty old ledgers.

In all my memories of my childhood in this town there are none that carry with them the comfort and security of that back room, with the crackling of the fire, the firelight coming through the cracks in the belly of the stove playing against the rough-sawn boards that covered the walls.

There was an unspoken feeling of being among those men there, of quiet strength and determination. Though I was no more than an orphan in many ways, I knew that each of these men would treat me as though I were the son of their best friend when I met them on the street. They gave me a sense of belonging that I desperately needed in my life.

Wherever they met, it was still the same talk. In the fall, they'd talk of the winter planting, while in the winter it was about getting the ground ready to sow the seeds in the fields for the summer harvest.

There were fields that needed to be cleared; fields that need-ed to be plowed; crops that needed to be planted; and crops that needed to be brought in. It seemed not one of these things could be done without first telling the other farmers about the plan.

I wasn't allowed to hang around the loggers on Saturday eve-ning—Granddaddy said their talk and their manners were things an innocent should not be subject to.

I suspect it had more to do with the fact that Granddaddy would be there—and it was not comfortable for him to think his grandson was watching him too closely.

I imagine it was sort of like how I felt about sitting in the front row at school. Whatever the case, I thought I understood and so I obliged him in this.

Besides, there were other places to go, and other things to see than my granddaddy making a fool out of himself on Saturday night.

I would usually come down the stairs to the feed store and slip in where the farmers would meet. The stories the farmers told weren't nearly as wild—or as fun to listen to—as those of the loggers, but theirs were generally more believable—and as the evening wore on, theirs were certainly more easily understood.

This had everything to do with the fact that the loggers gathered in close proximity to the tavern.

Also, Harley seemed to want to spend his Saturday evenings around the farmers—and Harley was sort of my hero then. He had little to offer in the way of stories concerning agriculture—or even horticulture, for that matter.

The old-time farmers tolerated him though, and even seemed to like him, although his ignorance of even the rudimentary knowledge of farming left them with their mouths hanging open and their cigars falling on the floor.

One time, Joe Lands laughed so hard at one of Harley's questions that he swallowed his chew. For a while, it looked as if he would never get his wind back. Thinking back on it, yes, I suppose they must have truly liked Harley.

It was seldom that any of the farmers would invade the loggers Saturday territory, and as rare that a logger would find his way to the feed store. Not that there was animosity between them. They just had different ways of looking at things—though I don't know why.

They were both involved in the same sort of business, in a way. The farmer planted and waited and reaped the crop. The logger did the same—it just took longer for his crop to become ready for the harvest.

———————

Chapter Five

Bill Getty was a logger, and a man who had always seemed to be a happy, go lucky sort. His practical jokes were legendary in the logging camps, and although he seemed to enjoy spreading his shenanigans liberally upon one and all, they had always seemed to be light-hearted pranks.

A person would need to look far and wide to find someone who didn't have a good story to tell concerning something that Bill had pulled on someone.

Of late, Bill had been directing his energy towards trying to provoke Harley Matthews. We didn't understand what was behind Bill's seemingly personal grudge. It was pretty obvious to everyone that it was there. We would come to understand what fueled it later on.

Now, Harley was as easygoing as they come and had just laughed off Bill's attempts to get a rise out of him in the past weeks—but a man can only do that for so long. There comes a time when enough is enough—and it just so happened that the time came on a Saturday evening.

It was a fine, warm evening in late August. The day had been hot, but the evening was cooling down nicely, with a little breeze gently coming in from the north. The air smelled of ground barley, oats, and corn that lay in burlap bags stored inside the building adjacent to the feed store.

Across the street were the smoke houses which were used by the butcher from time to time. They were filled with bacon and hams being cured—and the smell of them drifted across to us on the summer breeze, to mingle with the odors of the grain. It seemed almost intoxicating, though I doubt I could fully appreciate it then.

We were gathered in the area just off the side of the feed store, listening to each farmer giving his particular theory on plowing or reaping or what time of the month was the best to plant the winter wheat.

Harley was leaning against an old anvil which had been used, in earlier days, to form steel shoes for the horses.

As Bill approached Harley, there was a devilish twinkle in his eye—a look that said he had something up his sleeve that he'd been waiting to pull.

I could see it all clearly, as I was sitting on a shingle bolt facing Harley. Bill came strutting up behind him like some young rooster that had got out of the barnyard and had found someone's sour mash.

Bill had indeed been sampling—but more than likely it had been the beer down at Clancy's—and by the little swagger and slight shake of his head I could tell he was trouble as I saw him approach our group.

Making sure that we could all hear him, Bill spoke to Harley with a tone that said that he already knew the answer to the question he was about to ask.

"So, Harley, who's the woman you got livin' with you? Saw her as we was comin' into town this morning." He paused, looking around, to make sure that he had everyone's full attention—which he had.

"She sure is a pretty one— 'specially for some crippled rooster like you." Then he laughed and looked around and slapped his leg, looking as though he expected the rest of us to join in on the fun. No one said a word.

In the silence, though, which seemed to hang heavy in the summer air, everybody's eyes turned to Harley—waiting to see what his reaction would be to such a ludicrous accusation.

Harley pushed himself up straight from the anvil he'd been leaning against and, with a look of pure astonishment on his face, said, "I don't know what you're talking about, Bill."

And, from his look, and the tone of his voice, it was obvious that he was telling the truth.

Bill let his smug gaze travel over each of us before settling on Harley once more. "You heard what I said, Harley. I was just curious who you got living with you out there at your place. I don't think I've seen her around before."

I heard a couple of the older farmers clear their throats, and an expectant silence hung in the air, waiting for there to be some explanation.

Harley was still obviously puzzled. He tipped his head to one side and looked at Bill with a frown on his face.

"Bill," he said quietly, "I don't know what you're up to, but this isn't funny. You know I don't have a woman at my place—or anywhere else, for that matter. Anyone says I do is a liar."

"Well, I say you do," said Bill, obviously enjoying himself. "You callin' me a liar?"

His tone had been jovial a moment earlier—now it was menacing. He'd been working up to this from the start. It looked as if he thought he had Harley exactly where he wanted him.

I could see where this was going, and I tried to get Harley's attention, but he was focused on Bill and the challenge that Bill had just thrown down in front of him.

Not just in front of him, but in front of all of his friends—people he respected. There really was only one way that this could play out. At least that's the way it seemed.

I spoke out, loud enough for it to force itself through into Harley's senses, "Mr. Matthews! Harley!"

Harley turned and glanced toward me for just an instant. Bill saw his advantage now and stepped forward with his right fist beginning to cock.

At that very moment, though, another voice split the silence. "Mr. Matthews?"

The attention of the men—all of them, even Bill—was directed to the person who spoke. Bill put his fist down quickly, a malicious grin returning to his face.

"Excuse me; is there a Harley Matthews here?"

The speaker was a pretty, dark-haired, young woman about twenty-five to thirty years old. She could tell that she had just walked into something, but her instincts told her that interrupting it was not a bad thing, so she continued on.

She walked further on, into the midst of all the men, striding right between Bill and Harley as she did.

She looked around the group of men, with her gaze finally settling on old Dave Tompkins.

"Excuse me sir, do you know a Harley Matthews—and could you tell me where I might find him? It's really quite important."

Dave just looked at her for a moment, his eyes visibly growing larger, his mouth opening and closing, but with no sound coming out. Anyone around knew that although there wasn't a farmer in the county who could tell you more about running a farm than Dave Tompkins', his experience with women was woeful.

Being so tongue-tied whenever around women that he was virtually paralyzed, he had made it his lifelong ambition to remain a bachelor—and if possible, to not come close enough to enter into even the slightest of conversation with one.

Dave took his pipe—which had lost its fire earlier that afternoon—out of his gaping mouth, before it could fall out; and, never taking his eyes off the young woman's face, pointed the stem of his pipe in the direction of Harley.

"Oh!" she said, and turned abruptly to face Harley, ignoring Bill, who was standing there as well. "Are you Mr. Matthews? Mr. Harley Matthews?"

Harley just stood there looking puzzled—as he had earlier with Bill.

After getting no visible response from Harley, either, she turned back to Dave. "Is he alright?" she asked. "I mean, he's not deaf, is he? Or simple minded?"

Dave continued looking at her while his mouth moved up and down. He licked his lips, and his eyes got even bigger—as though he were suddenly in the grips of great fear of something.

Her eyes were big and round, as she asked, quieter now, nodding toward Dave, "Is he alright?"

She probably thought she had stumbled into a collection of confused lunatics recently escaped from the state mental institution.

Paul Anders, himself a farmer with a fairly normal back-ground—and able to carry on a somewhat intelligent conversation without embarrassing himself—spoke up.

He was chuckling a little as he said, "No honey—I mean, yes, he's alright—they both are. No, Harley's not deaf—and up till now we didn't think he was a blithering idiot either."

He looked at Harley in amusement. "He just seems to be a little confused right now. Don't worry; it'll pass in a minute. Can one of us help with something?"

"No, thank you. My business is with Mr. Matthews. Maggie, at the diner, said that I might find him here. It's between Mr. Matthews and me," she said.

Then, realizing that she was repeating herself, and recognizing that she had probably just made a fool of herself—and had definitely just made fools of a couple of innocent men—she decided it was time for her to leave.

Harley was beginning to show signs of intelligence once more, but by the time he was fully cognizant, the young woman was gone. But Bill Getty wasn't.

"That's her!" Bill shouted. "Don't you try to let on that you don't know what I'm talking about. She's the one I saw at your place! Call me a liar, will you?"

With that, Bill swung a right fist at Harley's head. Harley had seen it coming though, and stepped outside of the punch. On unsteady feet, Bill's swing missed its mark, and he landed in a heap on the ground.

Harley, side-stepping instinctively to his right, felt the strap which held the prosthesis to his leg give way, and he also landed on the ground.

A couple of the men went quickly to where Bill lay, brought him—none too gently—to his feet, and sent him on his way.

Then they helped Harley over to sit on a block of wood so they could assess the damage done. Inside the feed store were all the supplies needed to quickly mend the strap, and Harley was soon on his feet again.

Once things had calmed down, and he'd had time to think about it, Harley turned to me and said, "You were trying to tell me something, weren't you, Will? You called my name out just before everything happened. Do you know anything about any of this?"

I swallowed hard. "Yes sir, Mr. Matthews. I was trying to tell you that during this last week I seen something on my paper route—something you ought to know about."

I paused, because every eye was upon me now. I'd been a part of these Saturday sessions for quite some time, but only in a purely observational role. Children weren't supposed to speak. If they were allowed to be there at all, they were merely there to listen and learn. Now they were expecting me to say something—to explain something to them they did not understand.

"That big old chicken house on the far side of your place?" I said at last. "The last few times I've been by there, I've seen a woman there."

The chicken house was on the other side of Harley's barn, and not visible from the main house. I could tell this news came as a surprise to Harley—as well as the others.

I went on, "Sometimes there's a light coming through the window as I'm coming back in from delivering papers. Once, when I went by there in the afternoon, a woman was out in front of it beating the dust out of some rugs."

I paused for a second, and then added, "Looked to me like she was moving in."

Harley's face had been turning redder as I spoke. I could see that his anger was beginning to rise. His jaw was firmly set, and through clenched teeth, he said, "And?"

I cleared my throat and nodded my head in the direction the young woman had headed off in. "And that there was the woman, Mr. Matthews".

Harley stood there for a moment, trying to compose himself. "I guess maybe I'd best go down and have a talk with Maggie Davis," he said, and he turned and began walking down Main toward the diner.

Chapter
Six

The rest of the men stood there for a few seconds, and then Dave Tompkins cleared his throat, spit on the ground, and said to nobody in particular, "Well, I wonder what that's all about?"

That was all I heard as I lit out of there. I knew the talk about seeding, and harvesting, and such was over for the night—and that all the conversations from that point on would only be a rehash of what had just happened.

I didn't need to relive the last few minutes—I'd already seen it. What I hadn't seen yet—and what promised to be worth seeing—was going to be wherever Harley was now going.

Now, although Harley had only one good leg, that leg was long, and he could set a pretty good pace. There was a determination to his step now, and his stride was longer than usual as he stepped out with his good leg, followed by the bad one, which swung out unnaturally—coming down again just barely in time to receive his weight. The strap must have torn loose on one side again.

As determined as Harley might have been, I had no problem getting there ahead of him—running down the alleys which ran directly into the back of the diner.

As I passed the back of Clancy's, I had to leap over a couple of dogs who were in the middle of settling a dispute over the rights to a garbage can that had been knocked over.

Any other time I would have stopped to see how it turned out, but on this night, I didn't slow down—even when I reached the back door of the diner. I just burst in, unannounced, almost knocking over a blonde-haired girl with an armload of dishes.

Her eyes got big, as though she had just seen a spook of some sort, and then they got small—like glittering, icy blue stones, and her face began to flush.

"Hey!" she began, "What do you think…?", but her words trailed off behind me as I came through the door that divided the kitchen from the dining room.

"Sorry!" I yelled back over my shoulder.

As I came into the dining room, Maggie looked up from her job cleaning the counter, a smile on her face. "Hi Will, are you ready for a piece of pie? I've been saving this last one just in case you came in."

I was about to say yes when the door swung wide, as if a strong wind had just blown it open. Harley strode in, looking no less imposing than he had a few minutes earlier.

"Alright Maggie," he began. "Give me the straight of it. Tell me you haven't rented out my chicken house to some woman. Please tell me that!"

Maggie must have been expecting him, because she didn't even bat an eye. "Of course not, Harley," she said. "I haven't rented out your chicken house to anyone. That would be wrong—as well as being illegal."

Confused, Harley started to speak when his eyes noticed the pretty dark-haired young woman who was clearing dishes from a table in the back corner of the room. He closed his mouth and turned his attention from Maggie to the woman.

"You!" he cried. "You're the one who's been living out at my place!"

She just stood there with a frightened look on her face—her eyes traveling from Harley to Maggie, and then back to Harley again.

"Yes," she replied, swallowing hard, "My daughter and I…"

"Daughter!?" Harley exclaimed. "You mean there's a whole family that's infested my place!?"

His temper may have been on the rise, but if he thought he could win this confrontation through intimidation, he was about to learn a lesson.

"Now you just wait a minute!" the woman said. "You just back up and sit down Mister Mathews!" She was looking up at him now—and her eyes, which just moments before had been wide with apprehension, now became tiny, glinting sparks.

"I realize we may have taken liberties with your property—and I apologize for that—but there is no call for you to speak that way to me, or about my daughter! Infested?"

She emphasized each syllable of this last word. "How dare you speak to me like that? Didn't your mother teach you any manners at all?"

She poked Harley in the chest with her finger as she spoke each sentence—with the last poke sending Harley backwards into a chair. Now he was looking up at her.

By this time, I was sitting at the counter, on my second bite of pie, and Maggie was leaning on the counter beside me—a cup of coffee in her hand; while the girl was standing in the doorway to the kitchen, watching, with her hand covering her mouth.

This was probably the most fun and exciting Saturday evening I had seen in a long time—and it had the promise of getting better yet.

Harley was trying to fight off the counter-attack, but those of us who watched from the sidelines could easily tell it was of little use. Harley was over-matched.

"Now, hold on," he began. "I'm the....and, and you're the..."—but his words trailed off as it began to sink in that he had stepped into something that he was not prepared for.

Harley's shoulders sagged, and he sighed with resignation as he spread out his arms—palms turned upward. There was a look on his face that said to all that he knew he could not win this fight.

"Alright," he said, in a deflated sort of way, "if it's not asking too much, can you at least explain a little about what's going on? There are people who are talking in town about me having some woman out at my place living with me. That looks bad, and I have my reputation to look after."

"What people?" Maggie broke in. "Bill Getty? Are you worried about what the likes of Bill Getty says? Bill Getty is nothing but a loud-mouthed trouble-maker, and everybody knows it!"

"Of course, I'm not worried about Bill. But it's not just him I'm talking about. All my friends up at the feed store are right this minute wondering if they might have misjudged my character. Because of what Bill said—and the fact that it's partly true—a lot of people might question my integrity."

He looked at Maggie with worry in his eyes. "A man like me doesn't have much else to fall back on, if not his good name," he explained.

"What do you mean, 'a man like you'?" Maggie asked.

"You know," he replied.

"No, I don't know," said Maggie, "What is a 'man like you'?"

"A cripple!" he flashed at her. "I'm a cripple. I can't earn respect in the same way that others do. Bill Getty may be a loud-mouth, and he may be an obnoxious drunk on Saturday evenings, but he goes out and earns the respect of all the men he works with each and every day of the week.

"Why? Because he works hard, because he's not afraid to do things which require courage on the job—things which other people either won't or can't do."

"So?" asked Maggie, looking right at Harley as she spoke.

"So, my point is," Harley continued, "I'm not able to do the things which other people can do; things which give them their self-respect. All I have is the strength of my character."

Maggie smiled as she softly told him, "Harley, every man's respect is based solely upon the strength of his character. It doesn't matter if a man is crippled or not—and a man's character is determined not by what others might think of him, but by what he knows himself to be."

The young woman, having composed herself, now spoke. "Mr. Matthews, I'm afraid I owe you a huge apology. I knew what we were trying to do wasn't right, and if I hadn't been so desperate, I would never have dreamed of taking advantage of you or your situation. My daughter and I will go out there right this minute and get our things. I really am sorry," she said.

Harley had also been cooling down, and had allowed himself to think a little about what Maggie had been trying to explain to him. He didn't know if he completely agreed with everything she had said, but...

As the young woman turned around to take her leave, Harley jumped up. "Wait!" he called out.

"Listen, I suppose I might have overreacted a little. Why don't you sit down here for a minute and tell me about what you meant when you said that if you hadn't been 'so desperate' that you wouldn't have put me in this spot?"

Maggie had already gotten two cups out and was in the process of filling them with coffee while the young woman stood for a moment with her back to Harley, trying to decide what course to take. When she finally turned back around, Maggie had already set the steaming cups on the table next to Harley.

"You two young people have a seat. It looks as if you have some things to talk over," she said, as she motioned me into the kitchen with my pie. "I was just closing up, anyway."

The yellow-haired girl had been standing in the doorway to the kitchen, watching as the events had transpired. She looked worried as Maggie herded the two of us inside.

"What's going to happen?" she asked. She seemed worried and uncertain—a far cry from the temper she had shown me as I burst through the kitchen just moments before.

"Are we going to have to move? I like it here." She appeared to be about the same age as me, but for some reason, I felt a need to act protective.

"Aw," I said, "there aint nothin' to worry about. Harley'll figure something out. There aint nothin' Harley can't do."

She looked at me for a minute, studying me—as though trying to figure out if I had anything worth listening to. After all, I was just a twelve-year-old boy. She turned to Maggie, who had remained silent up to this point. She looked at her with big blue eyes that were searching for answers.

Maggie just patted her on the arm and told her, "You listen to Will here. Will might be just a boy, but he is much wiser than his years. If Will tells you that Harley can figure out what to do here, then you believe what he says."

Then that pretty little blonde-haired girl turned back to me, stuck out her hand, and said, "My name's Lucy—Lucy Prince—what's yours?"

As Maggie and the children scooted into the kitchen, Etta went to the table with the coffee and sat down across from Harley.

Harley asked again, "So, tell me what makes your situation so desperate that you have to sneak onto a person's property to live rent free—without him knowing about it."

"I hope you really do understand," she began, "I had no intention of doing any of this—and I apologize." She looked for signs which would tell her he believed what she had just said; yet his expression told her nothing.

"Lucy and I," she continued, "are from California, and we're trying to start over again. Her father passed away suddenly, and we just needed to get away—to leave the terrible memories behind us, and so we packed up, bought one-way tickets, and rode the bus as far as it would take us."

Her eyes fell to the floor. "I know it was a foolish thing to do—leaving without knowing where we were going, and without the means to take care of ourselves once we arrived—but here we are." She finished with a slight shrug of her shoulders.

Then she looked Harley in the eyes, and he saw the desperation she had spoken of earlier.

"We came in on the bus with no money or friends or job or place to stay. We were lucky enough to find Maggie—she's been a godsend." Etta's eyes went to the door of the kitchen as she said this.

"We just need a place to stay for a little while—that's all. If you could just let us stay there until I'm able to get my feet on the ground, I promise we will never bother you again. Please, we really need some help… please!"

Harley had sat there listening to her, sipping his coffee. His expression had never changed. When she finished, he sat there for another long moment, drumming his fingers on the table—as though trying to find the right words to soften the blow that would come. Etta's chin fell to her chest as Harley spoke, tears beginning to well up in her eyes.

"I spoke earlier about my self-respect—about how important it is to me to maintain it," he began. "I would lose the respect of myself, my friends, and my neighbors if I were to allow you and your daughter to live at my place like that. Respect is an important thing to me—I hope you understand that."

He took a sip of his coffee—waiting, allowing what he had just said to sink in. The young woman never raised her head from her chest. She merely nodded—and swallowed hard, trying to hold back the tears.

"Good," Harley said. "That'll make it a lot easier to persuade you and your daughter to move into the house and let me live out there in that old chicken house."

Etta looked up quickly, tears rolling down her cheeks, to see a broad smile on Harley's homely face. She smiled, and then she frowned, thinking that maybe this was his idea of a cruel joke.

She studied his face for only a few seconds before she decided that this was a man who wouldn't play with her emotions—that this was a man she could trust.

Her smile returned, and as she rubbed the back of her sleeve across, first one eye and then the other, she said, "Oh! You don't have to do that, Mr. Matthews! We'll be more than happy to live right there in that chicken house. We've been fixing it up to where it almost seems like a home. Oh! Mr. Matthews!"

Harley, still grinning broadly, said, "Well, since I'm the owner of the place, I reckon I'll be the one who says who lives where! If you don't like the accommodations, then I guess you can just go somewhere else."

He paused, studying her for a moment. "So, you've really fixed up that old shack, huh?" He shook his head in amazement. After all, it was just an old chicken house!

Then he turned a stern face toward her. "If this is going to work at all, we are going to have to get one thing straight right this minute."

She looked at him questioningly. "You're going to have to quit calling me Mr. Matthews. My name is Harley."

This time it was Etta who was smiling as she held out her hand. "Alright Harley, my name is Etta—Etta Prince."

If they had been listening closer, they might have heard Maggie chuckling behind the door to the kitchen. They might have heard Maggie say quietly, as if to herself, "This has been a good day—a very good day."

She was right. It had been a good day—and as far as Maggie was concerned, it had been a good day's work.

Chapter
Seven

Katherine Anders came to town with her husband on most Saturday evenings and spent her time with the other farmer's wives—as well as many of the women of the town—catching up on the "goings on" of the community.

Paul Anders affectionately referred to them as "the old biddies club". He would chide his wife, sometimes, for their "gossipy ways".

"And just what is it that you're a' doin' over at the feed store, I'd like to know?" she'd reply.

Paul always laughed good-naturedly, knowing that what she said was at least partly correct. Sure, they talked of farming, but much of the talk would be just as "gossipy" as the womens had been. The only actual difference was what they gossiped about.

When he picked up his wife later that evening to drive back to the farm, she could tell he had something on his mind—something he could barely contain.

She had a mind not to ask him—to show him she could wait longer to hear it than he could to tell it—but by the time they had crossed the city limits, her curiosity had gotten the better of her.

"Alright, Mr. Anders," she finally gave in, "what is it you're a needin' to tell me—and don't you try and tell me that you haven't been a sittin' there this whole time with something on your mind."

Her husband chuckled as he spoke. "It's a fact that I do know something that you do not—something that happened this evening that might be worth repeating. Not that it's gossip, mind you; even so, I'm not really sure I should spread it around. It may not even be worth mentioning. Maybe I should just forget..."

"Mr. Anders!" she broke in. "You're in danger of raisin' me Irish. Now, if you've somethin' to say, say it. If not, then quit your blatherin'. I'm sure I don't care one way or the other."

She was still having fun with her husband, but he'd lived enough years with his wife to know that the line which divided the fun from the fire could be so fine it could hardly be seen.

This wife of his had a wonderful disposition, but she was Irish born and Irish raised—and had the quick temper to prove it.

It was only the fact that her husband possessed both a gentle nature—and wisdom—that had allowed this marriage to not only endure, but to grow; and become something which could not be shaken.

He had learned long ago to recognize that whenever the clouds came the storm was never far behind. Where his wife was concerned, he watched those clouds with a practiced eye.

They had met while he had been in London, recuperating after being wounded in France during the war. She was but a lass then, and had come to London to work in the hospital there.

She was all fire and spirit, and it took a while for Paul to find that this young, slender, bright-eyed girl was also full of laughter, life, and love.

Looking across at her now, he had to admit to himself that she was no longer that young, slender girl he had brought back home with him. She had grown into a more "substantial" woman over the years—but she continued to be able to laugh at the trials which they had been called upon to endure over these past 18 years.

Oh, she still stormed and raged sometimes, but he'd always figured he'd made a good bargain—even though it had taken being wounded, while fighting in France, to find her.

There had only been once in all of those years when there had been a trial which neither of them had been able to laugh off, or work through. He didn't figure they ever would.

Anders began to tell his wife of the events which had transpired earlier that evening—as far as he knew—which wasn't nearly as far as they went, of course.

As he spoke, his wife listened—being drawn into the mystery of it all. In her mind, there was no mystery concerning Bill Getty—or as to why Getty had chosen to focus his malice on Harley.

She saw Bill Getty as a shallow, small-minded man who could only become big in his own eyes by making all others appear to be smaller than they actually were.

Katherine Anders figured Harley Matthews was ten times the person Bill Getty would ever be. She suspected Bill knew it as well, and that's what caused him to fixate on Harley.

On more than one occasion, Harley had been a topic of discussion for "old biddies club" on a Saturday evening. It was a natural thing for happily married women to want to see all the eligible bachelors in the area were happily married as well.

For some time, they had kicked around the idea of finding a wife for Dave Tompkins—but as that seemed out of the realm of capability even for this group of women, they had all but given up on him. Harley, however, was more to them than just another "bachelor in waiting".

With Dave Tompkins, it was more of a challenge than anything else. If they could have succeeded there, that would have been fuel for such efforts to continue for other unsuspecting bachelors for years to come.

But with Harley, it was different. Harley brought out the motherly instinct in them all. Each of them truly liked Harley Matthews. And they all felt a little sorry for him as well.

I doubt any of them even realized it—or would have admitted to it if they had—but they each saw Harley's disability whenever they thought of the reasons behind why Harley was nearing thirty years of age and still unattached. After all, Harley saw it that way, too.

However, their interest in Harley Matthews went beyond merely finding a wife for him. They would have loved to have had a free hand to arrange his entire life.

It was no surprise when Katherine dismissed the parts of the story which Paul had thought the most interesting—the brief scuffle, and how Dave had lost the ability to speak—not to mention Harley being accused of having a woman living with him.

Although they piqued her interest, to Katherine, those were nothing more than details; trivial matters to be brushed aside so she could focus on the issues of importance. The young woman now—she was a different matter altogether.

"I wonder who she is", she said. She could hardly wait until next week's session of the "old biddies club".

In the meantime, Katherine decided to pay a visit to her old friend in at the local diner. Katherine and Maggie had known each other for many years now, and had seen each other through the good and the bad.

They had sat, crying, holding each other following the death of Maggie's husband, and also when Katherine's son, Paul Jr. had died of influenza twelve years before. But they had also sat and laughed in the good times—each realizing her own blessings—not least among them the friendship they valued so greatly.

Katherine hadn't been able to stop at Maggie's on Saturday, but on Sunday afternoon—following the church services—she asked her husband to drop her off at the diner while he was conducting his business elsewhere.

As she walked into the diner, the first thing she saw was a little blonde- haired girl with an apron on, sitting at one of the tables eating a sandwich. The door to the kitchen swung open just then and Maggie came through it with a basin of soapy water and a dishrag.

"Kate!" she exclaimed when she saw her old friend. "How nice! I was just thinking I hadn't seen you for a while. How have you been?"

She didn't wait for a reply. "There's something that I wanted to tell you about."

As the two women met and hugged, Katherine said, "And me a' wantin' to talk to you too!"

Then she nodded toward the girl. "Finally, got yourself some help, I see. I've been a tellin' you for a long time that you need to get someone—free up your time a little—come out to the place and see me once in a while."

Maggie laughed, "She's a little young to turn the diner over to just yet, don't you think? I'll tell you about it in a minute."

She turned to the girl who was just finishing her meal and said, "Come on over here a minute, Lucy. Lucy, this is my good friend, Mrs. Anders—Katherine, this is my new friend, Lucy."

Lucy stuck her hand out and, with a big smile on her face, said, "I'm pleased to meet you Mrs. Anders."

Katherine looked at her friend, and then, while trying to keep a straight face, turned back to the girl and said, "Well, I'm pleased to be makin' your acquaintance too, Lucy."

Maggie turned to Lucy. "Why don't you run along home now, Lucy? I think I can handle it now—and I imagine your momma could be using some help right about now, too."

As Lucy went through the kitchen and out the back door of the diner at a run, Katherine turned to Maggie with a smile on her face.

"Oh, Maggie! She's a darlin', that one! And I'll bet she's a corker too! Wherever did you find her?"

Maggie then began to relate all that had transpired in the last few days. As she did, Katherine could almost see her friend's mind working out the intricacies of a plan already put into motion—and was thinking about what part in all of this she could play.

When she posed the question to Maggie, Maggie shook her head and said, "I think this is something that we need to stand back from now and just let it run its course." As if Maggie Davis had ever just let anything "run its course".

"I've meddled enough in it," she continued, "and I hope that nobody pushes any harder. Harley's a proud man—we don't want him to ever think anyone else even knows what's going on."

"Perhaps you are right, Maggie," she said, "but there are other things which Harley Matthews needs as well."

"I know," said Maggie to her friend. "Harley lacks more than just a wife. With the right woman, though, the rest will come of its own accord. Yes, the rest will come."

———————————

In the days and weeks that followed, Harley and Etta found themselves spending much of their time together. It was natural, of course, that they should because of the close proximity in which they lived. But Harley also found himself being drawn to Etta at other times as well.

Etta worked for Maggie, down at the diner, on the weekends to bring in a little money while she looked for more permanent work. Harley ate a lot of Maggie's dinner specials during those first few weeks.

Small, neat, and pretty, Etta had the same effect on more than just a few of the single men around town. She would always smile, being sure to only give each an air of cordiality—though many tried to read more into it—all the time giving Maggie's Saturday afternoon and evening business a definite boost.

Though friendly to all, it was Harley who appeared to have captured her attention.

Maggie, speaking with her old friend, Katherine Anders, remarked, "The world may see them as an odd pair—she being so small and pretty, and him so tall and homely; but there's something there I don't think even they realize—not yet, at least."

Her friend nodded. "Aye, they each have something that they try to hide. 'Tis easier for them to leave it hidden—because to bring it out into the open, I suspect, would cause them too much pain."

She stopped for a moment, considering her words. "I believe that in order for those two to heal from their wounds—whatever those wounds might be—each is going to have to learn to rely on the other."

"Yes," Maggie agreed, "I believe you are right. And that requires they trust each other. They each need someone to turn to—someone to help with their troubles. But it cannot be just anyone—it needs to be someone who can understand the other—someone who has suffered as well."

And so it was that—as Maggie and Kate so wisely understood—Harley and Etta, without ever realizing it was happening, were drawn toward each other by forces which were beyond their ability to comprehend.

People will tell you that opposites attract, but don't believe it. It's only that we aren't always privy to the things which they have in common.

Chapter Eight

Summer was in the process of coming to a close—and although that meant various things to a variety of people, to me and most of the other children in Hope Springs it mostly meant the fun was about to end and the school work was about to begin.

Now, as I've said before, I didn't really mind so much being in school—as that's where my friends were forced to be; but all things considered, there were other things which could have been of much more interest—and would no doubt have been educational as well.

This particular year, though, we all had heard of the dismissal of Mr. Kimble by the school board. The other kids didn't know why, and I didn't feel comfortable telling what I knew about it.

The walls which separated his room from Granddaddy's were mighty thin—you could almost hear him shuffling papers while he graded them in the evenings after school—and so I knew, but I kept it to myself.

The school board had begun to have second thoughts on their firing of Mr. Kimble—thinking that perhaps they had reacted too rashly—mostly because this left them without a grade school teacher just days before the beginning of fall classes.

It had been extremely fortunate that a young woman had arrived in town, needing a job, at almost the exact same time they had fired Mr. Kimble.

Lucky for them also, was the fact that she had taught school before. At least that's what they were told—and at this late date, that was good enough for them.

I had been spending a lot of time out at Harley's place, helping Mrs. Prince and Lucy move into Harley's house. Before anything else, there was a thorough house cleaning, which needed to be done.

I spent more time on my knees, scrubbing floors, than I had thought possible. It was certainly more than I thought was necessary; but then, this was the first house I'd ever helped clean.

They really didn't have much to move—just a couple of suitcases—so after the scrubbing, I was spending less time moving them in than I was moving Harley out.

Harley was away on his night watchman's job down at the sawmill, and had arranged with my granddaddy to sleep in our room during the day. This would allow for all the hustle and bustle of moving—as well as the beating of rugs, and the banging of pots and pans as his kitchen was being cleaned—something it direly needed—and rearranged to suit the ladies.

Etta had insisted—and Harley had wisely and quickly given in to it—that she and Lucy do the cooking and cleaning to help to offset their displacing Harley from his home and into the chicken house.

The truth was, Harley hadn't resisted the idea very much; only giving a token, "Oh, you don't have to do that Etta!" It was a good situation for Harley. The chicken house wasn't that bad, and the meals were great.

Since I had been spending so much time at Harley's place, I had looked around and found a board to use for a pitching target. It was the seat that had come out of the old outhouse that had been there when Harley and his mother had first moved in.

One of the first things Harley had done was to move the location of the privy, for reasons which were obvious to anyone who had used it back then. Besides digging a new hole in a new location, Harley had built a brand-new structure, too. The old one had been broken down, and the boards were stacked inside a storage shed.

Rummaging around for something to use, I had come upon what looked to be the perfect target. Propped up on the shady side of the barn, the level of the hole was almost exactly that of a strike zone. At first, I was just trying to keep my arm limbered up.

On the first afternoon, I had noticed Lucy watching me as I went about readying the old outhouse seat. When I threw the first pitch—which missed the board entirely—I saw her standing by the side of the house, and knew that she had seen my poor display of throwing a baseball, which for some reason bothered me more than it should have.

I was preparing to wind up for my next attempt when she asked me what I was trying to do. Girls! It should have been obvious, I thought. I had a baseball, a baseball mitt, and was throwing the ball at a hole in a board; what did she think I was doing?

After a few more throws, I figured that if she was going to stay and watch anyway, she might as well make herself useful by tossing the ball back to me. It would save me chasing after it after each pitch.

She threw the first one back and I'll have to say she wasn't too bad. Actually, she was good—almost a natural. She was better than a lot of boys.

From that day on, I began spending more and more time playing ball with Lucy out at Harley's place. She was small, but she could drive the ball just over the head of a shortstop consistently. She had a good arm on her, too. Yes, she threw like a girl, but like a girl who was really good at throwing a baseball. She would make a good left-fielder.

———————

Our schoolhouse and school yard encompassed the entire block on the north side of Main, between 7th and 8th. As schoolhouses go, it wasn't all that impressive I suppose, but our town was sort of proud of it, as it was the last big expenditure the community had made before the bottom fell out of the market, and everyone lost their jobs.

I know that by some people's standards it was fairly modest, and there were more impressive buildings in bigger cities, but it wasn't some one-room schoolhouse either.

Two stories tall, it was the largest structure in Hope Springs— if you didn't count the water tower, which stood on the hill on the west edge of town. The school was built of red brick; and it looked solid and somewhat foreboding, especially to a small child entering it for the first time.

The first day of school, a lot of the other kids were surprised to see a woman sitting at the teacher's desk. If they thought having a small, young woman for a teacher would be an advantage over Mr. Kimble, they soon discovered differently.

She was as inspirational—and as educational—as their former teacher had been. Though far from the austere, disciplined classroom of Mr. Kimble, Etta Prince still could conduct her class in an orderly and auspicious manner.

The real fun began after school, though. It had been a tradition for the past few years that when the first day of school had ended, the guys would get together and play a baseball game—of sorts. Sort of an "end of summer ball game". One could say it had become a "tradition".

There weren't nearly enough boys to field two complete teams—and so—even though we would choose up sides, many of those chosen would play on both teams.

Our field was not anywhere near a regulation field either. We played in the field which bordered the school building. There was only a small stream separating one from the other—and, at this time of year, the creek bed was dry, but in a couple of months that crick bed would be full—not dangerous, but difficult to get across without getting too wet.

We'd lay out the diamond—using whatever was at hand for the bases. Sometimes there would be an old flour sack at first base—sometimes a piece of wood—sometimes we'd use somebody's baseball mitt. The other bases, as well as home plate, would be designated by similar objects.

Often, second or third base was only a vague spot on the ground whose precise position was often debated when a runner tried to stretch a single or a double into an extra-base hit.

As unorthodox as our traditional game seemed to be, there was one rule which we had never weakened on—for that matter, it had never even been brought up—it had never needed to.

No girls were allowed in the game.

I guess we just naturally thought that some things don't have to be formally mentioned. After all, why would anybody in their right mind want to play baseball with a girl?

We had never worried about it though, because we each knew there was nothing in the world which would compel any of us to want to do such a thing. I know it had never crossed my mind—and I was sure that it had never crossed the minds of any of my fellow players either.

Imagine their dismay when I showed up at the game with a pretty little blonde-haired girl—a girl wearing a baseball mitt on her left hand. I know—it kind of surprised me too—and I was the one who had brought her.

The thing was, while I'd been teaching her how to play, I'd kind of been telling her stories of our "traditional" ball game. I had sort of focused on my great feats in those games, I suppose—trying to accomplish what all boys do when around little blonde-haired girls.

I guess I was hoping that she might want to come and watch me play or something like that. Instead, she had asked me the day before if she could play in our game.

Of course, I'd told her she couldn't; but then she said, "But Will, I thought you said I was good—as good as any of the guys you play with—good enough to play in your silly old 'end of summer ball game'. If I'm good enough to play, then why can't I?"

I didn't know what to say. It was apparent I'd said too much already. So, on Monday afternoon, after the first day of school, when I crossed the dry creek bed onto our makeshift field, Lucy Prince was walking beside me.

The boys stopped what they had been doing, and all looked at her as she walked along with me, carrying a baseball glove. Then they looked at me and then looked at one another—confused—as though they had just seen Sitting Bull walk up side by side with General Custer. Del Pruitt was the first one to speak up.

"Hey, what's the deal, Will? You know girls aren't invited to watch us play." There was some vigorous nodding of heads to this by the other boys.

"She's not going to watch our game," I said. I could see visible relief shining in their eyes.

Then Lyle said, "What'd she come for, then—she carrying your mitt for you?"

They all snickered at that one, so Lyle spoke up again, "Send her home, Will, so we can get this game going."

Lyle liked to think of himself as the self-appointed leader of our band of ball players, and I suppose that for the most part, he was. He was always ready to play a good joke on someone, and when he did, he was never short on giving them a good poke in the ribs about it.

He had red hair and freckles, and his blue eyes would almost begin to twinkle at such times. Lyle wasn't poking fun right now though. He was serious.

I didn't need to look at her to know that Lucy's eyes were starting to pinch down to where they were no more than mere slits, and she was probably biting her lower lip.

I knew her well enough by now to know that the girl had a temper—and that neither these boys, nor I really wanted to see it displayed—so I stepped forward and said, "She's not here to watch, Lyle—she's here to play!"

There was a long silence—as if what I had just said had sucked all the air out of the sky, taking all the sound with it. Then, almost in unison, they all laughed—big, horse laughs—"Ha! Ha!"

Del seemed to recover first. "Whew! You really had us going there, Will. That was a good one."

Then they noticed I wasn't laughing. I wasn't even smiling. Lucy Prince, standing behind me and off to my left, wasn't smiling either. She was glaring. Her glare held on them for a moment and then swung back and settled on me.

"Will...," she began. I held up my hand to silence her, and then I began to tell them how it was.

"Now boys," I began, "do you remember why we have the 'no girls allowed in baseball rule'?" I didn't wait for them to even try to answer.

"We all agreed that girls can't be here because girls can't play baseball. Not that they weren't allowed to play—but because they really *can't* play—and because of that, they are a pain to have around."

There was a lot of head nodding at this. A lot of these boys had sisters, and so they knew that girls in the game would mean that every time something happened, we would have to stop the game and explain it to them—or they would get hurt—or they would be afraid of getting hurt. But the main reason is, they just can't play well enough.

"That's right," said someone, "so send her home, and let's get this game going—she's already causing us problems."

"I'll tell you what," I said. "Lyle, you're a pretty good pitcher, right?"

Lyle nodded, with sort of a smug look on his face.

"Well, then, boys," I said. "If Lyle can strike Lucy out with his best pitching, then Lucy will turn around and walk home alone—right now."

"What if he can't?" asked one of the boys.

Lyle's head snapped around. "Who said that?" he asked. "Who says I can't strike out a girl?" Wisely, everyone kept their mouth shut.

"If he can't, then she plays—and no one says another word about it—deal?"

"Deal!" said Lyle, already walking out to the makeshift pitching mound. "If I can't strike out a girl, I'll give her my glove," he added.

I turned around to Lucy. "It's all up to you now, Luce. Just remember what I've showed you. Keep your eye on the ball. You can do it!"

The fierceness in her demeanor had slackened somewhat, and I could see that Lyle's bragging had begun to take effect. "Don't listen to what he says, Lucy. I've known Lyle Fletcher my whole life, and you can only believe half of what he says."

"Yeah," she said with a weak smile, "but which half?"

I could tell that I was going to have to be a little more convincing, so I said, "How well have you been hitting off of my pitching lately? Darn good, haven't you?" She nodded.

"Well, I taught Lyle Fletcher everything he knows—and he's still not as good as I am. Now go on out there and show em."

There was determination in her eyes when she stepped up to the chunk of an old tire that served as home plate that day. She drove Lyle's first pitch straight back at him so fast he hit the ground, barely able to get out of its way—a low liner over second base, into shallow center field. Base hit!

Lyle got up to raucous "Ha! Ha!'s" all around. The rest of the boys were already slapping Lucy on the back with "Man, did you see that?!", and "That ball was smokin!'—almost tore Lyle's head off!".

Lyle walked up to the group which had gathered around Lucy. He had a sober look on his face, and it was hard to gauge just how mad he was. He took off his mitt and held it out to Lucy.

"I meant what I said. Here, take it."

Lucy looked Lyle right in the eye and said, "You keep it, Lyle. I've got one of Will's old mitts. It fits just fine."

Then, realizing that she might have just added some shame to his embarrassment, she added, "That was quite a pitch, Lyle."

She continued, with a big grin on her face, "Will said that he's a lot better than you, but I never saw him throw that hard. I was just lucky!"

Lyle turned toward me, reached out, and jabbed me in the shoulder real hard. "Better than me? Why, I've been trying to teach this lunkhead how to pitch for the past two years!"

Turning back to Lucy, Lyle said, "I pick Lucy first."

"Can't," I said. "She's mine."

Lucy smiled big when I said that.

Nobody said anything for just a second, and then all the boys gave their big "Ha! Ha!" to me. Then I saw what I'd just said, and my ears started turning red. I knew they were because I could feel them start to burn.

Do you know what, though? It didn't bother me at all. I stood there and laughed with the rest of them—because I had just told them—and her, that she was mine, and she had smiled.

Chapter Nine

Foster Tilman owned and operated the sawmill that sat a few miles south of town. He was one of those self-made men from the old days that you seldom see anymore—a man who had started out with nothing but a pair of calk boots and an axe.

He'd had to buy his crosscut falling saw on credit and paid it off with the first load of logs he brought out; but his little one-man logging outfit had grown almost from the day his first tree hit the ground.

His success came not so much because he had big dreams—or dreams of being a big man—but because he just didn't seem to be able to stay in one place very long without doing something; and he seldom enjoyed doing the same thing year after year.

By the mid-thirties, it was suspected that Tilman was worth over a quarter of a million dollars—and probably closer to double that amount. He now owned a large logging outfit, as well as the sawmill—and kept a road building crew busy pretty much year-round.

Depression wasn't something he knew much about, and during the years that the price of lumber was down and other lumbermen were going out of business, he put on another crew.

He always said that if he was getting half price for his lumber, then he needed to turn out twice as much of it.

Though he had carved out a right to claim power and prestige over lesser men through his hard work and business savvy, Tilman never seemed to be anything other than what he was—a hardworking man, who never shirked his job, or felt that he had the right to loaf while others were called upon to pick up his slack.

Oh, it was true that he spent a good share of his time in an office which was at the mill site, but he was never happy to be there. If you wanted to catch Foss Tilman in a good mood, you'd have a better chance of doing so if it was on a day when he was out at the logging site—on one end of a "misery whip", teaching some man half his age the fine art of pulling a saw through an old growth log.

He had the knack of being a man who was comfortable with both the common working man and the wealthy power brokers of the industry. Not many men can pull that off—but Foss Tilman could—and he made it look easy.

He could walk into Clancy's at the end of the day, and easily buy a round for the house. Just as often though, a man who worked for him might offer to buy him a drink. Men would look up to him and respect him because of his position, but at the same time, they never felt that he was looking down on them.

Tilman's wife, Vera, had passed away several years before and he'd been left with only his son, Foss Jr., as family. People never had gotten to calling the boy "Foss", as it just didn't seem to fit once you had known his dad—and then got to know the son.

We mostly all just called him "Junior", unless he was close by. Junior never seemed to take too kindly to it; and maybe that was the reason that everybody seemed to latch onto it so easily. When

Junior was within earshot, everybody tried to remember to address him as Foster.

Junior was about twenty-five years old in 1936. He was a small man. I don't mean in size—Lord no! He was as big as most men around—physically. It's just that in the eyes of most of the people that I knew back then, Junior just didn't measure up.

As I look back on it now, I suppose he wasn't nearly as small as he seemed. It's just that everyone naturally held him up to his father, and, fair or not, the comparison always found him wanting.

Foss had seen his business grow and prosper, but to what end? Certainly not to grow old and rich, and be able to buy the best-looking headstone in the cemetery.

Nor was it for the power. Oh, he fully understood that it was a lot better to be the one giving the orders than the one taking them; but Foss Tillman's fulfillment in life did not come by throwing his weight around.

He just loved the work he did and wanted to be able to keep on doing it—and doing it in the way he wanted to. The best way to ensure that happened was to own the company.

Over the years, Foss had come to realize something else. Not only could he fulfill his needs by doing what he loved; he was helping a lot of other men meet their needs as well. He found great satisfaction in this—while at the same time realizing the responsibility it carried with it.

Early on, he had worried that when he was gone, not only would he be leaving his family with no one to see to their needs; but also, there were a lot of people who depended on him for their wellbeing. What would happen to them?

When Foss Jr. was born, Foss quit worrying. His son would be able to continue the business long after he was planted in the ground in a plain pine box.

Raising his young son on his own, he, like many in such situations, had spoiled the boy in a futile effort to make up for the loss.

Too late, he had learned that although it may be natural to want compensate a child for losing his mother, giving him everything he wants seldom has positive results; and it certainly didn't with Junior.

Over the years, he had grown into a pompous, spoiled, and just plain hard to be around young man. For the past few years, he had been away at some college, and had then traveled abroad—seeing places that most of us hadn't even heard of yet.

In the next few years, many of us would travel abroad and see some places he talked about. The second world war would cause the world to become a much smaller place; but in 1936, the places in Europe he talked about sounded more like places a child might find in fairy tale books.

He had a way of telling us about them that seemed meant to make us all feel small, ignorant, and insignificant.

Old Foss had always turned a blind eye to the things that were so clear to all of us. He didn't see—or didn't want to see—the person who Junior had grown into.

Looking back on it, it seems to me the biggest thing missing in Junior's raising was a sense of responsibility. His father had never made him toe the line after Vera's death. I suppose he would have had a hard time growing into any other sort of man than he did.

Etta had been working after school and on the weekends at the diner for about a month when a nice-looking young man came in and sat down at a table in the corner.

He was nicely dressed and clean shaven—someone who she hadn't seen before. He had a pleasant smile, and when he spoke, his voice was soft and his words were well spoken. From what she had noticed so far, he was different from most of the men she had seen in town.

She had been on her feet all day long, standing in front of a classroom and walking up and down rows of children, helping them with their schoolwork. She had begun feeling the effects of it long before coming to the diner to work the evening shift.

When she went to the man's table to take his order, he had smiled at her and his words seemed refreshing at the end of a day that had begun well before daylight had poked its head into her bedroom window.

She went back into the kitchen with a spring in her step, and wearing a smile on her face that hadn't been there just moments before. Maggie eyed her suspiciously as she came in with the man's order.

"Well," she said, as she raised an eyebrow, "where did our Etta get off to? Surely this isn't the same girl who could barely put one foot in front of the other a few minutes ago!"

Etta smiled sheepishly and hurried over to an old mirror that hung on the broom closet door. She began studying her reflection, and as she did, the smile disappeared and a small frown took its place.

Finally, she brushed back a loose wisp of hair and tried to pin it back. It was obvious that she wasn't happy with what she saw. That wasn't the only thing that was obvious—at least not to Maggie.

"So, what's going on?" she asked. "Why all of the sudden primping? Do we have a special customer out there?" As she was asking these questions, she was heading for the door that led to the dining area.

"Wait!" Etta said in whispered tones. "Don't go out there! He'll see you!"

Maggie couldn't help but laugh at the schoolgirl way Etta was acting. She had not seen this side of her before. She couldn't help but tease a little, and so she took another step for the door.

"Maggie!!" Etta was almost pleading by now.

"Alright" Maggie said, laughing. "But tell me what's going on. It is my restaurant, you know."

Etta moved up to the door and pushed it open a crack. She took a quick look and then turned to Maggie. "Can you see that nice-looking man over at the table by the window?" she said— even though there were no others in the diner that Maggie might confuse him with.

As Maggie peeked through the crack, Etta said, in hushed tones, "I haven't seen him before—have you? He seems so nice too. I think he might ask me for a date. Oh, my! What will I wear?!"

After Maggie closed the door again, and turned back to where Etta was standing, Etta said, "Well? Do you know who he is? Is he a nice young man?"

Maggie nodded as she looked at her young friend, sighing a little as she did.

"Yes," she said. "I know who he is—and yes, as far as I know, he is a nice young man. His name is Jun—umm—I mean Foster,

Foster Tilman, Jr. You've seen his father in here several times. He owns the sawmill that Harley is the night watch for."

"If he asks, what should I do?" Etta asked.

"Well, if I were you, I think I would answer him."

"Maggie! You know what I mean. Should I say yes—I mean, if he asks me for a date? I mean, is there any reason not to?"

"Etta," Maggie said, "You're a grown woman. You can answer him in any way that pleases you. As far as I know, there's not a reason in the world that you shouldn't be seen out with young mister Tilman."

With that, Etta brushed the front of her dress, smoothing it out the best she could, grabbed the coffeepot, and pushed her way through the door with a confident smile on her face.

For the next two weeks, Etta and Junior were often seen in each other's company. Many times, they'd be at the diner having dinner, sometimes out for an evening stroll.

They were the talk of the town—though it should be remembered that it was a small town, and that gossip flies through a small town like a bunch of crows—leaving a nasty mess everywhere they've been.

Harley had been aware that Etta and Junior were seeing each other—and for some reason he couldn't quite lay his finger on, it bothered him. For one thing, he was being asked to make sure that Lucy was fed and went to bed at the proper time.

It wasn't as if Etta was out all hours of the night, though. She was always in by nine o'clock—eight thirty most of the time. No—he didn't think that was the problem. But something had been bothering him.

Late one afternoon, Harley walked into town toward Maggie's diner. As he walked by the filling station, he noticed Francis Kimble, working on a tire in the garage.

Harley had taken a liking to Mr. Kimble and had begun calling him 'Frank', which seemed all right with Mr. Kimble. It's doubtful he had ever been called anything other than 'Francis' his entire life.

To Mr. Kimble, it probably seemed to be a sign of acceptance—that the people of the town were beginning to get comfortable with him. It had been a long time since he'd felt that.

Frank looked up from his work as Harley approached. I was in the back of the garage working on my bicycle right then. The way things were in those days, a person couldn't find new parts for anything—much less for a bike; and it was a continuous effort just to keep it in riding condition. Seemed sometimes as though I had to be a mechanical miracle worker.

As he came over to where Frank was working, Harley couldn't help but marvel at the change that had taken place in this man who, until recently, had been a distant sort of person—a man who, although being a good teacher, had been reserved, keeping to himself—shutting off the world around him.

Now, he was friendly, talkative, engaging. Harley had the impression that being around Maggie Davis had something to do with the change that everyone saw in the man.

Frank had stopped what he was doing and wiped his brow with the back of his hand. It was a hot fall day, and there was hardly any breeze to stir the air.

"Hello, Harley," Frank said, a big smile spreading across his face.

That was another of the changes we had all seen. Where Francis Kimble rarely smiled—Frank Kimble seemed to do it quite a lot. Harley supposed Maggie had something to do with that as well.

"Hi, Frank. How's business today?"

"Hot! How about joining me for a Grape Ne-hi, Harley? I'm buying."

"Hard to turn down an offer like that!" Harley said, and walked over to the shade of the garage while Frank opened up the back of the pop machine and took two bottles out. Popping the caps, he handed one to Harley.

"Maggie and I were talking the other day," Kimble said, as he sat down on an old lard bucket that now served as an extra seat in the garage. "It concerned you, Harley."

Harley glanced sharply over at Frank. "Oh?" It seemed like every time he turned around lately, Maggie Davis was sticking her nose into his business. It seemed that Frank agreed.

"I know, Harley," he said. "I told her it was none of our business if that young squirt, Junior Tilman, was trying to slip in here and steal your girl. I told her. I told her that if it was okay with you, then it ought to be okay with the rest of us."

Frank had been looking away from where Harley was sitting as he spoke, and now cut his eyes around so he could see Harley out of the corner of his eye. Nodding his head, he said, almost to himself, "Yes sir, that's exactly what I told her—uh-huh."

Harley's jaw had dropped as Frank spoke, and he poured a little Grape Ne-Hi down the front of his shirt when Frank had said "take your girl". Frank couldn't help smiling.

"'Take my girl!'" Harley sputtered. "What girl? I don't have a girl!"

"Sure you do, Harley," Frank returned in a calm, nonchalant sort of voice. "Why everybody knows that."

Harley took a deep breath and huffed, "Well, I don't know it!"

"Hmm," said Frank. "Well, I suppose you're the only one who doesn't know it then."

"Frank, what in the world are you talking about? And what does Junior Tilman have to do with me? I thought he was seeing Etta."

Frank sat there shaking his head, as though he had just realized the man he had been speaking to really didn't have a clue what he was saying.

"Harley, are you going to sit there and tell me you didn't know Etta was your girl?"

Harley shook his head, as though in a daze. There was a confused look on his face.

"Well, let me see if I can explain this, then. Do you like Etta, Harley? I mean, is she a likeable sort of girl? Good disposition, interests which are common to yours?"

Harley was nodding his head, though still carrying the confused look on his face.

"So, you enjoy being around her." This was said more as a conclusion than a question.

There was more head nodding from Harley. "And does she enjoy being around you?" This time, Harley merely shrugged his shoulders.

"Oh, for crying out loud, Harley!" Frank cried out. "Does it seem like she likes to be around you or not? It's not that difficult a question to answer!" There was exasperation in Frank's voice.

Harley thought for just second or two, and then said, "Yeah, I guess she does."

"Do you like being her friend, Harley?"

"Well, sure..."

"Would you like to be more than just her friend?"

"Frank...," Harley began. His friend was getting close to overstepping the boundaries of their friendship.

"Answer the question, Harley," said Frank. His tone was demanding, as though Harley was one of Kimble's students, and was being called upon to answer a problem in front of the classroom.

"Would you?"

"Well... yes."

"Then what's the problem, Harley? Why are you letting somebody else take your girl from you?"

"It's not that simple, Frank, and you know it. It's not just about what I want—it's not just up to me. She has to feel the same way."

"Are you blind, Harley, or are you just simple-minded? Every time that girl is around you, its pretty obvious how she feels. We all see it—why can't you?"

"You've been spending too much time around Maggie", Harley said, recovering his senses. "She's been wanting to marry me off to somebody for years.

"You only see it because that's what you want to see. Etta and I are just friends—and you and I both know that I'm no bargain as far as husband material goes. When times are hard, what woman in her right mind wants to rely on a cripple?"

And then, as if to bolster his case, Harley added, "Besides, if she wanted to be my girl so bad, what's she doing with Junior?"

Frank was looking off into the distance—perhaps through the years, and into the past. Maybe he was remembering a time when he had been given this same opportunity and had lost it because he had waited to make sure that her feelings were true.

He turned back to Harley and said, "A person wanting to leave town will only wait so long for a train to pull up to the platform, Harley. Eventually, they might just get on board whatever train pulls into the station. Don't wait until it's too late. Believe me, I know."

Harley seemed to notice, for the first time, that he'd spilled his drink on himself. He got up, sat the bottle on a workbench, grabbed a rag and began to clean himself off. It was then that he realized that the rag he had picked up had fresh grease on it.

With grease and grape Ne-Hi smeared on his shirt front, he strode off down the street toward home muttering to himself about "nosy people", "silly ideas", and "dirty rags that ought not to be left lying everywhere about".

Frank just smiled to himself and went back to work repairing the tire. He knew his friend was going to have a lot to think about that afternoon.

———————

Chapter
Ten

Later that evening, Etta fixed an early dinner for Lucy, me, and Harley, and then prettied herself up to go out for the evening. Junior was coming by to pick her up and take her over to the diner for supper, so we ate without her. I'd noticed that he never took dinner at Harley's place. He was missing out, as Etta was a fine cook.

Harley had come in while she was fixing the supper, and was in a rare mood. He had grouched at Lucy and me, and had hardly acknowledged Etta even being there—and when he did, it was only to complain about her going out.

"Etta," he began, "I don't think that it's a good idea you going out like this, all hours of the night. You've got Lucy to care for—and it looks bad for a teacher to be out running around like you do. You ought to be thinking more about your child and less about Junior Tilman."

He almost added that he was getting tired of being her built-in babysitter, but she had turned around from the cookstove and the look in her eyes could have peeled off what little paint was left on the south side of Harley's house.

"Harley Matthews," she started, "you've got no right to tell me what I can and what I can't do. We're not related. We're not married. We're not... well, we're not anything!"

Harley may have been ignorant about women, but he was a pretty quick study—and it didn't take but that one flash of anger for him to see that he'd just touched off a powder keg that was about to blow the roof off of his house.

I'd remembered reading somewhere that "discretion is the better part of valor". Harley must have read that same thing, because he discretely got up and left the house.

As he left, though, Etta called out from the doorway, "Harley Matthews, you and I have some things we need to talk about!"

Before he got out of earshot he called back, "Yes we do, Etta Prince!"

Lucy and I just turned and looked at each other. Her eyes were as big as two silver dollars—not that I'd seen that many—and I knew mine were as well.

Etta stood there for a few seconds and then said, "Well!" I could swear though, that as she turned back to the dinner cooking on the stove, I could see the beginnings of a smile touch her face.

———————

Etta didn't try to deny she had been thoroughly enjoying herself over the past couple of weeks. What woman wouldn't? Foster had been nothing if not a complete gentleman every minute they had spent together. The young man was attentive, courteous, and extremely interesting to be with.

The stories he told of the places he had been were like pages torn out of adventure novels. Not that he tried to get her to believe that he had done all those wonderful things himself—they were mostly stories he had been told by others. It was just that he had actually been to those far away, exotic places; and had a way of telling it that made it so she could almost picture it as she knew it must have been.

Although Etta's imagination might be easily excited by such stories, she was not the type of person to allow her head to be turned. As she pictured the far away adventures of people, in places she could only dream about, she knew her imaginings were probably much more exciting and romantic than what they had actually been.

She was also pretty sure that the times she had spent with Foster were more exciting and romantic in her imaginings than they actually would be if it were to ever become a day to day, real-life situation.

Although Etta could daydream right along with the best of them, she was—and always would be—a practical woman. Besides, it wasn't as if he had ever asked her to be a permanent part of his life—or likely ever would.

As these thoughts flitted through her mind, young Tilman was speaking. They were in the diner, in the semi-darkness of the room, waiting for Maggie to bring them their food.

The farthest light, hanging from the ceiling in the back of the room, had burned out earlier that evening, and Foster had chosen a table which was only dimly lit—but not as dark as the tables further back.

"Etta," he began, "I want to ask you something—something important." He reached across the table and took her hand in his.

She had only been half-way paying attention to what he was saying until he had taken her hand in his. She smiled at him now.

"What is it, Foster?"

He took a deep breath and cleared his throat before speaking. She noticed his hand was cool and damp. "I'm planning on leaving here shortly. I've got some things to tie up first—but then I plan to take a train to Frisco, and then sail for the Orient."

Etta frowned, trying to figure out what sort of reaction to this sudden news he was expecting from her. She took a sip of coffee and, in a somewhat guarded manner, said simply, "Oh?"

He explained further. "I'd like for you to come with me."

"What?" she asked, almost choking on her coffee. She had expected nothing like this—nothing at all.

"I realize that we've only known each other a short time, Etta, but I want to ask you to be my wife."

"I don't understand," she said.

"I asked you if you would marry me, Etta."

Etta had been expecting a nice dinner with interesting conversation—but she had expected nothing like this. Not in her wildest imaginations had she expected this.

Flabbergasted, and not knowing what to say, she searched for, and finally found some semblance of composure—enough so to say, "Foster, I'm not sure that you know what you're asking. This is an enormous responsibility. It's not just me—I also have a daughter to consider. Have you thought about that?"

"Yes, of course I have," he replied. "That is part of the 'things to tie up' that I mentioned. Lucy will be attending the finest girl's schools that money can buy. I expect to make sure that your daughter wants for nothing."

"The 'finest girl's school that money can buy'?" Etta said. "Why we wouldn't be able to afford anything like that? Not on my salary—and as far as I know, Foster, you don't even have a job.

Speaking of such things, I couldn't just pick up and go with you around the world, anyway. I have a class to teach."

He laughed at her apparent ignorance of the reality of the things he was talking about.

"First, you wouldn't need your salary. We couldn't travel and see the world if you were teaching at some 'podunk' school. I've got plenty of money. Don't you understand? I'm the son of Foster Tilman. He's the wealthiest man around."

He spread his arms out, as if to indicate the breadth of his father's massive holdings. "One of these days it will all be mine, and until then—well—let's just say I won't be in need of a job."

As he was speaking, her eyes had begun to see this man in a different light—recognizing something in him she had seen in another man, in another time. She shrank back, drawing away from him, as he spoke of his plans—and his entitlement.

"He actually believes he is better than the rest of those who live here—better even than me," she thought to herself. Even worse, he was basing this belief, not on anything that he had ever done, but on what his father had accomplished.

Finally, as he finished, she rose from her chair. With a look of almost horror in her eyes, she told the young man that she would not marry him—and for him to not come around anymore. Then she walked out the door of the cafe and on toward home.

Junior Tilman just sat there with a look of puzzlement on his face; astonished at what had just happened. For the life of him, he didn't know what could have caused this woman to change so drastically in such a short time.

At a table in a darkened corner of the room sat a man quietly eating his evening meal. At the conclusion of this little drama, he couldn't help himself—and began to chuckle quietly. It was loud enough, though, that the young man in the table ahead of him heard.

He turned around, furious at being laughed at, and said, "Listen, mister, you won't think it's so funny when I come back there in a minute!"

"I'm sorry, son," came the familiar voice. "It's just that I'd have been mightily disappointed in that young woman if she had accepted your offer. In time, I reckon you'd have been disappointed in her as well."

"Father? Is that you?"

"I'm afraid so, son," Foss Tilman said. "I wasn't trying to spy on you. We were both just caught in a situation we didn't know how to handle very well."

Old Foss chuckled again. "I suppose I should have spoken up a little sooner—and maybe you should have shut up a little sooner."

His son sighed. "I suppose you might be right, after all. Do you think I have a chance to win her back, Father?"

"Oh, I doubt it, son," his father told him. "I don't think you ever really had her to begin with. And by the way she marched out of here, you might be wise to leave it lay right where it is. Yes—might be best all around."

Then, turning serious, he said, "Son, we need to have a talk—one that I guess I've been putting off for too long now. How about you come into the office bright and early tomorrow morning? I understand you might need a job."

———

By the time Etta came walking up to the old farmhouse, her initial shock and anger had subsided. A good mile or so hike will do wonders for a person's attitude. For one thing, it allows a person time to think without the disturbances which come with the constant interruptions of life.

By the time she began walking up the short path which led to the front porch of Harley's house, she was a little embarrassed by how she had handled the situation. She suspected that her speedy assessment of the young man—though mostly accurate—may have been somewhat severe.

Her judgment of young Foster Tilman was formed by other things she had experienced at the hands of other people. She had a feeling she might have been too quick, and probably overly critical in her initial assessment of his proposal.

She realized, as her calm and rationality returned, it really didn't matter if her initial reaction to Foster's proposal was accurate or not—she would have refused it in either case. The fact of the matter was, she just didn't love him.

It was as simple as that. In matters of the heart, it always is. Either you do or you don't—and she didn't. She knew what she was giving up, and knew also that it was a fair trade.

Harley and Lucy were in the kitchen still. They had done the dishes, put them away, and were now engrossed in a game of checkers. They both looked up, surprised to see Etta come in the door.

"Home kinda early, aren't you?" asked Harley. She could see that he wasn't trying to bait her, but was genuinely curious.

"Dinner wasn't any good," she replied, as she sat down in one of the remaining straight-backed kitchen chairs.

Lucy looked up with a frown on her face. "Not good? I've never had anything bad at Maggie's. What was wrong with it? Was it spoiled or something?"

"You could say something like that," Etta said, smiling a little. "Lucy, I want you to get ready for bed."

"But…,"

"Now, Lucy. I need to talk to Harley."

Lucy looked from Etta to Harley, and then back to Etta once more. She could tell that this was an argument she wouldn't be able to win.

With an expressive shrug of her shoulders, and eyes rolled toward the ceiling, she said, "Alright—but I don't think it's fair. Just because you two want to talk, I have to go to bed early. I think my rights are being violated. I'm protesting!"

"Just as long as you do your protesting in bed," said Etta.

As Lucy got up and left the room, Etta smiled and explained to Harley, "We're in the middle of the American Revolution in our studies at school—Boston Tea party and such."

"Looked like the beginnings of another 'revolution' here, just a minute ago," observed Harley, dryly.

"Short lived, I'm afraid." Etta looked at Harley and then changed the subject. "Foster asked me to marry him tonight," she said abruptly.

Harley sat still, both of his big, bony hands on the table in front of him. He looked down at his hands and said, "Kinda sudden, don't you think?"

"I don't know, Harley," she said. "I don't suppose that the affairs of the heart are tied too closely to the calendar."

"Well, I think it's too soon. You hardly even know the man. Have you even stopped to think about what it will be like for Lucy?"

Then Harley stopped suddenly, aware that he was running the risk of angering Etta once more by sticking his nose in where it likely wasn't wanted.

"Foster plans to send her to 'the finest girl's school money can buy', so I guess that's what 'it will be like for Lucy,'" said Etta.

"Send her away?" Harley's voice was on the rise. "You can't just let him send her away!"

"Hush, Harley!" Etta looked at him sternly, as if he were one of her students. "I don't want Lucy to hear you."

"But Etta!" Harley's voice was still pleading, but quieter now.

"I didn't say that I accepted his proposal," Etta said. "As a matter of fact, I turned him down."

"Turned him down?!" Harley exclaimed. "Why on earth would you want to turn him down? He's what every woman wants!"

"You ought to make up your mind, Harley. Is it foolish to accept his proposal, or foolish to turn him down? It's got to be one or the other—but it can't be both."

And then she said, "By the way, when did you get to be the expert on what every woman wants?"

"It doesn't take an expert to figure out the advantages of having a man like Junior Tilman as your husband—and don't pretend you don't know what I'm talking about."

"Of course, I know what you're talking about," she said. "What you don't seem to understand is that there are things which are more important to some women than what they can get from a wealthy husband. Trust me on this one, Harley."

Harley seemed to accept this without further argument and decided to move on to the next battle.

"When I left earlier, the last thing you said was that we needed to talk. Well, O.K., let's talk. What was on your mind?"

She took a deep breath before she spoke. "There were some things that I learned about Foster this evening. Things which caused me to get up and walk out the door—things that I may or may not have been right about. It really doesn't matter, though."

"What sort of things, Etta?"

"That doesn't matter right now. What does matter is that his proposal helped me to get something straight in my mind; something I hadn't been able to figure out before."

Harley looked at her with a puzzlement on his face.

"What I mean is, I had already decided that I would not marry him if he were ever to ask."

Harley swallowed, and then asked, "Why not?"

"I guess it comes down to the fact that I just don't love him—and unless the man I love asks me, I doubt that I'll ever get married."

Harley sat there for a minute, fidgeting with a couple of the checkers on the table—stacking them and then unstacking them. Finally, he glanced up at her, and then back down at the table and asked, quietly, "Do you think that will ever happen, Etta?"

"I don't know, Harley—do you?"

"What do you mean? How would I know?"

"No reason," she sighed, shaking her head, as she started to rise out of her chair.

"Wait a minute, Etta," said Harley.

She stopped in the middle of standing up—frozen there for a moment—and then slowly sat back down.

"What is it, Harley? What do you want to say to me that hasn't already been said?"

"We…uh…that is, I…" He brought one of his hands up and rubbed the stubble on his jaw, and let his words trail off.

"That's okay, Harley. I think I understand." She sighed again and began to rise once more.

"No—you don't!" Harley said with more passion to his words. Then more softly, he said, "You don't understand. I don't even know if I understand."

Etta sat back down. "Try and help me understand, Harley," she said.

He looked at her and said, "You need to see the way things are, Etta. It may be true that a guy like me has the same wants that everyone has, but that's really about all that it can amount to—and I know it. That's all right—I mean, I'm used to it. I gave up on my big dreams a long time ago. A person needs to accept what they are—and what they can be."

"What are you talking about, Harley?"

Harley looked down at his hands resting on the table. Strong, capable hands. He was dredging up memories which had been long buried—of things which he had shared with no person. He had never intended to.

Finally, he looked up at her and spoke. "I never mentioned it before, but there was a girl—back home in Indiana—that was... well, we had talked before I left to play baseball. That was back— you know—back before..."

She nodded her head slowly, trying to follow the path of his thinking.

"Well, when I finally came home—and was recuperating— she came to see me, to support me while I got used to the new leg. I don't know what she thought. I guess maybe she thought it was something like a broken bone—given enough time it would heal—that with care it would get well.

"Then one day she happened to be there when I was strapping it on. I guess when she saw the stump which is all that's left, it must have hit her then. This was permanent, and if we ever got married, she would be marrying a cripple. And so, she left—just ran. Can't say as I blame her."

Etta—her eyes moistening—had been listening intently to his words, remaining quiet while he spoke. Now she looked into his eyes, with tears running down her cheeks.

"Do you mind if I look?", she asked; and before he could answer, she knelt down and gently rolled the cuff of his pants up on the right side of his trousers.

When she had rolled it high enough, she began to gently inspect the contraption strapped to his leg, and then with strong gentle fingers she removed the prosthesis and inspected the gnarled, calloused stump that remained.

Then, as surely as if she had been doing it all of her life, she reconnected the thing to his leg and then rolled the leg of the trousers back down.

She got back into the chair and looked at Harley with eyes that were soft and compassionate. She put small, but confident hands over his and said, "Well, I'm not running".

"But I'll tell you something right now Harley Matthews," and she continued, with some fire returning to her eyes, "If I ever hear anyone calling you a cripple—and that means you too—there will be a price to pay."

"Well?" Harley said, shrugging his shoulders as if to say, "what else can you call a man with only one leg?"

"The only cripples I know of are the ones who have convinced themselves they can't do anything. In their minds, they have crippled themselves. The man I choose will be a better man than that, Harley."

Harley looked up, surprised. "What are you saying, Etta?"

She shook her head and thought to herself, *"He may not be crippled, but Lord, he sure is dense."*

Then, with her hands still covering his, she sighed as she looked at Harley and said, "My answer is 'yes'."

For a moment, Harley felt perplexed as he tried to understand. He hadn't asked her anything. Then it began to dawn on him. She was answering a question he had been too slow to ask—would she be his girl? He shook his head and grinned.

"Well, it's about time," he said, and then he reached down and pulled her up into his arms.

Had they not been preoccupied right then, they might have noticed Lucy as she moved from the hallway and tip-toed back to her room—a big, satisfied smile covering her face.

Chapter
Eleven

Those who were new to the little community of Hope Springs—as well as strangers visiting our town—eventually would get around to asking where the "springs" were located. They would almost always be disappointed—and certainly surprised—by the answer they would receive.

There were no springs in the town of Hope Springs. This was simply because the town had never been intended to be built on its present site. The springs did exist, however—and as its name would indicate, the town had been planned to be built around them.

The springs were on the old Hope homestead, and as the Hopes were the first settlers in this part of the valley, they had the first opportunity to say where the town would be built.

Unfortunately for the Hopes, the springs were a combination of mineral springs and warm springs. Whereas that made them a matter of interest, it did not make them a place to build a town—and so the town was moved and rebuilt at its present location—off of Hope land.

Isaiah Hope could have moved it to any other place on his land, but using up choice farm land for the purpose of building a town would never have occurred to him.

In fact, for a Pennsylvania farmer, that would have been nothing short of sacrilegious. But Isaiah Hope was a prideful man, and in order to keep his pride satisfied, the town was to still bear his name.

So, even though the outskirts of our town were more than two miles from the springs themselves, our town would forever be known as Hope Springs.

In the late 1800s, long after Isaiah and Elizabeth had passed on from this life and into the next, their oldest son, John, seized upon a money-making idea that included these same springs.

It had been discovered—or at least strongly supposed—that mineral waters had healing qualities which went far beyond the explanations of the medical profession.

People who were ill—with what the doctors were unable to find a treatment for at the time—were often sent to a facility which would be built close to a mineral spring. Daily dips in the waters seemed to hold the answer for many of the people's woes.

Many of these were people who had the means which would allow them to stay for extended periods of time. I don't know how sick they were, or how well they got, but I remember wishing momma could go to one of these places for her tuberculosis instead of where she was right then. People didn't always come back from where she was. Even at my age I knew that.

Near to these springs was a warm spring as well. It was a large pool of water which was naturally heated by some mysterious force deep below the water's surface. At least, that's how I understood it at the time. It was, in fact, created from water which had seeped down, far below the surface, to be heated in the inner parts of the earth.

As it was heated, the water was then forced back up. Allowed to take a slow, circuitous route to the surface, the water cooled considerably, and created what we called a "warm spring".

If the water found its way to the surface quickly, and unheeded, then it would be very hot—sometimes even to the point of almost boiling; certainly scalding.

The warm springs were a natural complement to the mineral treatments which people needed for their healings. Folks could soak in those warm waters for hours and come out of them feeling better than when they had gone down into them.

John Hope saw an opportunity going to waste right here on his land. It was a fact that the acreage around the springs wasn't good for farming. It was too rocky to plow, and the ground had a strange, mineral quality about it which was not conducive to growing crops.

Unlike his father, though, John's world did not begin and end with the plow and the soil and the seeds. John Hope was forever a looking ahead sort of man.

By the 1890s, the stage road which ran from Sacramento to Seattle went right past his farm—within a quarter mile of the springs.

Capitalizing on a way to make the springs finally become a paying part of the old Hope homestead, John Hope had a hotel built nearby the springs; and then had a spur line run from the main stage road to the hotel.

He then hired some medical people—and advertised for paying customers to come and stay at his New Hope Springs Hotel and Spa.

It turned out to be an overnight success. People came from all over the world to stay there. Our town reaped some advantages from this as well, but for the most part, the people who came to use the springs stayed out at the hotel. The facility got some of its provisions locally, but mostly whatever it needed, the Hope farm could provide.

In 1909, though, disaster struck. The hot springs, which had always been one of the biggest draws to the place, began getting hotter. It had stayed a constant 105 degrees for as long as anyone had bothered to record the temperature. Then, within 24 hours, the temperature shot up to 150 degrees, and leveled off somewhere just over that.

"Seismic activity" was the explanation given many years later. The fault had shifted, allowing the water to rise unimpeded—too quickly to cool off sufficiently. But the cause didn't really matter; the damage was done.

Nobody could use the hot springs anymore—and no one wanted to trust the mineral springs either. No matter how hard John Hope tried to convince his customers that there was no reason to worry, people were just naturally reluctant to trust any water around Hope Springs.

Business fell off almost as fast as the water temperature had risen, and within six months, the New Hope Hotel was only a quiet reminder of days of glory forever gone.

However, to young boys who were looking for something to do, the old hotel—and the springs—were always a source of adventure. The hotel was boarded up to keep unwanted trespassers out.

They might just as well have hung a welcome sign from the front of the second story façade. We used the old building for our games of war, in which we would fight off the enemy—whether he was Indian, Mexican, or German.

Sometimes we would take our bed rolls with us so we could spend the night there—telling ghost stories, as the light from our candles shone eerily on the walls of the long vacant rooms.

We just knew that there were innumerable people who had died within this hotel, and that their ghosts were still there—waiting to feast on the flesh of young, innocent boys as they slept.

The springs were our playground as well. We would splash around in the mineral waters, and get closer to the scalding waters of the now hot springs, than we had any need to be.

If our parents, or my granddaddy, only knew what we were doing, we thought, they'd have tanned our hides. Though that was probably true, what we didn't realize was that our daddies had probably been doing the same thing when they were our ages.

Sometime in the middle of September, I borrowed Lyle Fletcher's bike, so I could take Lucy out to the springs to show her what I had been telling her about. I'd been telling her about the town—of how it had gotten its name, and such as that—and so of course I'd been talking about the old hotel and springs as well.

"Oh, Will, I'd sure like to see it!" she exclaimed. "Do you think we can? Will you take me? Please!"

I'd been taking some ribbing from the boys for the past couple of weeks, since our "end of summer" baseball game. It was all good natured, but I didn't want to add more fuel to their fire.

I'd already been doing enough of that by spending so much time out at Harley's place.

"No," I said, trying to come up with a good reason why not. "It's a guy's thing—not any girls allowed there."

I realized my mistake almost as soon as the words tumbled across my lips, so I thought real fast for some other—more plausible excuse. "Besides, it's way out of town—and you'd need a bike to get there."

"You could ride me double, couldn't you, Will?" she asked. She said it in a way that was hard to refuse, but I held fast. I could just imagine what the boys would say if any of them saw me riding around with Lucy on my handlebars—or worse, sitting in front of me with her arms wrapped around my neck.

The ribbing I'd get from that would never end. It would follow me to my grave. I could almost picture my tombstone— 'Here lies Will—caught with a GIRL'S arms around his neck. Died of shame'. It almost made me shudder. I had to think fast.

"I can't do that, Lucy," I replied. "It's too far—I mean for my bike. It's getting kind of old, and... and I don't want to put too much of a strain on it," I finished lamely. Even I could tell it was lame.

"That's alright," she said, not even seeming to sense that I was trying to evade her. I almost let out a sigh of relief. "I'll ask Lyle to take me."

"Well, maybe I could get Lyle to give me his bike for a couple of hours," I blurted out.

Too late, I saw I had been maneuvered into a corner—boxed in by a twelve-year-old girl! Looking down, I bit my lower lip, shook my head, and scuffed the toe of my shoe in the dirt. I had a feeling I'd be doing a lot of that.

Lyle was persistent in his wanting to know why I needed his bike the next afternoon. I made up something about breaking a chain on my bike, or some such foolishness, and that seemed to satisfy him—or so I thought. I should have known better.

He just went out and gathered as many other boys as he could find and waited behind the feed store.

When Lucy and I rode off—with a picnic basket hanging from my handlebars, and Lucy riding Lyle's bike—they all stepped around the corner to watch. I could still hear their "Ha! Ha's!" when we reached the highway, two blocks away and headed north out of town.

Nowadays, when people travel from California, north toward Canada, they use the Interstate. It's two or three lanes wide—both directions. Of course, we didn't have the Interstate yet, in the 1930s.

Back then, every car, pickup, and freight truck motored north—or south—on this same two-lane road that Lucy and I were riding our bikes on. There wasn't nearly as much traffic as there is today, but we needed to be watchful as we rode along the narrow shoulder we were on.

As we rode, we could see signs of the old stage road that used to carry the passengers and mail from Sacramento to Seattle in the early days. There were places where the new highway ran for miles right over the top of the old road—but it strayed away in other places.

Those were little more than old ruts, grown over by grass and small saplings and brush. Seldom would the highway and the stage road ever be more than a quarter mile apart.

When we had gone about 2 miles, I stopped so I could tell Lucy where we were going.

"The old hotel is a little way off of the old stage road," I motioned, with my arm towards the east, "no more than half a mile, as the crow flies."

"The problem is," I continued, "there isn't any road that goes across from here—so we made our own trail across this field," I pointed at the pasture by the highway which was a couple hundred yards wide, "then over that." I pointed at the timbered hill which sat on the other side of the field.

I'm sure that to Lucy, the hill I pointed to probably looked more like a small mountain covered with a thick, foreboding forest. It had, in fact, been logged off in the early days, but thirty or forty years later, it was hard to tell.

She looked at me with some doubt in her eyes. "Is this the only way?" she asked.

"No," I said, "another couple of miles up the highway, there's a road we could take." This was an old logging access road they had used when they came in and logged the other side of the hill. "It will get us there, too."

"Wouldn't that be better?"

"It's longer," I told her, "Three or four miles longer."

I really didn't want to go that way. It was an easier ride, but longer—and not nearly as much fun. The ride through the timber was always a little scary, but if you're going on an adventure, what's the point if it doesn't test your nerves a little?

"Me and the boys only go that way when we have to take someone's younger brother with us," I told her. The way I had said it made it sound like it was only for kids and sissies. I was pretty sure that would cause her courage to return.

So, where a minute ago doubt had sneaked and up and bit Lucy like a big old horse fly, she now brushed it aside—and, with the sparkle back in her eyes, she said, "Well? Are we going to just sit here and talk about it? Or are you going to show me how you guys get there?"

I set our bikes over the wire fence that ran along the highway and then held up the barbed wire so Lucy could slip under it. After I had crossed, I took a quick look around the pasture to make sure that there wasn't some mean old bull, or something, waiting to chase after us.

The boys and I had found two different trails through the woods. One trail pretty much went straight up the one side of the small mountain and then straight back down the other.

The other trail broke off from the first about halfway up and then veered off—circling in a wide arc until it wound its way around to the other side.

The more direct route went up and through the trees—snaking its way through the brush, around large boulders, and at one point going under a natural archway formed out of an old root wad. Down the other side, it was almost exactly the same—only quite a bit steeper—and therefore much faster.

This was the route the boys and I took when we came out to spend the day goofing off. Lucy and I took the other way.

I would never have admitted it to the other boys—even had there been torture involved, like burning pieces of bamboo shoved up under my fingernails—but I was really enjoying myself.

To do this, and not have my conscience burn at me later on, I told myself that I was only babysitting—that it would be good for Etta and Harley to spend a Saturday afternoon together alone. Even a boy could see there was something going on with those two. It was obvious that they liked each other.

Lucy and I arrived at the old hotel, with its façade beginning to break down, and its veranda showing signs of 30 years of neglect.

Still, one only had to use a little imagination to envision the splendor it must have been in the eyes of the people when they turned down the last straight stretch of road and saw it standing there, freshly painted and sparkling with the bustle of activity and the feelings of life and health that it seemed to generate.

Acting as tour guide, I showed her the hotel first, going from room to room, explaining to her the things which I only imagined, but sounding as though I knew what I was talking about. It seemed to have the desired effect on her. She was acting impressed—and so I continued on.

"And this is where they would put the honored guests," I told her, coming to a room which was much larger than the rest of them.

"Presidents, and Kings, and Dukes and such—they all stayed here." I was laying it on pretty thick—seeing how large her eyes were getting while I talked.

Many years later, when I went back to view the old hotel one last time before she was brought down, I realized that what I had been bragging about to that pretty little blonde-haired girl was not a master suite intended for Kings and Princes and dignitaries. Turned out it was only a laundry room. Even then my ears turned red, I think.

We went to the mineral spring first, and dangled our feet in the water while we ate our lunches which she had prepared for us—and then went to the hot springs where she got real scared looking when I did handstands on the banks of the scalding water.

All in all, it was a good day. I'd hate to have admitted it to anyone right then, but I doubt I had had such fun with the boys when I was with them there.

As I showed off in front of Lucy, on the banks of the hot springs, she acted afraid that I would fall into the caustic, burning water; while I acted totally fearless.

Little did either of us know we would meet here again, on the edge of this water, on a fateful evening not far in the future. Then we would understand fear.

Chapter Twelve

Etta was especially grateful to not have the children underfoot that day. She had something on her mind that she wanted to speak with Harley about. She had been teaching for almost three weeks now, and for the most part, it had been a wonderful experience.

But there was something that was bothering her. She didn't know if, or how, Harley might help—but she hadn't been in town all that long, and didn't know who else to ask. If Harley couldn't help, then she would ask Maggie—but she'd try Harley first.

The children had left on what had been explained to Etta as "showing Lucy some of the things around the outskirts of town". She had looked questioningly at Harley, when Will had asked, but Harley had only nodded, and smiled in such a way that somehow Etta knew it would be alright.

Harley had walked Lucy into town—though he didn't need to—and had spent an hour or so sitting on the bench in front of the feed store whittling on a piece of wood.

It was a time when Harley could see the town as it passed by—occasionally stopping to speak—sometimes sitting and visiting with him for a while. The children would come there too, and

Harley would fill their heads with stories of such things as they could only dream about.

When Harley returned to the house, he found Etta had coffee made, and was waiting on the front porch for him. He walked up the steps of the porch and sat on one of the two rocking chairs which faced the road at the front of the house. The other had belonged to his mother, but now Etta sat in it, gently rocking.

"Would you like some coffee, Harley?" Etta asked.

Harley nodded his head and, removing his hat, took out his handkerchief and mopped his brow. "It may be fall, but summer sure doesn't seem to know it yet."

Etta went into the house, and a minute later returned with two cups of steaming, hot coffee. She handed one cup to Harley and sat the other on a small table beside the other rocking chair.

"There's something that I want to talk to you about Harley— if that's ok with you," she started. Harley just looked at her, waiting.

Holding the cup in both hands, she began. "I really like my job as a teacher, Harley. You can't imagine how close I've gotten to the children in such a short amount of time—and I think they like me as well. Every day they come to school, eager and ready to learn—and mostly, they are bright, attentive children"

Her brow furrowed as she continued. "The problem is, in the afternoon, these same children seem to change. They aren't paying much attention to what I try to teach; it's as though they just aren't interested anymore.

"No matter what I try, I can't seem to get them to concentrate. I might just as well have sent them home at lunchtime for all the good it's doing me."

She paused and looked off toward town. "I keep asking myself what the problem is. Are they bored? Are my afternoon lessons not as interesting as the morning lessons? Is it them—or is it something I'm doing wrong?

"These are the same children that do so well in their morning studies. They are such good students part of the time. Could it be that I'm pushing them too hard?"

She looked at Harley then. "Do you have any suggestions, Harley? Can you think of why I can't reach these kids part of the time? I'm really at a loss about what to do. If you have any suggestions, I'd be more than glad to hear them," she finished.

Harley sat for a moment, gently rocking, and then took a sip of his coffee before he answered her. "Why Etta, the problem is food."

"Food?!" Etta exclaimed. Her brows furrowed together as she tried to understand the connection.

"Yes, food," he replied. "Or, I guess I should say the lack of food. What you're seeing in the afternoon is what happens when kids get too hungry. You may not realize it, Etta, but when a lot of those kids go home after school, they're going to get a mighty skimpy meal, at best.

"A lot of them have brothers and sisters—families too big for the support which is given by their fathers. Some of these men are working, but not all of them—and the ones who are don't make a lot of money. Times may be getting better—but we're not out of the woods yet.

"Some of those children will get a breakfast—and some won't. The ones who do won't get much—a piece of bread—glass of milk. There isn't a one of them who gets a lunch. Have you seen any of them carrying a lunch box?" he asked.

"No," she replied, "I guess I hadn't even thought about that."

"My guess is a lot of those children are trying to get by on just one small meal a day. That's not enough—not for a growing boy or girl, at least.

"Yeah, I imagine that they do have a hard time focusing—they're not thinking about their schoolwork, they're thinking about their bellies. That's not hard to figure out, Etta," he said, "What you're going to do about it is the hard part."

"I've already figured out what I'm going to do, Harley," said Etta.

"What do you mean?" he asked, a bit taken by surprise.

"I mean, I'm going to let you work this out, Harley," she told him. "I think that you're just the person to make sure that this problem gets solved. I'll help you in whatever way I can, but this is your problem now."

———————————

Harley knew the only real solution to the problem at the school, concerning the children's hunger, was to institute a hot lunch program.

He knew that in the bigger cities, which had more fiscal resources, they had already had success with this sort of thing. In those schools, the lunch program was funded through property taxes, which paid for all the school's expenditures.

Harley knew that this wouldn't work here. These people were already too strapped. To demand that they give more. When many of them were so poor that their children were the reason for the program, taxing them more was only defeating the entire purpose here.

He knew the only way this was going to work was for those who had enough to be willing to give of what they had.

This would require that he talk to the merchants in town—to convince them of the need—and to sell them on the idea that, with their help, this could be a worthwhile proposition. He would also have to go out to the farmers and do the same with them—convince them to give of their produce—whatever that might be.

But he also had to get the school board and the superintendent to agree to it. Harley had his work cut out for him.

Chapter
Thirteen

Edith Whittington was one of the wealthiest people in our little town. She came by her wealth honestly—she had inherited some of it, had worked for some of it, and had gained some by wise investments.

She came from pioneer stock. Her Grandparents, Isaiah and Elizabeth Hope, had come here from Pennsylvania by covered wagon in the 1840s. Crossing prairies, rivers, and mountains to get to our valley in the Northwest—in all types of weather conditions—they were among the first to settle in our area. The first ones to arrive, the land they chose to farm was the best there was.

The farm had been handed down to her father when the old folks passed away, and eventually would be given to Edith—there being no other children, much less any sons to continue the farm's lineage.

There was, however, Tom Whittington. Tom had grown up behind a plow, but being the youngest of three brothers had put him completely out of the running to ever own, and run, his family's farm.

A man who was ever looking to the future, he had cast his eye around the county and had discovered that there was a really nice farm which had a "farmer's daughter"—but not a "farmer's son".

Though Tom was older than Edith, it was generally thought to be a good match. It at least made sense. The farm would need someone to work it when her folks became too old—and Edith was going to need a husband.

From where Tom stood, it made sense as well. He needed a wife—and a farm. He was an ambitious man who had it in mind to own the biggest farm in the county.

For some time after Tom and Edith were married, they lived on her folk's farm, being little more than hired help. Tom though, ever with his thoughts on what will be, instead of what is, bided his time.

In time it became Tom and Edith's farm, with the old folks just staying on—almost as though it were for "old time's sake"; sort of transitional period. After a while everyone began to refer to it simply as "the Whittington place". And in time people began to call it "the old Whittington place".

Tom was a good farmer. He was up each day before dawn and worked each day until the sun went down—always looking for new, innovative improvements which would make his farm more productive. While Tom ran the day-to-day aspects of the farm, his wife ran the business.

Having instilled in his young wife the importance of property and wealth, it soon became apparent that there were few who were better at getting more out of a dollar than Tom Whittington's young wife. Edith Whittington was a shrewd woman.

One morning Tom went out to hitch up Sugar, one of the two mules he used for plowing the fields. In the back of the barn where Sugar and Jasper should be, he found Jasper down on his side. With his legs poking straight out—stiff as a board—it wasn't too difficult to see that this mule had plowed its last furrow.

Tom shook his head and sighed heavily as he let his shoulders sag. He'd been walking behind that old mule for a lot of years, and it was almost as though he'd lost an old friend.

Sugar was standing off a short distance away, looking as though she couldn't be less interested. He had bought the younger Sugar just recently in order to give the old mule a break now and then. He guessed now that decision had come a little late to be of much use to Jasper.

As he stood there contemplating what he was going to do with the dead animal—it being much too close to the main house to just let nature take its course—the thought occurred to him that just maybe he had been working his animals too hard, and for too long.

Sure, Jasper had a little age on him, but he'd never expected this. Sugar wasn't exactly young either.

Tom dug a hole deep enough and wide enough to bury a mule. Then, using his other mule, he drug the dead animal over to the hole he'd just finished digging.

After rolling him in, he began to shovel the dirt back in. As he worked, he considered what he should do. The more dirt he shoveled onto the old mule, the more certain he became of his next course of action.

After finishing the burial detail, he got into his Model-T Ford pickup and drove into the county seat. When he came back that afternoon, he was the proud owner of a brand-new John Deere Model D tractor.

The next morning, Tom got up before daylight, as always, and went down to the barn to do the chores. After the milking was finished, and the pigs were all fed, he went around to the back of the barn where his new tractor was parked.

He fired it up and listened to the 'pop, pop, pop' as the engine idled. He was sitting up on the seat, thinking proudly of all the crops he would be able to put in now—thinking to himself that he might even need to build more storage for all of those crops—when he felt a sharp twinge of pain high on his left side.

For a man who was always looking to the future, he never saw that coming. Tom Whittington's last thought, as he fell off the seat of his brand-new John Deere tractor, was how foolish he had been to worry about how hard he'd been working those two mules. After all, he'd been there too, walking behind them step for step.

They found him later that day, lying on his side—in almost the same place he'd found Jasper the day before. Tom was only 52 years old—his widow was 38.

They put Tom Whittington in the grave the next day, and by the end of the week Edith had the farm up for sale. The farm sold quickly. In 1928, the price she received for the farm was enough to set her up for the rest of her life.

Folks around figured the sale was more easily made with a new tractor thrown into the bargain.

With shrewd investing, Edith increased her capitol by one hundred per cent. After selling the farm, she moved into a nice, if somewhat modest, house in the middle of town. Though the house itself was no more—and no less—than anyone else's, it sat in the middle of three large city lots.

I suppose it would have been difficult for a person used to living on a farm to settle in town on just one city lot. It might seem too confining. I could understand that—since I lived in a two-room apartment above the feed store.

The people in town said that she was a shrewd businesswoman, and I suppose she was. That's how she got her wealth, they said. They also said that she was thrifty and frugal—and that's how she kept her wealth.

Us boys, though, we figured that what the people of the town recognized as thrift and frugality was nothing more than being tightfisted and cheap.

Each of us had, at various times, worked for Mrs. Whittington. I might stack her firewood and split her kindling. Lyle might paint her fence. One time Del Pruitt spent the better part of two days with a hand scythe clearing the grass off those three lots.

When the job was finished, she would come out to inspect the work, looking almost disappointed if she couldn't find some fault. She'd then take out her purse—a small change purse, made out of satin with a drawstring at the top—and stick a finger down into it and begin to stir the coins around, like a boy might do when trying to find just the right marble to shoot.

Finally satisfied, she would pull out a dime or a quarter (and that, on rare occasions) and offer it forth with these words of wisdom, "Any job well done is worth more than mere wages".

Maybe so, but for me, the only reason I ever did any job for her was if I needed that dime really badly.

Anyway, that's the way it seemed at the time; but, like many things, what we thought we knew was not necessarily how it really was.

Chapter Fourteen

Not long after moving into Hope Springs, Edith Whittington took a portion of her money and donated it to the newly developed fund, which had been designated for the building of a new schoolhouse.

It was an ambitious project for our small town, and the merchants in Hope Springs—as well as many of their patrons—had been attempting to give a little here and there.

And, even though they had done the best they could, the new school fund was growing at an abysmally slow rate.

With the Whittington donation, however, the school fund was completed, as was the new school, within the next year. The depression struck about then, and so the town felt blessed to have gotten their school built in time.

For a while, everyone thought of Edith Whittington as a blessed benefactor. Had it not been for her, they told themselves, they'd still be trying to teach their children in that rundown, leaky old building that served as the Odd Fellows Lodge on Saturday evenings.

The only ones who were disappointed were the Odd Fellows, who now were forced to do all the maintenance which they had previously shared with the school district.

I don't know about all Odd Fellows members, but the ones around here were short on upkeep, and long on complaining. Other than that, the general consensus seemed to be that she should be nominated for sainthood.

And then they began to learn what the new building would really cost the town. There had been a deal struck between her, the school board, and the city council.

For her generous "gift", she would be given the job as School Administrator. She would also be granted a seat on the board.

This would literally ensure that she could run things at our school the way she deemed necessary. Without an override of the entire school board, her word was law—at least as far as the school was concerned.

Harley could have spent the remainder of his life trying to get everyone in the area to come to a decision concerning the idea of a hot lunch program at the school. It's not that the people were against his idea. As a matter of fact, an overwhelming majority of them thought it was just dandy.

The problem lay in that nobody would commit to it. Jim Clancy, over at the tavern, said he'd be glad to contribute (money—not liquor—of course), if everyone else did. Tom Girvan, over at the grocery store, said the same. The rest of the merchants were about as noncommittal also. Harley had about the same reaction with the farmers.

A lesser man might have thrown up his hands in frustration and given up at that point. Harley, though, had the bit in his teeth and was determined to find a way. He realized if he could get everyone together to talk about it, then he might have a good chance of getting this idea off the ground and up and running.

———————————

It was no secret that Mrs. Whittington was not one of those favoring Harley's plan. She was from the old school of thought—believing that what the community owed the children was an education. Nothing more, and nothing less.

It was with some surprise that she volunteered the school's gymnasium for the community meeting the next Saturday evening. We were so naïve.

Being more of a military tactician than we understood at the time, Mrs. Whittington understood that on the battlefield, choosing where to fight your battles—and that, being the "high ground"—would almost always ensure success. I suppose it's a lot like 'home field advantage' in baseball.

As this meeting was at the school—and she being the school administrator—it seemed natural for her to take control of the entire process. There were chairs set up, from half court on back, for the people of the community to sit in. Facing them, at about the foul line, was a table with five chairs behind it.

The meeting was to begin at seven o'clock in the evening. Harley gathered up his courage to get up and speak before the whole of the community. He turned so he could face the crowd, and yet still not have Mrs. Whittington and the other board members who were sitting at the table at his back.

When he glanced over to where Etta, Lucy, and I were sitting in the front row of chairs, Harley had a nervous look on his face. I'd tried to offer words of encouragement earlier.

I'd told him, "Just remember, this won't be any worse than the first time you got up to pitch in the minors. You did fine then, didn't you?"

He'd looked at me, a little weakly it seemed. "Yeah," he said, "after I threw up in the dugout." He reached out and tousled my head, showing me he appreciated my effort. I kept my mouth shut after that.

Etta smiled a smile at him that told him she had all the confidence in the world that he would succeed. It appeared it was all he needed. With his resolve restored, he walked up to the front and turned to face the group of folks who had come that evening. There was quite a turnout.

"Ladies and gentlemen," he began. "The reason we're all here this evening isn't a big secret. I've been making a pest of myself over the past few days—talking your ears off about a lunch program here at the school." He paused to take a big gulp of air before continuing on.

The crowd nodded, and a quiet laughter could be heard around the room.

Before he could continue, however, he was interrupted. "On that subject, Mr. Matthews," cut in the voice of Edith Whittington, "I'm sorry, but the school just can't allow that to happen."

Harley was caught completely off guard, and stood there for a moment with his mouth half open, the words which were on his lips falling back into his mouth. Instead, his brows knit together and he half-turned toward the school board with confusion on his face.

"What did you say?" he asked, shaking his head as if he had just been slapped. "Did you just say the school won't allow a hot lunch program?"

"You understood me quite correctly, Mr. Matthews," she replied. "This school won't be enacting any programs which go beyond the necessary curriculum. It would be fiscally irresponsible to do so—especially at this time."

"But Mrs. Whittington," Harley responded, "We aren't asking for the school to fund this program. This will be an entirely volunteer program, using donations from the charitable people of our community. It won't cost the school a penny."

"It always costs the school!" she replied, as if she were exasperated at having to explain such a fundamental fact of life. "The education system is set up to do just one thing—educate children.

"We can't be diverting our attention from our job of educating these children every time some do-gooder with a cause comes along or some new welfare program is suggested. We barely have enough money for the essentials as it is."

"Now," she began, with an air of authority, "as there's no more to be said concerning this matter, I suggest that we all retire to the comfort of our homes."

It became clear then that the only reason she had agreed to this meeting of the community—and had allowed it to take place at the school—was so she could put an end to this idea once and for all. She underestimated her foe.

"Mrs. Whittington!" Harley spoke sharply as she turned to walk away—probably sharper than he had intended.

Still, it caught her off guard, and she stopped mid-stride and turned—her mouth opening in obvious surprise. She probably hadn't ever been spoken to with that tone of voice.

Harley took advantage of her momentary astonishment. "I've heard it from others—though I tried to think better—that you were a stingy and miserly woman, Edith Whittington."

He was looking at me when he said this last part. I guess I must have given him my opinion of Edith Whittington sometime in the past.

He continued then. "Now I guess I may have to change my mind about that. Am I to understand that you oppose giving children the food they need because you want to make sure that you can balance the books?"

"Mr. Matthews, I believe you misunderstood me. I'm certainly not against children having food. Don't be ridiculous! I just don't think the role of the school is to be the one who feeds them. That, Mr. Matthews, is the role of their parents."

Then she turned again to leave, as if she had just dismissed a recalcitrant child, and was going on about her business.

Harley wasn't done yet. "You seem to have forgotten that life is more than just figures on a blackboard—or numbers in a ledger, Mrs. Whittington—and so is a child's learning. What kind of lessons will a child learn from a school that doesn't seem to even care if he's hungry or not?"

This time he didn't stop to catch his breath, but continued on. He had learned that lesson fast.

"Now, I agree with you—it is the job of the parents to see that the child is cared for. But you seem to have forgotten, Ma'am, that many of the parents just aren't able—for reasons which are beyond their own control at this time—to put the necessary food on their tables so that when their children get to your school, they can think about something more than their empty bellies!"

Harley had spoken with such a passion we were all a little taken aback. Where there had been much murmuring only a moment before, now there was complete quiet.

Mrs. Whittington seemed to chew on what Harley had just said—though it may have been that she was just trying to recover from the shock of being spoken to like that for perhaps the first time in her adult life.

Suddenly, a voice broke the silence from the back of the room.

Surprisingly, it was the voice of Dave Tompkins. He had come in just before Harley had begun speaking, and had been leaning against the wall, not far from the doors that opened into the building.

He took the pipe out of his mouth and slapped it against the palm of his hand until the ash fell from it. Its fire had probably been dead for several hours. He bent down and poured the ash into the rolled-up cuff of his overalls. He stood up and cleared his throat before he spoke.

"Let me ask you something, Edith," his voice ringing loud and clear. When a person spoke in those old gymnasiums, the voice would bounce off the walls—almost like shouting in one end of an old hollowed-out log.

Dave's voice continued. "Do you remember back here a few years ago, when Tom got hurt by that ornery old bull you owned? Tom had a fine crop of winter wheat that year—wheat that he'd need for the next year.

"He couldn't even get out of bed right then—much less bring in his wheat—and wheat don't wait till you're ready. Now, by all rights, harvesting that wheat was Tom's job, but do you remember what happened?"

Dave stopped, took his pipe back out of his shirt pocket, began reloading it, and waited patiently for a response.

Edith's face had noticeably softened a little as she was remembering a time of good neighbors and good will—a time when Dave Tompkins and Paul Anders had set their own harvests aside for a few days so they could bring in the Whittington's winter wheat. She hadn't thought of that in years.

It had been more than 'a few years ago'. It had been a lifetime ago.

"Yes," she said quietly, "Yes, I remember." Then she seemed to realize where she was, and how quiet the gymnasium had become—and she became a little embarrassed.

She stood a little straighter, cleared her throat, and then announced, "I believe I see what you mean, Mr. Tompkins—thank you for reminding me"

Seldom would you hear that many words pass Dave's lips in an entire week, unless he was talking about his farm—and he hadn't spoken that much to all the women in the county in the last thirty years. We could only sit there—utter disbelief showing on our faces, I suppose, at what we had just seen and heard.

She turned to face the rest of us and said quietly, "The school—that is, I—have no further objection to your proposal, Mr. Matthews."

Then she seemed to become less commanding, and more vulnerable, as she turned and walked past the crowd of people to the door which Dave Tompkins held for her. Then Dave followed her outside.

As soon as Mrs. Whittington left, the Chairman of the School Board turned to Harley and said, "Well, I guess it's all right if you go on ahead and outline your proposal, Harley."

So, Harley looked over to where we were sitting—me and Lucy were still on the edges of our seats—and Etta sitting there, eyes glistening, smiling like she was really proud to be where she was—and he cleared his throat once again and began to lay it all out.

Oh, there were some who still thought it a waste of time and resources, but by and large the entire community got behind it—accepting it with open arms.

There was a kitchen, of sorts, which they set up in the basement of the schoolhouse—and as the aroma from the soup or stew or beans wafted upwards into the classrooms above, the children could barely contain their excitement.

As they wiggled in their seats with the anticipation of the first good meal that many would have had since the day before, Etta thought to herself, *"I've only traded one problem of keeping their attention for another."*

Still, she was more than content with the trade.

Chapter
Fifteen

Tinker Bellum owned the farm that bordered the old Whittington place to the north. Though Tinker may have been land rich, as far as his bank account went, he was as poor as the rest of us.

When Tom Whittington died several years before, Tinker had gone to the bank to see about a loan. More than anything, he wanted that farm added to his. The bank, however, didn't share in Tinker's passion, and so his loan was denied.

A nice family—the Bakers—was able to secure a loan from the bank, and so it was they—and not Bellum—who had purchased the farm from Edith. Tinker fumed and stomped around and said enough things out of anger to turn the Bakers solidly against this neighbor of theirs.

I suppose each of us can think back over the course of our lives and pick out a particular year which stands out from the rest, as being filled with just plain bad luck. This past year had been a terrible one for the Bakers.

Not the farm, mind you. That farm was as rich and fertile a piece of ground as a person could ever hope to find. It had been said that a person could take a hoe and a stick and go out and raise more crops off of that land than off of any other in the county.

No, the troubles which came to the Baker farm were internal struggles. They had begun when the new Black Angus bull, which Charlie Baker had just purchased to improve the bloodline in his cattle, decided to walk through a muddy bog instead of just going around it.

While trying to free his prized animal—and beginning to become frustrated in his efforts—Charlie had allowed himself to do a foolish thing. He got on the downhill side of the bull.

The bull, breaking free of the muck, lunged up the steep bank. Charlie had been pushing from the back of the animal, and when the bull broke free suddenly, Charlie fell face forward, into the mud.

Unfortunately, the sudden lunge only partially freed the animal, and it fell back onto its haunches—right atop Charlie Baker.

Although death from the impact of the animal falling on him was probably instantaneous it was several hours later that his oldest son, Alvie, a solemn faced fourteen-year-old, found the bull grazing not far away from the bog.

Continuing the search, he finally happened to look in the bog itself and discovered his father's body, still pushed face down in the mud.

Mrs. Baker had four children—none of them old enough to run a farm—so she hired a man to come out and finish harvesting the crops her husband had planted, and to do the things a four-teen-year-old boy wouldn't be able to do.

For a while she toyed with the idea of staying on and running it on her own, but soon realized there was more work than she could ever hope to get done; and she couldn't afford to hire the work to be done for her year in and year out.

All things considered, she put the farm up for sale.

Tinker Bellum had already been by the farm to see the grieving widow. He knew then what she had soon learned: she could not run the farm on her own. Recognizing that the new widow Baker was in a bind, he made her two offers.

The first, a proposal of marriage, caused a combination of rage and disgust. Enough so, that when Bellum got around to the second offer—this time to buy her farm—she would not have sold it to him had it meant the difference between prosperity and the poorhouse.

Edith Whittington had never grown overly fond of "city life", as she referred to life in Hope Springs, and so when the widow Baker called one day to present an offer of reselling her old farm, she found herself more than a little interested.

She didn't know what she would do with the old place, but even if it was only a sanctuary away from the town, it would be worth it, she thought.

So it came to pass that Edith reclaimed the old farm. She still planned to live at the house in town—at least for a little while; and so, the Baker family was allowed to continue living there while they set about trying to figure out their future plans, which were far from secure without a breadwinner in the family now.

For the last couple of months Tinker had been trying, without success, to court Mrs. Whittington. Us kids couldn't figure out why anyone would want to woo someone as old as Edith Whittington—though, in truth, she was a widow of about forty-five years of age. To twelve-year-olds, though, that seemed downright ancient.

Bellum figured to have that farm one way or another—even if it meant marrying Edith Whittington. After all, he told himself, that was how her last husband had acquired the farm—and besides, she could do a lot worse.

He had a good farm, which he devoutly worked at each day. He had most of his teeth, bathed once a month (twice, now that he was in the courting frame of mind), and was reasonably healthy—which was a site better than her last husband had been. From where he stood, it looked like a pretty good match.

It surprised him considerably when she turned him down after he first approached her with the idea of matrimony. He'd gone home, regrouped and rethought his strategy, and come back two weeks later—freshly shorn, shaved, and bathed—and carrying a bouquet of flowers.

He had even taken his hat off this time when she had come to the door. On this occasion, as on the first, she had stood in the doorway and listened to his proposal—then politely said, "No thank you, Mr. Bellum,"—and closed the door in his face.

He had been back four times since, with the same results. He was a little aggravated—but not too worried. As he recalled, his father had needed to coax his mother a little too, before she had accepted his proposal. He could wait. The Bellum's were patient when it came to matrimony.

On his last trip to town, however, when Edith opened the door for him, he looked past her—to her kitchen table—and saw Dave Tompkins sitting there with a fork in his hand. It looked as if he was eating a piece of squash pie!

Tinker couldn't help but notice how the corners of Edith's mouth were drawn up into a tight smile as she said, "Hello Mr. Bellum. What can I do for you?"

Bellum's mind was trying to grasp what he was seeing, but all he could think was that once again he had been denied that which he had so desperately wanted. Not the love of a good woman, but the title to the best farmland in the county. And he didn't understand it at all. Why would she choose Tompkins over him?

Could it be she was somewhat reluctant to accept his offer because there had been no declaration of love to go along with it? Could it be she felt it was just what it was—a business transaction, with some other benefits attached?

So, what if it was? What about Tompkins? His property bordered hers to the south. It was obvious to Bellum that Tompkins was trying to accomplish the same thing he was. Surely, she could see that!

"I...uh...never mind, Mrs. Whittington," he stammered. "I think that I'd best be on my way. Goodnight!" He turned on his heel, and briskly strode down her path to the street, got in his flatbed truck and drove away.

Chapter Sixteen

Edith closed the door, chuckling to herself, and turned back to where Dave was washing down his pie with a glass of milk. "What was that all about?" he asked.

Dave had only stopped by earlier, on his way to the weekly farmer's gathering, so he could deliver a dress Katherine Anders had altered for Edith. He thought it a little odd that Katherine hadn't delivered it herself, but being a good neighbor, he was happy to oblige.

He had been at Edith's for only a short time when Bellum had knocked on her door. When he had arrived, Edith gladly invited him in, saying that she was expecting him—that Katherine had called ahead. She had then asked if he would care for a slice of pie and something to drink.

Because of his social inadequacies when around the opposite sex, Dave had few such offers, and so had gladly accepted. Besides, Edith Whittington was just an old friend whom he had known for the better part of twenty-five years. He could talk to her as easily as he could talk to anyone. He was more than glad to accept the invitation.

Edith couldn't suppress her smile as she turned around toward Dave. "Tinker Bellum thinks that you have come courting me, Dave!" she said with a laugh.

Dave's eyebrows shot up, and then his broad face broke out in a great big grin. He began to chuckle until he was laughing so hard that his sides shook and his eyes were watering.

"He thinks…he thinks…he thinks that I'm…," but he couldn't finish because he was laughing too hard.

Edith had joined in at first, but soon the humor of the situation had vanished, and her face took on a more contemplative look. In truth, over the past couple of weeks, she had been doing a great deal of what some liked to refer to as "soul searching".

She didn't know if she would go that far—but since the night of the community meeting over at the school gymnasium, Edith Whittington had been doing a lot of thinking—re-evaluating her life.

What was her purpose here in this community? What were her priorities? Was she motivated by greed? Ambition? Concern for others? Or had she ever shown concern for anyone other than herself?

What kind of person was she? What kind of person had she been twenty years ago? She knew, as we all do, that no one remains the same through the years—everyone changes.

Still, she knew the Edith Whittington who came to that meeting would have been an unwelcome stranger to the young girl who had married Tom Whittington almost twenty-five years ago.

She was a miserly, stingy, bitter woman—and with that realization came another, also; she didn't want to live the rest of her life that way—and somehow, she would find a way to grow past the bitterness that had formed a shell around her heart.

She was smart enough to know that her life could be so much better if she changed, and strong enough of character to make that change happen.

Edith knew that Dave Tompkins was as old of a friend as she had, and that if she couldn't gain his approval, then what chance would she have of ever changing anyone's mind?

For some reason, acceptance was more important to her right now than she could ever remember it being. It was this which had caused her to become more reflective lately.

Dave seemed to notice her mood had changed, though it was some time before he was able to wipe the tears from his eyes. With some effort, Dave controlled himself finally.

"Well," he explained, as if he thought perhaps Edith had only lost the absurdity of the situation somehow. "It just seems kinda funny that anyone would think you and I…you know…"

But then he stopped himself as he realized Edith didn't think it was funny at all.

"And why not?" she asked. "Am I such an old, mean, miserly woman who you can't see yourself courting? I know what other people think of me, Dave." She was sitting across the kitchen table from him now.

He reached his big, calloused hand across the table and put it over Edith's small one. She was so startled by the move that she actually had to catch her breath.

That was something which had never happened before. Her eyes seemed to grow larger, with obvious surprise—but she didn't move her hand.

He looked her in the eyes, and when he spoke to her, it was in the softest, kindest voice she had ever heard. "I don't know—nor do I really care—what other people think about you. I've known you for twenty-five years—and Edith—I know what kind of woman you are."

He cleared his throat, beginning to get a little nervous now that he had dived off into such uncharted territory.

"As far as you being miserly—well, I guess it all depends on what you mean. Sure, you can squeeze a dollar—but I've also seen your generosity. Why, this very minute you're letting people live on your farm rent free. Why?

"Because life has dealt them a hard blow. I know you've probably done some things which have caused people to doubt that you are a kind and generous woman—but I know the truth—because I know you, Edith.

"And as to being 'old', Edith, neither one of us can claim to be anything other than what we are. I don't worry too much about it—and I'd suggest you don't either."

Then his ears got beet red, but he said it anyway. "Edith, as far as I'm concerned, you are—and always have been—a fine-looking woman. And, if I'm not being too forward, Edith, I'd be proud to court you!"

Edith's indignation had evaporated as Dave had talked, and at the end of his little speech her mouth was open a little, and there was a look of wonderment on her face. She couldn't seem to find the words that she needed right then.

When Dave had finished, he sat there for a moment—waiting for some response—wringing his big hands as he did. Finally, thinking the silence that filled the air, like smoke from a clogged flue, meant he had overstepped the boundaries of their friendship, he reached down in the chair sitting next to him, picked up his hat and started walking to the door.

He had almost reached the door when Edith called out behind him, "Dave!"

Dave froze, and then turned to face her, his hat being crushed in a pair of very large, very nervous hands.

"Don't go, Dave—please!"

"Alright, Edith," he said, still not quite understanding what his place was there.

"Come back over here and sit down, please. I need to talk to you about what you just said."

"Alright, Edith," he said again, and made his way back to the chair he had just left.

When she had reseated herself, she looked across the table once more at this big farmer.

"I need to get something straight in my mind, Dave," she began. "Did you just ask if you could court me?" Even at her age, she couldn't help blushing.

Dave was looking down at the table, so he didn't notice the pink on her cheeks. He merely nodded his head.

She waited a moment before asking the next question. "Dave, this is very important to me, so you had better tell me the truth! Do you want my farm?"

His head snapped up. "Want your farm? Why, for the love of God, would I want your farm? I've got a perfectly good farm already! Why, that's the silliest question I ever heard! Want your farm!! Huh!!!"

It was apparent his indignation was real. Edith had her answer, and she smiled to herself, and breathed a sigh of relief.

"Then why?" she asked.

"Why?" he said, puzzled at her question. "Why what?"

"Why, after all of these years, do you suddenly want to court a dried-up old prune like me?"

Dave chuckled a little and said, "The fact is, Edith, I've admired you since the day I first saw you. I was just too scared to say anything then. And then Tom came along and you two were married, and, well, I guess I just started thinking of you as more of a neighbor and friend."

He cleared his throat and looked up at Edith, and then shifted his gaze to the table in front of him again.

"After Tom's death, I guess I had been so long just a friend, that I hadn't considered anything more—and then, well, I am getting a little old to start thinking about matrimony."

"God's honest truth," he continued, "if it hadn't been for Tinker Bellum coming here tonight, I guess I might have kept all of this inside me. I probably would have taken it to the grave. But... well, now you know—so what do you think, Edith?"

Dave looked up from the table as he asked her this, and he saw the tears glistening on the cheeks of this woman before him. He didn't realize it, but he had just given her something she had never believed she would ever have—a man's unconditional love for a woman.

Oh, she had grown to love Tom Whittington over time, but it had been a marriage of convenience—for both of them. She supposed Tom had loved her too—but never like he loved the farm. Tom needed a farm, and the farm needed Tom. The only role available was that of being a husband to the farmer's daughter.

She had known from childhood that she would marry a farmer and that they would run the farm together. As the only heir to the Hope farm this was her expected role.

Just as other girls do, she had dreamed of her handsome prince arriving on his mighty steed to sweep her off her feet. Instead, Tom Whittington had come.

Rather than riding a mighty steed, he had arrived on an old farm wagon pulled by two plow horses. Tom Whittington would never have swept anyone off their feet, but he was young, and he was strong, and he was willing to work. He had the makings of a good farmer and her father had seen advantages she didn't realize at the time.

Up to this moment, she had believed that the closest she would ever get to her handsome prince was Tom Whittington. She had resigned herself to the belief that she was destined to be without what other women had in that respect.

In part, it was that resignation which had caused Edith to become the woman she was.

She dabbed at her eyes with the corner of her apron—drying the streaks which ran down her cheeks. It left flour smudges on her face, giving it an almost girlish look.

She sniffed, and smiled at Dave, and said, "Why, I'd be happy to have you court me, Dave!"

As Edith prepared to go to sleep later that evening, she laid her head down upon her pillow, thinking how fortunate it had been that Tinker Bellum had shown up at her front door while Dave was there.

As her thoughts mingled with sleep, she began to wonder why Katherine hadn't brought that dress to her instead. Her last thought as she was lost to slumber was that if she didn't know better, she would think Katherine and those other women had…

When Dave left that evening, his head was filled with thoughts of the future, the same as any young man might have had when coming home from a night with his girl.

Not even thinking of it, he drove right on past the feed store—and the farmer's weekly meeting—and on out to his farm.

The "old biddies club" had pulled off its greatest triumph!

Chapter
Seventeen

After the evening when Bill Getty had tried to make a fool out of Harley in front of all of us up at the feed store, Bill had surprisingly backed off.

He had never gone so far as offering Harley an apology, but then a person like Bill wouldn't have considered such a thing. That was all right by Harley. He wasn't wanting—or expecting—one.

As time went on, it became apparent what had prompted Bill's animosity toward Harley. Tom Girvan's only child, Alice, a mousy young woman who worked at her father's store, was behind it all. Not intentionally, of course.

Alice was a quiet, timid woman—the kind of woman who was easily overlooked by most men. She spoke little—except to conduct the business of the store—and when she did speak, it was soft and quiet—as though she was afraid that what she said might be heard.

Still, she was nice, and she was young, and she was single—and so the "old biddies club" had been busy trying to get Alice and Harley together for some time. They had gone to dinner together a couple of times—and they enjoyed one another's company—but that was as far as it had gone.

Bill had been trying to catch Alice's eye at the store on Saturdays when he came in from the logging camp, but had not seemed to have been having any luck.

Then one Saturday evening he happened to walk past the diner and, looking through the window, he had seen his Alice eating dinner with Harley. To put it quite simply, it was jealousy that was really behind Bill's feud with Harley—nothing more—nothing less.

Since the evening he had tried to goad Harley into a fight, Bill had noticed the same thing everyone else had—Harley Matthews wasn't interested in any girl other than Etta Prince.

Alice had noticed this also, and had breathed a very soft, very quiet sigh of relief.

It's not that Alice didn't like Harley—because she did. Everybody liked him. It was just that Alice only liked Harley—nothing more. There was someone else, though, who had caught her eye—who had caused her heart to race a little when he came in on Saturday afternoons.

The trouble was, she didn't know how to act charming and interesting and colorful, and so she had just remained quiet and distant and rather bland while he was in the store.

As soon as he would leave, she would bite her lip and wish she had said or done something—anything—to show him she was more than just an uninteresting, overly shy, and socially stunted storekeeper's daughter.

On a Saturday afternoon the bell that hung above the store's front door tinkled, and she looked up to see this young man come in. By now, she knew his routine by heart.

He would putter around, spending his time looking at items that could hardly be thought to interest such a person. Finally, he would raise the courage he needed to take his items up to the counter so he could talk to the young woman who ran the cash register.

This time, however, as the door closed behind him, he walked straight up to the counter that separated the customers from the clerk and stopped. He stood there, just looking at Alice, until she finally spoke—in a soft whisper— "Yes?"

He stood there for a moment longer, gathering his fortitude, and then launched into his business. "Alice, I would like the pleasure of your company for dinner tonight."

He had taken a deep breath before he spoke, and the words had tumbled out—expelled along with his breath—leaving him a little out of wind for a moment.

When he caught his breath once again, he continued, less formally now, "I thought maybe we could get a bite to eat over at the diner—you know—if it's okay with you." He gave her a weak, but hopeful, smile.

Her eyes, which had gotten larger and more apprehensive as he spoke, had stayed on the ledger which was lying on the counter in front of her. Her lack of a response could only be interpreted as a lack of interest in his invitation, and merely waiting for him to finish and leave.

At least that's how Bill Getty read it—but Bill had trouble reading the menu over at the diner, much less the intricacies of a woman's heart.

So, he stood there, licking his dry lips, shifting his weight from his right foot to his left, and back to his right again, and waited for her to reply. This was a different Bill Getty than usually came into the store.

The other Bill Getty would come in, look around till he found something to bring to the cash register, and then make some funny comment concerning something irrelevant and unimportant. He'd usually wait a few seconds, and then he would turn around and leave, saying that he'd see her next time he was in.

Finally, she looked up. Bill was still there—he hadn't left. She didn't know what she should do—or what she should say. And so, she swallowed hard, and with obvious fear and trepidation showing in her eyes, she finally said, "Okay".

From that moment on, it was clear to everyone that Alice was Bill Getty's girl—and that Etta was Harley's. Also, from that time on, the trouble between Bill and Harley disappeared as quickly as fog lifting out of a canyon on a sunny October morning.

Although Harley and Bill never became fast friends, there was never any animosity between them either—and in times to come, each learned that he could depend upon the other if the need should arise.

As shy as Alice Girvan had been at the beginning of their courtship, we were all surprised at how quickly she gathered herself and took control of the relationship that had begun that day at the front counter of her father's store.

She seemed to be fully aware of what she was getting when she entered into it, and set about to salvage the best parts of Bill, while at the same time working at disposing of the worst. She went about the task like a woman tearing weeds out of her prized flower bed.

To begin with, Bill's days as a logger—living in the rough confines of a logging camp—were a thing of the past. After a brief, and rather forceful, discussion with her father, she was able to impress upon him that this "wild, uncivilized, and probably untrainable logger"—as Tom Girvan referred to Bill—was probably going to be his son-in-law someday.

She further explained to her father—as he sat with his face resting in his hands, and a look of defeat in his eyes—that it would be in his best interest to see that Bill receive the necessary education and training to work in, and someday be able to take over, the running of the family business.

It wasn't all that difficult to convince Bill of the need to leave a career of arising before daybreak each morning in a cold room with a number of other dirty, odiferous men, and prepare himself for a long day hanging onto the working end of a crosscut saw.

Bill wasn't a fool, and could easily see the advantages of town living, and a job that didn't require that a man freeze in the winter, roast in the summer, and be soaking wet most of the rest of the year.

Besides, Tom Girvan's store was just catty-corner to the tavern, where Bill was used to spending much of his time on his brief stays in town on Saturdays.

Although this was a problem which Alice had foreseen, Bill was not as easily trained as she might have hoped. Still, as the days and weeks passed, Bill was spending more and more time at the store, and less and less time at Jim Clancy's tavern.

Chapter Eighteen

Fall blustered and blew, and before we knew it, it had turned into winter. As December wore on, I began to feel the excitement that always came during the holiday season.

There had never been such a thing as presents around our house on Christmas; at least not that I could remember—and certainly not since Daddy had left, and Mama had taken the consumption—but there seemed to be just something about all the things that surround the season that had always gotten me to feeling good. It still does.

By now, Etta and Lucy had moved out of Harley's place and into a small cottage that had become available, so as to allow Harley to move back into his house again.

The old chicken house was fine during the summer months, and most of the fall, but in the latter part of October the hard freezes began, and Harley would have frozen to death out there, with no heat in that drafty old building.

Harley had invited Etta and Lucy, and Granddaddy and me, to come and celebrate with him on Christmas day. Sometime during the week before, he had made a deal to buy a cured ham off of Paul Anders.

With that ham in the oven when Granddaddy and I got there, I do believe that I had never smelled an aroma so heavenly in the entire twelve years I had been alive—nor have I since. I doubt I ever will.

There were mashed potatoes, gravy, green beans—and some sweet potatoes with thick, sweet, gooey stuff on top of them. I found out later that those were called marshmallows. I ate like I would never eat again.

I ate and ate until my belly was round and tight as a tick. I could hardly even move afterward.

After dinner, Harley went into the bedroom and came back out with a gift for each of us.

"Santa Claus stopped by here last night," he said, with a grin on his face, "and he brought these presents for you."

I had gotten to where I really didn't believe in Santa anymore. I don't know if I ever did. What I knew was if he did exist, he sure hadn't ever stopped at my house before. The parcel I held in my hands right then was the first Christmas present I believe I had ever received.

Still, I couldn't help teasing a little. "Why did he drop our presents off at your house, Mr. Matthews?" I asked him. "Why didn't he take them to our houses?"

Everything in the house seemed to stop, and everybody looked at Harley then, waiting for an answer. Etta and Granddaddy had amused looks on their faces as they cast their eyes on Harley. Lucy, I believe, looked as though she were truly curious.

Harley looked a little worried for a minute, but recovered nicely by saying, "When I told the old fellow that you would all be here today, and that he could just leave them with me to pass them out, he appeared to be happy to do so—said it saved him from making two more stops."

I can't begin to remember what anyone else got for their Christmas present on that day, but I'll always remember what I got. Harley had wrapped it with brown butcher paper and had tied it with a piece of old bailing twine. He'd stuck a holly twig under the twine for decoration.

I had that string and paper ripped off that Christmas present quicker than lickety-split. Just because I'd never had one before didn't mean that I didn't know what to do once I got my hands on it.

As the paper fluttered to the floor—and I gazed down at what was left in my hands—I know that my mouth must have been hanging open. I couldn't say anything for a minute. I'd never imagined that getting a Christmas present would be this good!

Right there in my own two hands—freshly oiled, rolled tight, and tied with a pigging' string—was Harley's old baseball glove. Harley had used this when he played professional ball. I couldn't believe my eyes.

I looked at him, and I know that doubt must have shown in my eyes, because he said to me, "It's yours now, Will. A good ball player deserves to own a good mitt. Yes," he said, smiling, "it's yours now. If you take good care of it, it'll last you a good long while."

Then he nodded at me, saying, "Untie that string for a minute. There's more inside."

I undid the piece of string that bound the mitt so tightly, and as it came open, a baseball fell out of the pocket. I reached down quickly with my right hand and snatched it from mid fall before it could hit the floor.

I turned it over and over—not a blemish anywhere—a brand new, white leather baseball. I don't know if I'd ever seen one that was new before.

I had finally closed my mouth and could speak once again. "Harley! Really? It's mine? Oh, Harley! I promise I'll take good care of it. I'll be real careful with it! Maybe I ought to just show it to the boys, and then put it up and use my old mitt." I was talking faster with each sentence I spoke.

Harley sat there listening to me rattle on excitedly, chuckling to himself—but then said, "No, Will, this is a gift that needs to be used. A baseball mitt is made to play ball with. It was never meant to sit on a shelf in some old closet, gathering dust. This one's been doing that for far too long now."

It was around this time that we all realized that our town constable was busy building an addition onto his house—a fact which struck everyone as a little strange, for Homer Long had been widowed for several years now, and lived by himself.

That being the case, it was an oddity that he was expanding a house that had seemed to be plenty big enough for one man for as long as I could remember. As the holidays passed, and the new year began, we all soon understood.

Back during the late fall of the year, after the bull had sat on Charlie—and Tinker Bellum had tried to gain the farm from Charlie's widow by whatever methods he thought necessary—Homer had been called upon to intervene.

After Charlie Baker's widow had refused Tinker's advances, he had allowed his anger to override any good judgment he might have once possessed; and had bellowed and raged and had said things—some of which were meant to discredit the Baker's reputation—and other things which, if taken a certain way, could be seen as threatening.

Edna Baker would not have worried about any of this had her husband still been alive. Charlie would have taken care of a pipsqueak like Tinker Bellum.

Fate, however, had taken that security away from her and so she told her oldest boy, Alvin, to stop by the constable's office the next day after school and ask him if he could come out to the place—that there was something that she needed to talk to him about.

Alvie was a boy who had already seemed to be old before his time—and seemed to be even more so now that he was the man of the family—being the oldest of the Baker children.

The next day he made sure to stop by Homer's office after school let out to pass along his mother's message. He had the other three Baker children with him, the youngest—Lenny—who was just in first grade, and the others scattered in between.

Homer listened to Alvie and merely nodded his head when the boy had finished. He then turned and walked into the back room that he had been in when the Baker children had entered his office. Alvie shrugged his shoulders and turned to usher the other littler Bakers on toward home when Homer reappeared with his hat and coat.

"Where are you kids going?" he asked them. "If you want a ride home, you shouldn't be so quick to take off. Just wait around for a minute or two."

He shook his head and rolled his eyes to the ceiling. "Kids!" he exclaimed, as if he had raised a dozen or so of them. In fact,

Homer and his wife had never been blessed with children. He was around them so seldom anymore, they almost made him nervous.

A couple of the younger children giggled, and Alvie smiled. It might have been the first smile to cross Alvie's lips since his father had died—maybe even longer than that. Homer put his hat and coat on and turned to the children.

"Let's load up!" he called out. Homer smiled, thinking to himself how he sounded more like a rancher taking some animals to the auction than a lawman. Well, he guessed he was neither right now. It looked as if he would be posing as a school bus driver.

Homer had been both rancher and lawman in his forty-odd years of life. He'd started out as a cowboy, and had herded his share of cattle and horses, but events beyond his control pushed him into the life of a lawman.

Though he had served in a variety of capacities in the law, he was content to work here, in this small northwest town, for the rest of his life.

The town supplied him with an automobile, and so when the children had all squeezed in, tight enough that none could pop out, he pulled out from in front of the town hall and began driving out to the old Whittington place.

Chapter Nineteen

Edna Baker looked up as she heard the sound of Homer's car coming up the long drive toward the house. She was busy getting the evening meal started.

One of the good things about living this kind of life, she had often thought, is that there was never a shortage of good food to eat.

They had fresh vegetables and fruit in the summer and fall, and they canned enough of it to last them through the rest of the seasons. Meat had never been a problem either—until recently.

They had always raised hogs for butchering, as well as a steer or two. They still did, but most of what they were raising now was sold to the butcher in town.

Money had been really short for the last several months, and it didn't look as if that situation was going to change anytime soon.

"We'll make do," she thought to herself, "we always have somehow. The Lord provides."

The car pulled up outside, and she realized who it was—Homer Long—the town sheriff. What in the world?! She had told that boy to stop and tell the sheriff that she had something she wanted to talk to him about—not to bring him home with him.

"Lord!" she thought, as both hands went up to her face, "I must look a fright!"

She rushed from the kitchen to her bedroom, where there was a mirror and a basin with some water in it. There was a cloth there as well; and so, she began to inspect what she saw in the mirror, quickly dabbing here and there with the damp cloth, removing smudges as best she could in the time she had.

When she was finished, she sighed at what she saw reflected back at her. *"Well,"* she thought, *"you can't make a silk purse..."*.

A woman in her late thirties, she, like many people do, had begun to show the wear and tear that comes from life. Now, although she was certainly not the woman of her youth, she also was far from being ready for the grave—and there hadn't been another man in the house since Charlie had died—and that was months ago.

She was suddenly overcome by how much she had missed having a man around. It wasn't the romance, she told herself—as she looked in the mirror for the last time, shaking her head at the final product—it was just the strength and the sense of being able to depend on another that she missed so much.

"Edna Baker," she said, "get hold of yourself. Homer Long hasn't come out here for any other reason than business—and that, only because you sent for him."

She sighed and shook her head at her own girlish foolishness as she went back through the house to the kitchen, where her work still lay undone.

Homer was following the kids into the house, through the back door, as she entered the kitchen. Her hand started to go to her hair to brush it back, and then to the front of the old gingham dress she was wearing—an involuntary motion—which she stopped in mid brush.

A little embarrassed—and a bit out of breath from coming so quickly through the house—she stopped and said, "Hello, Sheriff, there wasn't any need for you to rush out here right away."

She turned to Alvie. "Alvie, didn't I tell you to say that it wasn't so important as to make a hurry out of him coming?"

She had said no such thing, but Alvie just nodded his head and said, "Yes, Mama, I must have forgotten. I'm sorry."

Homer had stepped forward, sweeping off his hat in a grand gesture as he did so. Motioning to young Alvie with it, he said, "I believe he did say something about it not being all that important—but I always figured there was no good reason in putting off an unpleasant task."

He smiled, admiring the quickness of mind he possessed which had allowed him to step up and save Alvie's bacon. He stood there for a moment in the silence that followed until it began to dawn on him what he had just said.

His ears began to turn red, and he coughed a couple of times, and then said, "That's not what I meant. No Ma'am! What I meant was that going out to talk with Bellum is unpleasant—not being out here, with you…that wouldn't be unpleasant," he finished.

He looked up, smiling at the way he'd covered up his blunder—and then noticed that they were all still staring. "And the kids," he hurried to add, "With you and the kids."

He looked around at them, pleased now with how it sounded. They were all still just standing there—staring at him. With uneasiness, he looked from side to side, then up and back down.

In what seemed much longer than it actually was, he stood there, waiting until he noticed, finally, a smile which was forming on Edna's face.

They all seemed a little amused, for that matter, but he was looking mostly at Edna. She was trying to hide the smile that had come to her lips. There wasn't any hiding the smile in her eyes, though.

Finally, she reached out and took the hat from his hands and said, "Well then, sheriff, if we're not too unpleasant after all, come on in and sit down."

She turned to the four children—three boys and a girl. "You kids go on about your chores now. The sheriff and I have some things to talk over." She said it in such a matter-of-fact way that Homer could tell there would be no arguments.

"Now, sheriff," she said, "why don't you sit down over here while I work on getting dinner ready?"

As he sat down, he said, "Call me Homer, Ma'am—if you will?"

"If you'll call me Edna," she returned, over her shoulder.

"It'd be my pleasure, Edna. Now, tell me what it is that Tinker has done this time?"

––––––––––

It was only a few miles from the Bakers to Bellum's place, and Homer's thoughts revolved around how best to solve the issue at hand. Homer's success as a lawman was at least partly due to his philosophy that it was always preferable to be a peace officer than just a keeper of the laws.

This was partially responsible for Homer's jails being empty most of the time. If he could find a reasonable solution to a problem—one that would achieve desired goals for all the parties involved—then Homer bent over backward to make sure that happened.

Over the years, Tinker had caused him to do a lot of bending. Oh, Tinker was a law-abiding citizen of the county, who caused no one any trouble—unless there was something he wanted that he couldn't get.

When that occurred, his methods of attaining what he felt should be his were sometimes unorthodox—even unlawful. Take something away that he had decided was rightfully within his grasp. He could get plain ornery.

That's what had happened with the Bakers. A few months ago, Bellum had tried, by a couple of different methods, to gain the old Whittington place.

Had Bellum not made such a horse's rear end of himself when he had first approached Mrs. Baker—not even trying to conceal that it was the farm he really wanted, and that he would even be willing to marry her in order to get it—he might have been able to buy the farm from her.

As it was, she made it plain to him, and to anyone within earshot, that selling her farm to Tinker Bellum was about as likely as their old milk cow jumping over the moon—and she was a very old milk cow.

Bellum held a grudge like most people hold their child. He fed it often so it could grow strong and was careful to never leave it alone for any length of time. His grudges were very healthy grudges.

Her refusal of his offer of wedded bliss held against her, Bellum had made disparaging remarks about her in front of people down at the feed store a few months back.

Homer had found out about that only after the fact. Dave Tompkins had straightened Tinker out on the spot, telling him that talk like that could wind up getting a person in trouble.

Dave had gone on to tell him that if he heard of any more such talk, he'd go down to the bank and talk to Jason Paulson, the banker, and get him to call Tinker's loans in.

Tinker feared that wasn't just some idle threat. He was having a hard time making his payments as it was right now, and Paulson wouldn't need much talking to.

Homer figured the problem was resolved, and so he told Dave to try and not threaten people with wreck and ruin any-more—and had pretty much forgotten about it—chalking it up to just another one in a long list of things that went into his mental file on Tinker Bellum.

Tinker, though, hadn't forgotten. He had next been rebuffed by Edith Whittington in another attempt to gain the farm through matrimony. Angry now, he was taking it out on everyone he could.

Fortunately, he knew that most folks would not put up with much foolishness out of him. The widow Baker and her children, though, could do little about it, and so he began to concentrate his meanness on them.

The last thing which had happened—what had finally prompted Edna to call upon him—was that one of the Baker's sheep had gotten out. It had pushed itself through a spot in the fence somewhere, and had been feeding in one of Bellum's fields when young Alvie had spied it.

Alvie had gone over onto the Bellum farm to retrieve the animal—as anyone would have—and had been ordered off, at gunpoint, by Tinker.

"I've just come to get our sheep, Mr. Bellum," said Alvie, staring with big eyes at the shotgun in Tinker's hands. "I'm real sorry, Mr. Bellum. I don't know how he could have gotten in here."

"You just turn around and go back the way you came!" said Bellum.

When Alvie made a move toward the ewe, Bellum took a step forward menacingly, and said, "Leave the sheep! She's mine now! She's been in here eating my feed, getting my care—costing me money. If you have the money to pay for all that, then pay me—and then take the animal. If you don't, then get!"

"But, Mr. Bellum…," Alvie began, not understanding. Tinker leveled the shotgun at him. He understood that.

As he left, Alvie heard Bellum say, "Maybe that'll teach your Ma not to be so uppity in the future!"

Alvie walked back empty-handed—but before he went back to tell his mother, he walked the entire fence line, looking for breaks in the fence—any place that looked as though a sheep could squeeze through. As far as he could tell, the fence was solid.

When he returned home and told his mother what had happened, she made up her mind that it was time to get some help. Some things people can handle on their own—some are best left up to others.

Although she had never really gotten to know Mr. Long, the sheriff, she remembered her husband saying that he was a good man and a good lawman.

More than that, he had said, he was a throwback to the old days when what was right and fair was always more valued than what was legal and binding. He'd always said that if there was ever anything he figured he wasn't up to handling on his own, he'd have no problem asking Homer Long to help.

Chapter Twenty

Homer pulled up in front of the small rundown house at the Bellum place. There was more than enough work to be found on a farm—especially for a man alone—but it sure seemed to Homer that Tinker could find time to at least clean it up a little.

He'd been out to almost all the places in this part of the county a time or two, and all the other farmers found time for a little sprucing here and there. All but Bellum. Well, he figured, it's his place.

It was still early evening and Bellum was just coming back from the barnyard, carrying a two-gallon pail of milk in each hand. At least he wouldn't have to go track him down, he thought.

"Hello, Tinker," Homer said.

"Sheriff," Bellum replied. He always spoke in a manner which made a person think he was in a hurry—and mad, too. His words came out short and clipped—as though they were bitten rather than spoken. He was a small man—perhaps taller than Homer—but slight of build.

His face always seemed to have a week's growth of beard—never more, never less—and Homer, who shaved each morning, had always wondered how that was even possible.

He was always dressed in a flannel shirt and bib overalls; and as far as Homer could tell, they very well could be the only pair he owned—and there might be some of the original dirt still on them from the first day he pulled them on. Smelled like it too.

"I need to talk to you, Tinker," he said.

"I'm busy. Come back later."

"You're not so busy you can't talk, Tinker." He fell into step with the man.

"Suit yourself," he said, as he marched on with his load.

"I hear that you had a little run in with Alvie Baker the other day—something about a sheep. Is that so?"

"That his name? Yeah, I had to chase him off my place—caught the thief trying to steal one of my sheep."

"That's not how Alvie tells it, Tinker," Homer said. "Alvie says that you threatened him with a gun."

"Well, what am I supposed to do when a boy comes sneaking around here stealing livestock? If I see a varmint trying to steal one of my animals, what do you think I'm going to do—let him take it?"

"No," said Homer, "I expect you to come into town and fill out a complaint—if that 'varmint' is a man—or a fourteen-year-old boy."

"That's the difference between me and you, sheriff. You handle things your way; I'll handle things mine. Now, don't let me keep you."

Homer looked at him for a moment, and then turned around and went back to his car.

Tinker looked at him as he was leaving, then said, "Humph!" and turned back to his chores. The next thing he heard was the lever action on the sheriff's 30-30 rifle as Homer put a shell in the chamber.

Tinker stopped, sat the buckets down, and said, "What do you think you're doing, Long?"

"Why, I'm 'handling things my way,'" Homer replied, and he pulled a set of handcuffs out of his coat pocket. "Turn around, Bellum! Put your hands behind your back!"

"Wait, a minute! You can't do this!" Bellum exclaimed, astonished by Homer's actions.

He took a step toward Homer, and when he did, the short, stout sheriff—in a move that was so fast that Bellum didn't have the time to protest—had him down on his belly, and handcuffed.

Homer had been throwing calves at branding time when he was barely fourteen years old and Bellum didn't weigh nearly as much as some of those calves, nor did he put up anywhere near the fight. If he hadn't had the cuffs with him, he would have been just as comfortable using a pigging string on him.

"Now," said Homer, "I can take you in and let you stay as a guest of the city until the JP comes by next week, or we can settle this right here, right now. Which is it going to be? It's your choice, Tinker. Would you rather sit in jail or have a nice talk right now so that we can settle the issue?"

Bellum blustered. He tried to say something, but he was too mad, and when he got his voice back, it wasn't a 'nice talk' voice that he was using.

Homer shrugged his shoulders and said, "If that's the way you want it, it's alright with me. Do you want me to turn your animals loose so they can get to water and feed while you're gone?"

Though he was seething inside, Bellum used considerable will power, and was finally able to gain some control over his senses.

"Alright! Alright, Sheriff!" he said. "I won't be any trouble. Just get these things off me."

"That's more like it, Tinker," Homer said with a smile on his face. He had never raised his voice, nor seemed to have even become excited.

As he removed the man's shackles, he said, "I always like it when people are willing to work things out peaceably."

"Now," he continued, "back to the matter at hand. Let's take a look at the sheep, Tinker." Bellum frowned, looked at the ground for a moment, and then looked off to the east.

"Where's the sheep, Tinker?" This time, Homer's voice had a little edge to it.

Bellum winced a little. "I ate it," he mumbled.

"You what?" Homer exclaimed.

"I ate it," Tinker said again, louder. "Well, some of it, anyway. The rest of it is hanging up in the shed around back, cooling out."

Homer shook his head and sighed. "I'll tell you what I'm going to do, Tinker. I'm going to file this under "theft" in the office in town. Then I'll put that file away—for now; but if I ever hear of you so much as looking at any of the Baker family, I'll pull that file out and throw your sorry rear end in jail. Do you understand me, Tinker?"

Bellum nodded his head, a surly look on his face.

"I can't hear you!" the sheriff said with authority.

"Yeah, I understand."

"Good—and one last thing—you will pay the widow Baker for the cost of that sheep, and I want you to get what's left of it and put it in your flatbed right this minute, and take it to the Bakers."

"Sheriff—" he began to protest, but Homer gave him a look that threw water on whatever fire he might have been building. He shut his mouth and headed toward the shed to get the remains of the sheep.

———————

As he drove away from Bellum's place, Homer couldn't help thinking of how old Tinker sure put him in mind of some horses he'd been around in his younger days. Some just had a better disposition than others.

He had broken a lot of horses when he was a young man, and some of them turned out to be docile creatures, while others were highly spirited—but there were a few that were just downright mean.

Oh, sure, you could ride a horse like that—and do just fine—as long as it knew who was boss; but you never turned your back on a mean horse. If you did, you were liable to get a plug bitten out of you somewhere.

Yeah, he thought to himself, Tinker was a lot like some mean old horses he had known. It would pay to keep his eye on him.

As he drove back toward town, he decided he would stop by the Baker place so he could settle Edna Baker's mind on all of this foolishness.

"That Edina Baker, now," he mused to himself. "It's a wonder that I hadn't noticed before, but she's a right handsome looking woman—good woman, too.

"It's too bad that she and these kids have been saddled with this. The farm's too big—too much work." He shook his head as he turned off the county road and onto the drive that led up to the house.

Edna came to the door when Homer knocked, and, as he swept off his hat, she opened the door a little wider in a gesture of welcoming, and invited the sheriff inside.

"We were just sitting down to dinner, Homer," she said. "We'd be pleased if you would join us."

Tempted by the invitation, as well as the welcome aroma that came from whatever was for dinner, Homer looked past her at the children gathered around the old oaken table. There were two empty chairs—Edna's and what had served as Charlie's not all that long ago.

It was almost as though Charlie was expected to show up at any time—come in and sit down with his family. Homer didn't know if it was a proper thing to be doing—sitting down at another man's table, with the other man's family, eating the other man's food.

He saw the children were all looking at him expectantly. For what, he didn't know. "No ma'am," he said. "I just wanted to stop by and let you know everything is settled now with Tinker."

"Nonsense!" she said. "You haven't had your evening meal yet, and we have more than enough! Now, give me your hat and go sit down while I get another plate." She reached out and took the hat from his hands, hanging it on a peg on the wall by the back door.

"Probably Charlie's peg, too!" thought Homer. When he stood there, as if trying to decide, she said, "Go on now! Your dinner will get cold."

Homer finally decided that, as she already had possession of his hat—and the food did smell awfully inviting—he might as well do as she said. Besides, he hadn't been ordered around like that since his wife had been gone.

He'd kind of missed that. She used to boss him around a lot—inside their home. Anything outside the house was his to be in charge of—but the house had always been her domain. He supposed it had been the same with the Bakers.

"Yes, Ma'am," he said, as he went past her to the two remaining chairs and sat down. The children were all grinning, and he figured it was probably fun for them to see their mama scold someone other than themselves.

Even Alvie seemed to enjoy the little scene—though a smile didn't really come to his face. Smiles rarely came to Alvie's face these days—but Homer sensed he was pleased, none-the- less.

"You can expect to see Tinker drive up pretty soon," Homer said, as she set the plate and silverware in front of him. Everything in the room sort of stopped right then.

He figured they might be a little uneasy at the thought of Bellum coming over here after all that he had said and done, so he explained, "He's going to bring the cost of the sheep over—and what's left of it."

"What's left of it?" Alvie said. "What do you mean?"

Homer turned to Alvie and said, "Well, it appears that Mr. Bellum thought he ought to dispose of the evidence—but he was too practical, or too cheap, to just bury the thing. He was trying to eat his way through it."

He reached for another biscuit. "Only got started on it though—so he figured that the neighborly thing would be to bring the rest over and share with you good people."

That did raise a smile to Alvie's face—and his mother's as well. "He figured it would be 'neighborly', did he?" she said. "Well, that would be a first."

Just as she spoke, they heard the sound of Bellum's old flat-bed truck as it pulled up outside.

Edna arose and started for the door and then turned back to the table. "Homer," she said, "would you mind…?"

"Not at all, ma'am," Homer said with a smile.

He got up from the table, and they both went out on the porch as Bellum was getting out of his rig.

Tinker took the remains of the sheep's carcass to the porch and deposited it there. He looked from one to the other, and there was a sullen anger that was hard to miss; but he said nothing other than "Here!" as he put the money in Edna's hand.

Then he went back and got in his truck and drove away.

Edna's mouth was hanging open in wonder, and she turned to Homer and said, "Why, never in all my born days did I think I'd ever see the likes of that! Sheriff, I'd like to thank you for all that you did for us here. Without your help, I doubt that this would have ever turned out this well."

"I thought I asked you to call me Homer."

"I wasn't thanking 'Homer'," she replied. "I was thanking the sheriff."

Homer stood there a moment, chewing on what she had said, and then he cleared his throat and said, "Edna, do you suppose it might be all right if one of us comes out to see you once in a while?"

"I doubt I'll be needing to see the 'sheriff' again," she said, "but I'd be pleased if you came out to see me, Homer—anytime you want to."

She turned then, and smiling at Homer in the growing dusk of the evening said, "In fact, if you would like, Homer, you can come to dinner tomorrow evening. I believe we'll be having mutton, if that's okay."

Once we had heard a little of all of this, it was pretty easy to understand the new addition which was being built onto Homer's house. Homer was going to be a father—four times over!

.

Chapter
Twenty-One

To the amazement of us all, Dave Tompkins turned out to be a regular romantic. Maybe not a Valentino, but still… it was on Valentine's Day that he proposed marriage to Mrs. Whittington—although that may have been purely coincidental. The day, not the proposal itself.

The wedding—was to take place toward the middle of March. It was sure to be an event to rival any that our small community had witnessed in its nearly one hundred years of existence.

This was not because of its size or pomp, though it would be bigger than any event of its sort in many years. It wasn't because everyone had such a fondness for Dave Tompkins, though we all did.

No, it was from the sheer amazement of it all. It had happened so quickly that we were still completely astounded by it. No person in this part of the county would even think of missing a thing like this.

It was like when Neil Armstrong stepped onto the surface of the moon a few years ago. Nobody wanted to miss the first man setting foot on the moon.

We all watched with feelings of awe, amazement, and gladness, and a little disbelief when Armstrong stepped down onto the surface of another world. It was much the same feeling we all had at the approaching wedding.

The entire community was invited to celebrate the joining of these two old friends in the state of matrimony. Because of the expected number of friends and acquaintances, it was decided that after the wedding, a reception would be held at the old Hope Valley Grange Hall.

The change we witnessed in Dave was stunning. Everybody had liked Dave—even when he was trying to keep from choking on words that couldn't seem to get past his own throat when a woman approached him from time to time. The fact was, this had only added to his unique, and somewhat charming, personality.

Yet as amazing as that was to each of us—the transformation which took place in Edith Whittington was even more remarkable.

Maybe it was because of how it affected us all.

I mean, we had known Dave to be a good man when he was tongue-tied, and we fully expected him to be the same good man now that he had pulled that knot free. He had gone from being a bashful, inarticulate, confirmed bachelor to a confident, almost loquacious groom-to-be.

Edith, however, was a different story. For years we had been under the impression that Edith Whittington was a bitter old woman who would rather be left alone.

It seemed to us she had been content to just remain in her house, or at the school, attending to her own business—and expecting everyone else in town to do the same. She was a bit like old Ebenezer Scrooge in that book by Dickens.

And we hadn't misjudged her either. She had been all of that. What most of us didn't realize, though, was that she was more than that as well.

As things progressed, we came to see more of what Dave had known for many years. Edith Whittington was a kind, loving friend—though one who had long ago withdrawn herself into her own interests in an attempt to escape her troubles.

Dave had breached the wall she had built around herself, and now she was free to enter into the accepting arms of our town.

Had it not been for Dave Tompkins, Edith would probably have died a miserable, sad old woman. Now, however, she was beginning to involve herself in the things those other women of the town did.

Edith was now an accepted member of "the old biddies club" on Saturday evenings. She visited with other women in town—and out on the farms as well. She and Katherine Anders seemed to have struck up a fast and strong friendship.

Even I had to admit that I might have been a little harsh in my original assessment—though for a while, at least, I wondered what had happened to Dave's judgment.

In the end, though, it was obvious even to me, she had truly become a valuable part of our little community, and the only woman who could ever have caused Dave Tompkins to get past his lifelong insecurities.

Everyone seemed to figure that anyone who could do that had to be alright. So, finally, even I said it was OK.

———————————

A couple of days before the wedding, a stranger came to town. He was driving a late model car, wore nice clothes (though not too nice), and was friendly (though not overly so)—like a salesman might be, except he wasn't selling anything.

No, he was looking for something—or someone, I should say.

He began asking questions around town—discretely at first—about a sister of his who he had lost touch with years ago. He had been serving in the military, he said, and had only recently been discharged after ten years of service.

During his time away, he said, his parents had died and his younger sister had moved on. He didn't know where she was and was trying to find her. He had heard she might have moved north—into Oregon, or maybe even Washington. Her name was Etta Johnson, he said.

Maybe small towns are just naturally suspicious of strangers—or maybe it was because, although his clothes were nice, and his manner was friendly, his eyes just didn't seem to make a person feel like opening up and sharing.

Whatever the case, when asked about a woman named Etta Johnson, people just stared at him blankly and told him they didn't know of anyone by that name—never even heard of anyone by that name. They also didn't volunteer any information outside of what he had asked.

Not that people necessarily thought the man was actually looking for Etta Prince—though the time of her and Lucy's coming to Hope Springs did coincide with the time frame the man gave of his sister's disappearance.

It wasn't really that at all. No, it was just that they didn't figure their Etta was any of his business—and they figured there was no good reason to send the man out to Etta's asking a lot of fool questions of her.

Small towns can get a little protective of their citizens. Besides, Etta had been here for several months now, was well liked, and had mentioned nothing about a brother. It was obvious to everybody that this was some other Etta.

On the day of the wedding, Tinker Bellum came to town. This being a Saturday, it was not an unusual thing—as he would often need to come in to buy supplies for the coming week. Tinker was the only farmer who was in town that day to buy supplies.

All the other farmers were home, getting their chores done ahead of time so they could attend the wedding and the reception later that evening.

There would be dancing and laughing—as well as a little men's talk outside; and no doubt some things kids weren't supposed to know about.

Everyone was invited—even Tinker. His pride was still pretty sore, though. He felt that Dave Tompkins had sneaked in and stolen that farm while his back was turned. If they thought he would go and wish them well on their marriage, they could think again.

"Yeah, I'll wish them something," he thought to himself. "I'll wish them all the trouble they deserve—that's what I wish."

He was just throwing the last sack of ground barley feed onto the back of his old flatbed truck when a stranger approached him. Ignoring the man, Tinker walked around to the driver's side and opened the door to get in. The man spoke quickly, before he could step up into the cab.

"Excuse me, sir—I wonder if I could have a moment of your time."

Tinker looked at the man with belligerent eyes. "Well, what do you want? You're wasting my time here!"

"Yes, sir," the man replied. "I just wanted to ask a couple of questions."

He paused, but then quickly continued as he saw the impatience growing in the man who stood on the truck's running board.

"I've been looking for my sister, and I have reason to believe that she may have passed through your town. I would like to ask if you might have heard of, or seen, anything of her. Her name is Etta Johnson."

"Never heard of her!" he snapped back at the stranger as he began to climb into the truck. He paused, his left foot still on the running board.

"Wait a minute—how much is it worth to you to find this 'sister' of yours?"

The stranger's eyes narrowed as he saw that this dumb farmer had shrewdly seen through his little ruse. "Ah," he said, half to himself. "I see that you're not as stupid as the rest of these rubes around here."

"I'm not stupid at all. How much?"

"Fifty dollars—if it's the right woman."

Bellum nodded. "Alright. I don't know if she's the one you're after, but there is an Etta that lives here in town. She doesn't go by Johnson though—it's Prince—and she has a little girl."

The stranger allowed himself a smile as he listened to Bellum's description. It gave him a sort of sinister look. "Where can I find her?"

"I have no idea," said Bellum. "Now, give me my money and let me get on with my business."

"In due time, my friend—if she proves to be the one I'm looking for."

He thought for a minute and then turned back to Bellum. "Who, in this miserable excuse for a town, would know where I can find this woman? If I can just see her—or the girl—I will know. Then you can get your money."

"Ask anybody in town—they can tell you," replied Bellum.

"I've already asked everybody in town—all that I've gotten so far is stonewalling. I doubt anyone is going to offer up anything now."

"There's one place I know she will be—a little later on," Bellum said. Then he explained about the wedding and the gathering afterwards.

"If you want my opinion, that'll be your best chance to see her without raising any questions. It's an open invitation. You can walk in, look around, and leave with no one even noticing. Now, give me my money!"

"When I'm convinced that it is her, my friend—and only when I'm convinced," he told him. "If you want to get paid, then be there when I see for myself. If you're not..." He let the implication hang there with the rest of the sentence.

It aggravated Bellum, being forced into having to be somewhere that he swore he would not go—but fifty dollars was fifty dollars. "I'll be there!" He climbed up into his truck, slammed the door, and drove away.

Chapter
Twenty-Two

The little church was crowded that afternoon as one and all—with the exception of Tinker—came to pay tribute to, and to celebrate, the marrying of Dave Tompkins to the widow, Edith Whittington.

I was there, in the back—with Dell, and Lyle, and a few other boys. We'd all had our hides scrubbed and our shirt collars starched and were about as uncomfortable as twelve-, or thirteen-year-old boys can be. Even at that, I wouldn't have missed it for the world.

As I looked around, I could see heads wagging, and head scratching, and downright looks of amazement. At first, I was sure that everyone must still be trying to cope with the shock of the whole concept of the two of them being together.

Then I saw the bride, as she began to walk down the aisle—with Paul Anders walking beside her, as he was to "give away the bride"—and I realized what those looks of wonder were born of.

This woman who was walking down the aisle, toward Dave and the preacher—she was not Edith Whittington. I mean, she was, of course—but not the same Edith Whittington we all knew.

Gone from her face was the bitterness and severity—the austere countenance which had caused us all to think of her as a mean, hateful old woman with a sour disposition.

As she came down that aisle with Paul Anders, she seemed to glow. I knew she wasn't, really; but the happiness was so clear in everything that was Edith Whittington on that day—at that moment—radiated from her as though she had something warm and bright inside that was escaping into the room around her.

From the sparkle in her eyes to the blushing of her face, from the smile that she couldn't—and didn't seem to want to—suppress, to the spring in her step. If I hadn't known better, I would have sworn this was Edith Whittington's long lost, much younger, and far prettier sister.

I remember it clearly, for in that moment I was to glimpse something I did not fully understand until many years later; something about how the love between a man and a woman is a beautiful thing. And how that beauty is very real and very tangible, and at certain times—like this—can actually be seen with the naked eye.

The children were invited to go to the wedding—but were not necessarily encouraged to attend the reception later that evening. There would be dancing, and toasting, and, when the men went outside, there would be some drinking—and, occasionally, there might even be a fistfight or two.

In other words, it was bound to be a normal Saturday evening dance at the grange hall. It was generally accepted that this was no place for children, and the parents saw it as a good excuse to leave the kids at home and get away for an evening without them.

I, of course, didn't live my life with any such restraints and so when the reception began, I was there—enjoying the fun, but staying back and out of sight as much as possible.

I knew from experience that if I became bothersome, I'd be chased off. If I minded my "p's and q's", I wouldn't have to worry.

After the toasting of the bride and groom, I mostly just stayed outside with the men. As they smoked and drank and told some of the longest, windiest stories ever told, I stood and listened and thought to myself, "This couldn't get any better".

I don't know what I was thinking.

Harley was outside the grange building, along with Jim Clancy, Tom Girvan, Bill Getty, and me. Etta was inside with the other women, serving punch and cookies, and dancing with every man—married or not—who lived within twenty-five miles. Not a one of them wanted to miss an opportunity to dance with the pretty new school teacher.

Harley would have liked to have been in there himself, but with his leg the way it was, dancing was a little too adventuresome. No one could know—not even Harley—what dangers might arise if he got out on the dance floor and started swinging Etta around.

Someone might get hurt (at least that was Harley's excuse), and so he was happy to let Etta enjoy herself while he just watched from the side. For the moment, he had stepped outside to get a breath of fresh air. I had too.

Since Bill had been sparking Tom's daughter, Tom had put him to work in his store. Almost as unbelievable as the transformation which had overtaken the new Mrs. Tompkins was the way Bill had been molded into the model of perfection for a future storekeeper and husband.

We all suspected Bill's ambitions had less to do with becoming a younger version of Tom, and more about creating an impression that he was pointed in that direction. In reality, we all knew that

Bill had never actually been interested in anything more than Tom's daughter, Alice.

We could all see through Bill's pretense at wanting to change from the fun loving, wild logger to the responsible storekeeper and husband. Looking back on it, I suppose Tom could see through it as well. Everybody just sort of quietly laughed about it, though.

We all knew—and Bill would soon find out—that as soon as they were married, Alice would take care of any foolish notions Bill might have fostered up to this point in his life.

She would see that he became the responsible family man and civic leader that her husband ought to be—no matter what Bill might have in mind.

Bill wasn't married yet, though; and so, for at least this evening, he was doing his best to see that he hadn't given up all the vices he had for so long cultivated and so greatly enjoyed. This was no doubt the main reason Tom and Bill had become inseparable of late.

In order to successfully monitor the actions of a man such as his future son-in-law, Tom would need to remain alert as well as resourceful.

Tom should have approached this duty with more caution, though. As much as he wanted to keep Bill on the straight and narrow—socially, at least—there was a fair chance that Bill would drag Tom off into some social miscue.

Tom had gone inside for a moment and had just returned with a glass of punch in each hand—one for himself, and one for his future son-in-law.

While he was inside, Bill had pulled a small flask out of his inside jacket pocket and had taken a quick swig. Capping the flask and wiping the back of his hand across his mouth, he then returned it to its concealed position once more.

He turned to the rest of us and, with a grin, held his index finger to his lips—a signal to us to keep it to ourselves. There was no need, as he had been taking a nip all evening long, and thus far, no one had said a word. It was doubtful we would start now.

Tom returned and handed one of the punch glasses over to Bill. "Now, where was I?" he asked. "Oh, I remember," he continued. "This fellow came into the store yesterday. I didn't like the looks of him—looked like some city man."

He said it as though being from the city was a crime—or at least something to be ashamed of.

"And he was a little too slick—something just not right there. You were there when he came in, weren't you William?" Tom had taken to calling Bill "William" lately.

I suppose he thought it sounded a little more respectable that way. It seemed that Tom was trying just about anything to bring Bill more respectability

"Yeah, I was there," Bill replied. "Tom's right about that. There is something wrong with the guy. Hard to put your finger on, though. Seemed nice—but he was too nosy for my taste."

Bill turned to Harley then. "He was wanting to know about someone—said she was his long, lost sister. Maybe so, but I don't know. He kinda reminded me of these detective types you see in the movies. He's looking for someone alright—but I'd bet it's not his sister."

As Bill was talking, he had casually pulled his flask out of its hiding spot—when Tom wasn't looking—and without missing a beat, had reached behind Tom, who was standing next to him, and poured a liberal amount into Tom's glass of punch.

Then he slipped the flask back into its hiding place as he finished what he was saying. The rest of us were facing Tom and Bill, and so we were watching everything—with our minds only half on what Bill was saying.

I noticed that Jim Clancy was having a difficult time keeping a straight face. I know I was.

Almost absent-mindedly, more to keep the conversation going than for any other reason, Harley asked, "Who'd he say that he's looking for?"

"A woman named Etta Johnson," said Tom, as he took a drink of his gin-laced punch. He smacked his lips and said, as if to himself, "Umm, that's good!"

Harley's attention was jerked fully back to what was being said, and away from the little comedy that was playing itself out before us.

"Who did you say?" he asked.

"He said it was someone named Etta Johnson," said Bill.

"You don't suppose…?" Harley began.

"Oh, I doubt it," said Bill. "Etta is a common enough name, and, besides, if it is her, he's after—she's better off if he didn't find her. Believe me."

"Still…," Harley said, his brow furrowed in thought.

"Ah! Put it out of your mind," Bill counseled. "He's probably gone by now, anyway. If there was trouble, it's gone now."

At that very moment, a car pulled up into the field beside the hall that passed for a parking lot—followed by Tinker Bellum's old flatbed truck. A stranger got out of the car, and Bellum climbed out of the truck.

"I didn't figure old Tinker would come here tonight," observed Tom. "He swore up and down that he'd not give them his blessings, or his good wishes."

"Maybe that's not why he's here," said Harley. "Maybe he's here to cause trouble. Let's make sure that doesn't happen, alright?"

He looked around, and all the men nodded in agreement—even Tom, who under normal circumstances was as kind and peaceful a person as you would ever find. Of course, unbeknownst to him, he had already had more liquor that evening than he had in the past thirty years.

About then, as the two men approached, Bill said, "Hey! That's the man we were just talking about. That's the man who has been hanging around asking all those questions. I wonder what he's doing here."

It didn't take long to find out. Bellum walked up to the open door of the hall, and then back to the corner of the building where the stranger had waited.

We could hear Bellum say to him, "That's her. Out there dancing with Homer Long—the guy in the gray shirt. Now, do I get my money?"

The stranger walked over to the doorway, looked at her for a few seconds, and then he pulled what appeared to be an old photograph from his shirt pocket and looked down at it.

Then he looked back at Etta, being whirled around, with a big smile on her face. Then he walked back to where Bellum had waited.

"All right, Bellum," he said finally, "here's your money." He reached into his other shirt pocket and pulled out a money clip, drawing a fifty-dollar bill from it.

He reached out and handed it to Bellum. "You earned it."

Bellum walked off looking at the new, crisp bill. He probably hadn't seen one like it in a long while. His eyes were narrowing as he walked away, and his face got a weasel-like quality about it.

Bill looked at Harley. "Does he act like he just found his 'long, lost sister'?" Harley shook his head slowly and moved toward where the stranger stood.

"Hey, mister," Harley said.

The man had taken a little black book out of his jacket pocket and had begun to write something in it. "Yeah? What is it?"

"What do you think you're doing?"

"What do you care what I'm doing? It's none of your business what I'm doing," the man replied with an obvious tone of unfriendliness.

"That woman is a friend of mine. That makes it my business." Harley had spoken softly, but I could tell things were beginning to heat up.

"I'll ask you again, what do you think you're doing here?"

By that time, Harley had walked over to where the man stood at the edge of the dim light that shone from the single bulb above the doorway.

The man took a step back out of the light and into total darkness. Harley stepped into the night after him just as Bill yelled, "Don't, Harley!"

We could all hear a dull "whack!"—and then the sound of a body falling to the ground. The stranger stepped back into the light once more—still holding what appeared to be a piece of leather—about a foot long and a half inch thick. It was black and sinister looking—and sort of put me in mind of the man who was holding it. He just smiled at us.

"Your friend should have been a little more courteous. Don't worry though—he'll wake up in a few minutes. I didn't hit him very hard. He'll be alright—except for the headache." He gave a little laugh, as though it was all some kind of joke.

As smart as this man probably was in whatever place he came from, there was a world of things he didn't know about here. One of those things was that Harley Matthews' head was as hard as a piece of granite. Oh, he had been dazed, briefly—but only briefly.

Another thing he wasn't aware of was that just a little farther into the darkness stood the well from which the grange hall got its water supply. That wasn't really all that important to know, I suppose.

What might have been significant, though, was that the crank handle had broken last year, and someone had taken an old, broken axe handle and fashioned it so that it could be inserted into the crank in place of the old, broken handle. When not in use, it stood propped up against the side of the well.

I suppose the other piece of vital information which he didn't have—but he soon came to find out—was that, when motivated, Harley could swing an axe handle like a ballplayer could swing a bat.

We didn't know it either, I guess, and were taken completely by surprise when, right in the middle of the man's little laugh, we heard a dull "whump!"—and then the stranger just collapsed into a limp heap on the ground.

And then Harley took a step forward that brought him into the light, axe handle still in hand.

"Well, I hit him hard!" he said. "Maybe not as hard as I could, but I hit him hard enough. He ought to be out for a while."

Bill whistled and said, "Remind me never to get on the wrong side of you, Harley!" to which Harley reminded him he had already tried to do so once before.

Tom, the gentlest of souls, was still having a hard time getting past what the stranger had done to Harley, and couldn't even begin to imagine what Harley had just done. If he hadn't seen it with his own two eyes, he would never have believed it. Even yet, it didn't seem possible to Tom.

"Harley! What have you done, boy?" he said in almost a whisper.

"Now, Tom," Bill said, "it's not nearly as bad as what you're thinking. Harley just brought an end to a discussion that was getting a little out of hand. All that we're going to do is to take him back over to his car so he can sleep it off for a little while, and then when he wakes back up, he can leave, and that will be the end of it."

Harley and Bill went over to where the man laid, each taking one end of him, and packed him over to his car.

Harley looked at Bill and said, "Bill, you know as well as I do that this won't be the end of this. When he wakes up, he's going to be mad. I just don't want him taking it out on Etta."

"I've been thinking about that," said Bill. "He's not going to wake up…"

Harley's head swung around, and he said, with shock in his voice, "Bill! I won't be a party to that kind of thing. I'm surprised that you would even think of it yourself."

Bill couldn't help laughing. "You didn't let me finish, Harley. He'll wake up—he's just not going to wake up here. I've got a plan!"

About then, there was a commotion out in front of the hall. Tinker Bellum had returned. He was in a belligerent mood. He'd been drinking some—though he didn't need liquor to cause him to be difficult. Bellum just had that sort of nature.

Jim Clancy was trying to keep him from entering the hall, and when we reached them, Bill pulled out the blackjack which he'd just taken off of the stranger, and whacked Tinker across the back of the head. Bellum dropped like a steer on butchering day.

"Oh, my God!" said Tom.

The poor man had had quite a night so far. I thought for a minute that he might actually faint right then and there; but he regained his composure finally, and said, "Bill, what in the world are you doing? You can't just go around hurting people like that!"

We all noticed it was no longer 'William'; it was just 'Bill' now.

"Oh, he's not hurt," said Bill. "At least not bad hurt. Anyway, he was about to go in there and spoil Dave's and Edith's night. Couldn't just stand here and let that happen, could I?"

"Well…" Tom began. He was beginning to soften a little. "But what are we going to tell the law?"

"I don't know, Tom," cut in Clancy, "what are you going to tell the law? The rest of us don't have anything to tell—how about you? It's a mighty poor thing when a man's future father-in-law is thinking about getting him into trouble with the law—especially over a trivial matter like this."

He had put extra emphasis on "father-in-law".

It was well known that, although Bill Getty was no prize, it was unlikely Alice Girvan would get many more chances at matrimony. It wasn't as if the young suitors had been fighting their way to her doorstep.

Unless he wanted to continue supporting his daughter for the rest of his life, he had better be willing to make some concessions. Tom seemed to understand this only too well.

"Alright, Jim," he said with a sigh of resignation. "I don't like it—but I see your point."

Point won or not, there was still the immediate problem of two unconscious bodies that would awaken sometime—and when they did, it would be like the time Lyle and I were taking turns shooting our slingshots at a hornet's nest.

They were confused for a minute, but as soon as they got their bearings, we wished we were somewhere else.

The next best thing to our being somewhere else when these two men woke up would be for them to be somewhere else. Bill had figured that one out a long time ago. So had I (the hornet thing). Harley was beginning to see the light, as well.

Jim Clancy didn't care one way or the other, as he had only been a bystander, mostly. And Tom? Tom had wandered back inside the hall and sat down next to the punch bowl. He reloaded his glass, took a sip, and wondered why the punch tasted so ordinary.

It had been a lot better earlier.

Chapter
Twenty-three

"Well?" said Harley, when Tom had gone back into the reception area. "What's your plan? It had better be a good one, because the way it looks, we might be in a bit of trouble here. The law might even get involved, Bill."

Bill took in Harley with a sideways grin, winked at me, and said, "If I can talk Clancy here into getting involved with a couple of dangerous desperadoes for just a little while, I think we can maybe salvage the evening for everybody—with a little luck."

He turned to Clancy. "Jim, do you think you can drive Bellum's old truck?"

"Sure, I can, Bill," Clancy replied. "Where do you want me to take it?"

"We're going to take these two somewhere so they can sleep it off—but not so they'll be close enough to cause any trouble when they wake up."

Bill turned back toward Harley and me. "Harley—do you think you can drive that man's car?"

"I don't think so, Bill—not with this bum leg of mine. I'd probably just wind up putting us off in a ditch. Why don't you drive it yourself?"

Bill shook his head and said, "No, I've got to drive Tom's old car. We've got to have a way of getting back here, you know."

I spoke up then. "I can drive it for you, Mr. Getty. I'm a good driver!"

"Yeah, I'll bet you are!" snorted Bill. Then he looked at me again and said, "You really think you can drive that man's car, Will?"

"You better believe I can!" I shot back, with more bravado than I had any right to. "If you can get it started for me," I finished, with a little less confidence.

It evidently suited Bill, because he reached over, tousled my head, and said, "That's good enough for me." I wished people would quit doing that.

Then he said, "We better hurry and get this show on the road. Who knows when these two yah-hoos might wake up?"

Bill's plan was simple, and if it had worked, it would have been effective enough—at least we had hoped it would. Foss Tilman's sawmill was about two miles off to the south of town. It sold and shipped a part of its lumber to California interests.

Each Saturday evening, shortly before ten o'clock, a freight train would come rolling through town, grind to a halt, uncouple some empty boxcars, and hook up the loaded cars.

Bill's idea was to go on out to the empty cars which were sitting on a side rail, waiting to be loaded the following week—put the two men in one of the empties—and drive off with their automobiles.

We'd park them on the outskirts of town, and hope that by the time they walked those two miles back from the sawmill, their disposition would improve.

As we looked back at Bill's plan later on, we could see that there were a ton of holes in it. We should have known better. Well, Harley should have known better, at least.

Bill had been drinking some, and so his judgment was a little suspect—and so we shouldn't have expected anything else. Clancy had already shown that he really didn't care one way or another, and as for me—well—after all, I was just a kid.

We couldn't blame Bill too much, though. I mean, who could have known that there was a severe shortage of boxcars in the state of Washington?

———————

When we returned from our trip to the boxcars, Bill parked Tom's car back where he had taken it from earlier in the evening. He was fumbling with something—trying to pull his flask out of its hiding place.

When it finally came free, something else came out of the pocket with the flask and fell to the ground. I reached down to retrieve it for Bill, and when I did, I couldn't believe my eyes.

It was a roll of bills big enough to choke a horse! I had never even seen that much money at one time—much less held it in my hands. I must have said something in my surprise, because Harley stopped to turn and asked, "What's the matter, Will?"

Harley's eyes fell on the wad of bills. He turned to Bill and said, "What did you do, Bill? Did you rob that man?"

"Naw," said Bill, "I'm just holding his money for him for a while. I relieved old Tinker of that brand new fifty-dollar bill, though."

Harley looked as though he were going to put up an argument. Bill held up a hand, laughing a little as he did.

"I just figured that it wasn't right for him to hang on to ill-gotten gains, like that. It's not right to sell out your neighbors like he done, so I figured I would take that temptation off his hands."

He looked down and winked at me. "I'm merely helping old Tink stay on the straight and narrow."

"And just what did you think you were going to do with it.... once you 'straightened and narrowed' old 'Tink'?" asked Harley, with more than a little suspicion. "Were you planning on 'donating' it to Clancy's saloon?"

Clancy was standing there watching as the two of them tried to work out this recent development. Finally, he spoke up. "I think it would be a mighty fine gesture if you were to donate that money to the lunch program down at the schoolhouse—but it's entirely up to you, of course."

Bill, who had indeed been trying to think of some way that he could have some fun with the money—while appearing to be philanthropic at the same time—had actually begun to lick his lips before he heard Clancy's suggestion.

It took a moment for the beer and the friends and the back-slapping and all to disappear from his imagination, but when it did, he could clearly see the wisdom and the decency of what Clancy had just said.

"Why," he said, lifting his hands in an expressive gesture, "that's exactly what I was planning to do. Doing anything else never even crossed my mind!"

"Good," said Harley. "That being so, you probably won't mind letting Jim hang onto it until it gets to the schoolhouse, will you, Bill?"

He handed the money over to Clancy, but I swear, it was a long time slipping out of Bill's fingers.

"Now that's settled," Harley said, "what about the rest of that wad?"

"Well, you see, it's like this. I figured this fellow owed us something for all the trouble he put us through tonight. This probably ought to about cover it. What do you guys think?"

It turned out that the man had over three hundred dollars in that roll of bills. After we all whistled, even Bill could see that it would be wrong to keep the man's money.

"I'll go back and put it in the glove box of his car tomorrow," said Bill. "If I put it there before he walks back in, then he really shouldn't have anything to complain about."

"I think that's a good idea, Bill," said Harley. "It might just keep him from getting the law involved and causing us some headaches later on. I wonder how Bellum's going to take it, though."

"I don't think Tinker's going to say a thing—at least not to the law—maybe not to anyone," said Clancy.

It was true that even Bellum might figure out it would be beneficial to him if no one found out that he sold out Mrs. Prince to that stranger—or that he was trying to cause trouble for the new Mr. and Mrs. Tompkins on the eve of their wedding.

"No," he finished, "I wouldn't worry any about him. Now, let's go back inside and hope that no one missed us."

Chapter
Twenty-Four

Tinker shivered and drew his knees up, trying to get warm. For some time, his foggy brain had been trying to work out just why he was having such trouble with his blankets. Why was his bed rocking back and forth?

He had drifted in and out of consciousness and was just beginning to realize that he wasn't home in his own bed—or anywhere else he had ever been. Finally, he shook his head clear enough to push himself up into a sitting position.

It was dark where he was—and damp, as well as cold. It was loud, too. In fact, if he didn't know any better, he would swear that he could hear a train.

His mind finally focused enough for him to realize that he was on the train! He was in a boxcar going somewhere, and he didn't have any idea just where the boxcar was, how he got into it, or where it was going.

He got up onto his knees and scrambled over to the boxcar door. He pulled hard, trying to slide it open—hoping to see a glimpse of something that would give him some clue to what was happening to him.

"Don't bother," said a voice from the other side of the dark car. "I've already looked. There's nothing to see out there but darkness. We'll have to wait until daylight to see just where we are."

The voice was familiar, but Bellum couldn't quite place it. Then he remembered. It was the voice of the stranger who had been looking for that Prince woman. But...how did he...how did they...?

Then it all started coming back to him. He'd been struggling with Clancy, trying to get past him and into the grange hall, when something had hit him in the...

He reached a hand to the back of his head and felt a knot about the size of a goose egg. Someone had hit him with something from behind—and then loaded him onto this train bound for—well, bound for somewhere; and when he got off of it, and got back home, somebody would pay for this!

"What happened to you?" Bellum asked the other man. "Why'd they put you on this train?"

The other man sat silent for a moment. "I underestimated a man back there," he said, finally. "I let him get the jump on me. It won't happen again; I can tell you that."

"What man?" asked Bellum.

"I think I heard someone call him Harley."

"Harley?" Bellum started to laugh.

"What are you laughing at?" the man snarled at Bellum.

"Nothing—except that you let a one-legged man get the drop on you. I'd think it would be hard to underestimate a cripple."

"I doubt he hit me with his leg. It felt more like a tire iron."

"Where do you think we are?" asked Bellum.

"Don't know," replied the other. "Won't know either—not till morning. My guess, though, is that your hogs will wonder where you are for a few days."

Then Bellum remembered the money the stranger had paid him the night before. He reached his hand into his pocket, but there was nothing there.

He muttered something unintelligible under his breath. He looked over toward the other man. "Hey! Give my money back!" he said.

"It wasn't me who took it," the man said. "You can chalk that up to whoever loaded us on this boxcar. You've got some real nice friends and neighbors, pal. They took everything I had, too."

The man laughed then, and said, "Well, not everything. They missed this." Even in the noisy boxcar, the sound of a revolver's hammer being cocked was distinctive.

"Hey! What's the idea?" said an incredulous Bellum.

"While you were laying there, I went ahead and relieved you of your watch and chain," the man said in a matter-of-fact way. Bellum's hand went to an empty pocket.

"I'm hoping that it's worth something—though I doubt that a dumb farmer like you would own anything worth stealing. I'm hoping, though, that between this gun and my new watch, I ought to be able to get back to L.A. Thanks."

The man's nonchalant manner evaporated into coldness as he said, "Alright, pal, get up and pull that door open, it's time to get off."

Bellum gasped, "But—but the train's still moving!"

The man laughed, "Well, what do you know, so it is. I'd try to roll when I land—if I were you, mister. If you do, you might not break too much."

"But I can't see anything! It's still dark!" Bellum was pleading now. He knew that when he jumped, he might land on anything—or nothing at all, for that matter. There might be a tree, or a fence post, or he might fall off of a cliff.

For that matter, even landing in soft ground could kill, or cripple him just as easily as not. He reached deep down inside for the courage to face the man with the gun, but came away empty-handed.

With a trembling hand, Bellum pulled the boxcar door open, and after one last pleading look toward the man with the gun, he turned to face the open door.

He opened his mouth for one more attempt to save himself when he felt a foot in his back push him hard—and then he was falling, striking the ground, and rolling over and over. Then the darkness came over him.

———————————

The boy had been walking the railroad tracks down to where they passed by a small pond—hoping to bring down a duck or two for Sunday dinner—when he had seen the body of the man lying, half hidden, in the bushes a little distance from the tracks.

At first, he had thought that the man was a dead hobo. Although he had never seen one, he knew it was not an uncommon thing in that day and time. Upon closer examination, he could see that the man's heart was beating strongly.

Though not bright, he was a practical boy. He told himself that if this man had lain there all night long without care—and still seemed to be a long way from expiring—then it wouldn't hurt anything to let him lay there a little while longer.

Since he and his mother lived alone, Jamie had been called upon to shoulder more and more of the responsibilities that would normally be a father's.

Bringing in meat for the table was one of those responsibilities. He had a strong sense of duty to the family. Next to that was a sense of duty to his neighbor. He didn't figure that this man was either.

He walked on another quarter mile to the pond, and after waiting for a short time, was rewarded with two fine mallards. After collecting his game, Jamie walked back to where the man still lay.

Jamie was a strong young man, and the injured man wasn't very large, and so he put him over his shoulder and carried him home.

When Tinker opened his eyes once more, he knew instantly that he was not where he had fallen. Everything was white and clean and smelled of starch and soap.

There was an overriding aroma that reminded him of his childhood—when his momma used to cook chicken broth when he or his brother was sick. He hadn't thought of that in years.

For an instant, he had the thought that perhaps he had died— and this was actually heaven. However, even in his condition, he wasn't so delusional that he really thought he'd see heaven when he died, and so this must be someplace else.

Wherever it was, it sure looked and smelled like what heaven should, he told himself. And then he saw what he was sure must be an angel.

"I'd better go back to sleep—see if I can make sense of this later," he told himself.

Hours later, when he awoke again, his mind was clear enough to convince him that this was not heaven—or hell, for that matter. It was obvious he had been found and brought to this house by someone—someone who was nursing his wounds.

As he shifted his weight on the bed, he began to explore what those wounds might be. His head throbbed—but that could be from the blow that had been struck from behind back at the grange hall. He could move his arms, though his right shoulder was extremely sore. He had probably landed on it, bruising it badly.

He wiggled his torso, making sure that it still worked, and pain shot up from his right leg. His left leg seemed to be fine, but his right one hurt so badly that he almost cried out from the pain. He was able to move it a little, though, so he figured it must only be a bad sprain.

His movements had attracted the attention of someone in the room. He turned his head and saw his 'angel' walk up to him with a cautious look on her face.

"Well, it's about time! I was starting to think you might sleep on through another day."

"Another day? How many days have I been here?"

"Jamie found you on Sunday morning, and it's Tuesday evening now. I reckon you've been here almost three days."

"Where is 'here'?" he asked.

"You're a little south of Woodburn—in Oregon," she replied. "Are you hungry?"

He was, he thought—in fact, he felt as though he was starving. He nodded his head, and then asked, "Who are you—and who is Jamie, your husband?"

"My husband?" she exclaimed, "No! Jamie's my boy! My husband's been gone for three years now. That's one man who won't be coming back. You can call me Myra."

Chapter
Twenty-Five

It took Doug Blackman almost two weeks to get back to Los Angeles and when he did, it wasn't the way he had expected. After he had pushed the farmer out of the boxcar and into the black of night, he continued to ride until the boxcar was dropped off at a rail yard somewhere in south Washington state.

Waiting for the coast to clear, Blackman hopped down from the boxcar and made his way out of the yard. He needed to get back to Los Angeles as soon as possible. Until he made his report, he wouldn't get paid.

By this time hunger had set in, as had thirst, and he was ready to find a new mode of transportation, anyway. Those yokels had taken every cent he owned back in that cesspool of a town in Oregon, and all he had to his name was his gun and the watch and chain he had taken off that greedy farmer some hours ago.

In the broad light of day, the watch and chain didn't appear to be worth much, and so he decided he was probably going to need to pawn his gun, too. With the money he could get from it, he was sure to get home.

When he got to the first pawn shop though, it struck him that he'd be a fool to take a gun into a pawn shop just to pawn it for a few dollars, when he could take that same gun into that same pawn shop and take all the money they had.

Reflecting on this decision later that evening, while sitting in the jailhouse in Vancouver, Washington, he decided perhaps he had been a little too greedy as well.

This was not the first time Blackman had been behind bars. In fact, he had been a guest of the state of California for almost seven years on an assault conviction. He had been out on parole for only about six months.

Although Doug Blackman wasn't the brightest person in the world, it didn't take a genius to see that he would soon be back in the California penal system. He was sure that they would extradite him so he could serve the rest of his sentence in California for breaking parole.

He was allowed one phone call—which he made to his current employer. After five long rings, during which he began to think he had wasted his call, he could hear the receiver being picked up on the other end of the line.

"Yes?"

"Hello—this is Blackman."

"Blackman! Where have you been? I've been expecting to hear from you!" The voice on the other end of the line sounded anxious. "You're supposed to stay in touch. Where are you, any-way? Still up in Oregon?"

"I'm in Washington!" came the reply. "Vancouver, Washington."

"Washington? She's in Washington?"

"No. I'm in Washington! Listen, it's a long story, and I don't have time to go into it. I think I've found her up there in some tiny backwater town in Oregon called Hope Springs."

"Hope Springs? Never heard of it! Are you sure?"

"Yeah, I'm sure," Blackman replied. "Now listen. I'm in a jam here with the law, and I need a good lawyer—your lawyer! You hear me?"

"Just calm down, Blackman," he said. "Tell me more about where she is—is she alright? What is she doing up there?"

"Not so fast," said the other. "First, you help me out of this, then I'll help you."

"If you don't tell me everything you found, you won't ever hear from me again. Remember, I can send another man to find what you found. Do you really think there's anyone else who's gonna be willing to help get you out of the bind you've gotten yourself into?"

Blackman thought it over, and quickly decided that the other man had the upper hand. He realized that his only hope here was to give him what he wanted, and hope the man would keep his word to help him in his trouble.

Blackman then began to lay out all that he had seen and heard during his stay in the little town in Oregon.

When he had finished, the other man said, "Alright, Blackman, it looks like you've given me everything that I need here. As soon as I return with my property, I'll send my lawyer to see what can be done to help you. If my lawyer can't get you off, then no one can. I'll be talking to you later."

After hanging up the phone, Blackman sat back in the hard, straight-backed chair, clasped his hands behind his head and smiled to himself. He had absolutely nothing to worry about.

Chapter
Twenty-Six

In the days that followed, Bellum was content to sit back and let the woman, Myra, wait on him hand and foot. Watching her, he thought to himself, "this is pretty nice"—a man could get used to this.

He'd been doing his own chores for so many years that he hadn't really considered the advantages of having someone who would take care of all of those menial tasks—such as cooking and cleaning, washing and mending.

Looking around the place, he could tell it wasn't much. It was maybe five acres of bare ground, with the railroad bordering the back, the county road in front—and somebody else's bare ground on either side.

The house was small—cramped—no more than a shack, really. He knew the house he lived in wasn't much either, but this one made his seem like a mansion.

He began thinking to himself that maybe the woman would be willing to come with him when he went back home. For that matter, the boy could come too. He looked strong, and Tinker could always use a hand—especially one that he could get for room and board.

Having the boy plowing his fields and the woman cooking meals—yeah, he thought to himself, that sounds pretty good. If she insisted, they could get married, but he'd rather not be that tied to her.

As he looked around the place and saw what she would be giving up, he was pretty sure that she'd jump at the chance. Anyway, they'd done right by him—it was the least that he could do.

Myra was just coming in the house and so he decided to give her the good news.

"Myra," he said, as she set an armload of kindling down in the wood box by the cookstove, and looked his way.

"Do you remember me telling you about a farm I own just outside of Hope Springs?"

"Sure," she said, as she stood up—dragging a forearm across her brow.

"Well, I've been thinking," he continued. "Maybe you and the boy would like to come with me when I go back here in a few days. What do you say?"

"Come with you? What do you mean 'come with you'?"

"You know—come back with me, live at my place. It's a lot better than this one. Why, it's the best farm in the county."

She looked at him shrewdly. "You mean come with you to do all of your cooking and cleaning, right? And you want my boy to come so you can put him to work on your farm—isn't that it?"

"Well, sure—everybody has to pitch in and help out," Bellum explained.

"No thanks," she said, shaking her head. "I've got plenty to do here. All a bigger place means is a bigger mess for me to clean up.

"Besides," she continued with a sly look about her, "it can't be that good, or you'd already have a woman—wouldn't you?"

"Not good?" Tinker blustered. "Why, it's better than anything you'll find around here!"

"Oh? How much is it worth, then?"

"It's hard to say," he said. "It's difficult to put a money value on a place like mine."

"Well, try" she said dryly.

Bellum pulled a figure out of the air. "Ten thousand."

"I'll bet!" she said. "It's probably not worth half of that! Anyway, I'm not going anywhere with anyone without a ring on my finger."

"Now, why would you want to complicate an opportunity like this by talking about something like getting married?"

"It's not a complication as I see it," she returned. "Try to think of it more as a…" She paused, as if trying to find the right word. "Try to think of it as a guarantee," she finished.

"Guarantee?" he asked, trying to sound as though he didn't know what she was talking about. "My word is my guarantee. Anybody will tell you that!"

"Yeah," she laughed, "I'll bet. At any rate, that's the deal—take it or leave it."

Bellum thought for a minute and then seemed to resign himself to the woman's demand. "Alright," he sighed, "but get your stuff together fast—it's time I got back."

"Not so fast," said the woman. "Marriage first—then we go. We got a JP in the town just up the road. We get the marrying over with, then we'll see about the leaving."

Bellum had been afraid of that, and he didn't like it, but he figured he'd still come out ahead on the deal—after all, it was just a piece of paper. He really had nothing to lose.

———————

When the newlyweds returned from town later that after-noon, the new Mrs. Bellum insisted on a celebration. After all, she said, a girl doesn't get married every day. Bellum was in a hurry to get back to his place, but figured that it wouldn't hurt to spend one more day.

Earlier, while they were in town, he had sent a telegram to Homer Long, letting him know he'd be returning in a couple of days, with a new family in tow—and demanding that he investigate, and arrest those responsible for shanghaiing him.

Myra cooked a nice meal, and after it was finished, the boy went outside to allow them time to themselves. Tinker knew what that meant and smiled to himself, thinking that perhaps this plan might have some advantages he had failed to consider.

After she had cleared away the food and had done the few dishes they had, Myra went to a cabinet in the kitchen and pulled out a bottle of wine.

She turned to Tinker, and smiling sweetly, told him, "I've been saving this for just this moment. It was my first husband's favorite. I thought that maybe you'd like it too. After all, it is our wedding night."

Tinker thought it was a little strange to be drinking from the old husband's private reserve—but then again, he was wearing the man's clothes—and was now married to the man's wife—so what difference did it make to him if he sampled the man's wine as well?

"Sure," he said. "Go ahead and pour me a glass. Pour one for yourself too, if you'd like."

"No," she said. "I'm not much of a drinker—and besides, this is really more of a man's wine."

He shrugged his shoulders. He had never heard of a "man's wine" before—but he was willing to try it. "Suit yourself," he said.

"Oh, I am," she replied. As she poured, a smile crept across her face. "I am."

Chapter
Twenty-Seven

Myra couldn't help but think how easily this had all fallen together. It was almost providential. Had she believed in the Almighty—and had she been a praying woman—she would have said this was God's way of answering her prayers.

However, Myra had never put her faith in anything, or anyone, other than herself. She was confident that the good things which came into her life were there because she had arranged them that way.

She was confident that God's hand wasn't in any of her newfound fortune. In that, she was correct. It wasn't God who poured the poison-laced wine for her new husband to drink that afternoon.

No, it was Myra—Myra who had used the same device before. That wasn't the first time she had disposed of a husband. The first time had been about five years earlier. She could still remember how easy it had been—and how, when it was over, she had wondered what took her so long to think of it.

Jamie's father had been a drunk and a lay-about—and had used her and the boy as objects to take out his frustrations on. And he had been a very frustrated man.

For years she had resigned herself to the belief that her life would continue on in this manner—that there was nothing she could do but to hope that perhaps he might contract some sort of illness, influenza, TB, or such—and die from it, leaving her and the boy to escape the life they were stuck in.

However, although worthless, the man proved to be made of durable cloth. Then one day she read an article in the paper about the men in their small community who were leaving to find work elsewhere.

They were leaving their families behind for the time being, planning to send for them later on. What a relief it would be, she had thought, if her man would do the same. Maybe he wouldn't ever come back—or send for her and the boy.

As nice as that thought was, it didn't look to ever become more than just a wish; because her man—as durable as he might be—had no obvious ambitions beyond eating, sleeping, and drinking. Other than those—which he excelled at—he also yelled at, and beat upon, both her and the boy.

A thought had occurred to her right about then.

There were men who left their families with plans of coming home later—or sending for their families to join them; men who were never heard from again. No one ever really knew what happened to them. No one ever really knew...

Many of those men rode the rails across the country to look for jobs that were only rumors. There was little safety in that sort of travel, and men sometimes disappeared along the way—without a trace left behind of where they might have gone to, or what might have happened to them.

Her husband, however, hadn't traveled nearly as far as those men who had gone off seeking work. She forced herself to wait until a time when her husband was in a stupor.

She really hadn't needed to wait long; it was, after all, his normal routine. As usual, he had slapped her around a little, shoved the boy against the wall, and continued to shout at them both until he passed out on the bed.

Myra had gone out into the backyard that night, dug a hole, and rolled him into it. She then laid the sod back over the fresh dirt, and within a short time, there was no visible evidence of the deed.

Burying a man alive was a horrible thought, but she only needed to recall the way he had treated her and the boy to get past the horror of it. If any man deserved such a fate, it was him—at least that's what she continued to tell herself.

For weeks after that, she had suffered nightmares. In her dreams, she could see the hands of her husband clawing through the dirt of the freshly filled in grave—fighting to free himself.

Finally, he would push through, and sit up—half in, and half out of the grave—pieces of dirt falling from around his hollow, soulless eyes.

Each morning, she would arise and go into the backyard to assure herself that the ground was still undisturbed. In time, though, the nightmares went away and she hardly ever thought of it anymore.

Myra had passed the word around that her husband had gone in search of work elsewhere. That would explain his disappearance to anyone who wondered. It wasn't as though the people in the town would care enough to wonder much about a man like him, anyway.

Eventually, she and the boy made their way out west. The man who owned the place where they now lived in wasn't as bad as her husband had been, but he wasn't what a person might call 'good husband material' either.

Within a short time, she realized they could get by without him just as easily as with him, and she went about the task a second time.

Myra would not go through the nightmares of burying a man alive again, and so she went about discovering a new method. She learned that with the right household goods, mixed in a bottle of cheap wine, the man could be dealt with once and for all.

This time, Myra slept just fine.

As time wore on, she told people that her man had gone on a trip to Montana to seek a job he had heard about—and that she didn't know why he wasn't back yet. She said that she expected him to come home any time.

Well, time wore on and people began to wonder. She would shrug her shoulders and simply say that she didn't know any more than they did. After a while, it was assumed that he must have met with some bad luck along the tracks—a lot of men did back in those days.

She had him declared 'legally dead', and it was then that she realized her mistake. She had never become the man's wife and, therefore, was entitled to nothing.

All that the man owned reverted to the bank, which held the loan on the property. Had she been able to sell, she wouldn't have seen a dime of the money.

The banker, a kindly man—and knowing it was nearly impossible to sell the place in the middle of a depression, allowed the woman and her son to remain on the place for a time. After all, it was better to have someone there than to allow the house to stand empty.

The disposal of the second man had been easier than that of her first husband. She thought that possibly it was because she wasn't all that attached to this one; not having even been married to him.

But that was a mistake she would not make again, she told herself. When the opportunity arose the next time, she would make sure of her assets before she disposed of her liabilities.

She had done all the work the first time, when she had buried her husband. That was only natural, she thought, as Jamie had been but a small boy at the time—and also considering the man had been his father. After all, she told herself; she wasn't a monster!

That wasn't the case the next time, however. Jamie had been almost fourteen years old then, big and strong for his age. He didn't seem to be able to figure things out very well, usually depending on his mother to tell him what needed to be done.

Well, she had told him to dig a hole—having lined it out for him on the ground—and then she had gone on with her part of the scheme.

He hadn't realized what was happening until after the fact, but his mother had seemed pleased with what he had done, so he figured it must have been alright to push the man's body into the hole and shovel the dirt over it.

A deeper thinker would certainly have had misgivings about what his mother was asking of him, but Jamie's strength was not in his ability to reason.

Long ago he had learned the value of obedience. His father had taught him that lesson, and it was the one thing Myra could thank the man for.

His mother had said he must never say anything to anyone about what they had done. Now, although Jamie wasn't clever, he was dependable—and his mother knew that once told, he would never forget what she had said.

Myra didn't have to tell Jamie anything this time. He seemed to read her mind, and so he went out after dinner that evening—leaving Myra and Tinker alone in the house.

He walked out to the old tool shed in back of the house and grabbed a shovel, then walked out into the field between the house and the railroad, and began to dig.

Although she didn't know what Tinker's place was going to be like, Myra knew that it now belonged to her. It was the first thing she had ever owned. She felt a little quiver of excitement at the thought of it all. Of all the places he could have fallen off a train, it was almost in her backyard.

When she thought of it now, she shook her head in amazement. She couldn't help thinking that maybe there was a God after all.

They would wait a few days, pack up what few belongings they had, and buy bus tickets to... where was it... Hope Springs?

Then, with marriage license in hand, she and the boy would move onto Bellum's place—wait for her husband to return from the 'business trip' he'd gone on after their wedding—and then go through a proper mourning period as the 'widow Bellum'.

It was as simple as that. No one would ever know the difference.

After all, men disappeared every day.

Bill Getty had been getting plenty worried by the time word arrived from Tinker. He had been staying out at Bellum's place since the day after Dave and Edith's wedding reception—when we all became aware that something had gone wrong with the plan the night before.

Word had gotten around the night before, about what we had done to Bellum and the stranger, and by the next afternoon there wasn't a person in the county who hadn't had a good laugh about it.

Even Homer Long had to chuckle—but duty, and common sense, told him something had gotten out of hand, that someone would have to pay a price. There was also the matter of Bellum's farm. It had to be tended to.

In order to kill two birds with a single throw, Homer went to Bill and impressed upon him that when Tinker did finally get back from wherever he was, it would go a lot easier on Bill if he was to go out and take care of the place in Tinker's absence.

Harley and I both had volunteered to help, but Bill allowed as how it was really his job, in that it was his idea in the first place to give Bellum and the stranger their little vacation trip. We didn't press the issue.

I think Bill figured it might be a good idea if he were to get out of town and away from his future wife for a while, as she was still a little put out with him—and he was probably figuring that a few days away from his future father-in-law was needed to bring his 'William' status back once more.

It was almost a week before we heard anything from Tinker. At that, it was only a wire that came through to the sheriff's office. In the wire, Bellum named Clancy, Bill, and Harley as the men who had "viciously attacked him" and "shanghaied" him onto a train. It said he was recovering somewhere outside of Woodburn.

I could not imagine where Tinker had learned all those big words.

Ten days later, a tall, thin woman and a huge, simple looking boy got off the southbound bus after it rolled to a stop in front of Maggie's diner.

The woman looked to be a hard worn thirty-five years of age. Each carried two suitcases. We would all soon learn these people were Tinker's new family.

Bellum wasn't with them though, which seemed odd to us—but she explained that she and Tinker had met briefly as he was passing through Woodburn, and had quickly fallen in love. Theirs was a "marriage arranged in heaven", as she put it.

He'd decided, since he was already away, he would continue on to Washington—saying that he had a man he wanted to talk to about farming equipment. He had told her to take the boy and go to his place. That way, she said, she could have the house set up just the way she liked it by the time Tinker got home.

But Tinker didn't come back home.

After a few weeks, Homer started looking into it—trying to determine what might have happened to the man.

Homer may have looked like a somewhat over the hill lawman out of one of those old western novels, but there were few people at any level in law enforcement who were sharper than he was.

Nor were there many who had the determination he had. He was like a hound dog on a scent.

It didn't take long for him to discover that nobody had ever seen Bellum leave town. This was interesting, because he would have had to buy a ticket on a bus, drive an automobile, or hitch a ride.

There was no record of him buying a ticket or an automobile. Although it was possible that he might have hitchhiked to Washington, Homer found the chances of it so remote that he didn't seriously consider the possibility.

No, to Homer's way of thinking, something had happened to the man. Where to start looking? You start looking in the last place that a person was seen.

In this case, Homer could find records of a Tinker Bellum and a Myra Felton being married in a civil ceremony in Woodburn.

It really wasn't a difficult case to solve when it came right down to it. Homer contacted the local authorities in Woodburn, then told them what he knew, and sat back to let them do all the work.

Yes, they remembered the woman—and her boy, who seemed a little slow. They remembered they had been in the area for about three years.

They had lived with a man outside of town a little way. It appeared they'd had some bad luck, the local law told Homer.

The man they were living with had left to find work and never returned. The bank owned the little place, but had been letting the woman and her son remain there for a while.

With a little more digging, Homer found where Myra had lived in Oklahoma, talked to the police there, and found a similar—if somewhat more grisly story.

At Homer's urging, they had investigated, and found, where a body had been buried in the backyard of the house where Myra and her husband had lived.

The Oklahoma authorities told Homer that from evidence found at the site of the burial, it would appear that this one had actually been alive when he was buried.

They figured he must have been subdued, somehow, and had only been able to work at freeing himself after the grave was filled in. His fingers had almost dug through to the surface when he was finally overcome by lack of oxygen.

Homer got back in touch with the law in Woodburn and explained what he had found. He then talked them in to going out to the place that she and the boy had lived—taking shovels with them—and had them look for freshly dug ground.

It took only a short time to find the right place, dig up the body, and see that, yes, this was indeed the missing Tinker Bellum. They also found, quite by accident, the remains of another body, which would later be proved to be that of the other missing man.

Although it would be impossible—in that time—to prove anything with the first two victims, it was a simple task for a capable doctor to determine that Tinker had been poisoned.

Myra had hardly gotten the house settled to suit her by the time Homer pulled up outside Bellum's place with an arrest warrant in his hand.

He said later that she had cried all the way back into town— saying repeatedly how it just wasn't fair that some people had everything, while she had nothing.

He said she asked him why that was. He said that he didn't know for sure; said he supposed it had a lot to do with how God blesses good people, while others—well, not so much.

Chapter Twenty-Eight

It had been one of those spring days that we wait for all winter long; one of those days that gives kids a chance to use up a lot of the energy they've been building and storing up during the long winter months.

It was toward the end of April. The dogwoods were beginning to bloom—the birds were beginning to sing—and baseball season was arriving right on time.

Not that it had ever really ended for some of us diehards—but it was more official now that we could get out onto the field in back of the schoolhouse without having to ford the stream that had separated the field from the school during the winter months.

That stream couldn't have kept us out—really—but the field had a bit of a dip in it, which held the rain. During the winter months, our ball park was more of a shallow lake than a ball field—so until the sun had a chance to dry things up a little, it really was too soggy to go out on and play ball. Believe me, we'd tried.

The boys and I—and Lucy—had spent the afternoon out there playing a little ball and generally goofing around, as young boys (and apparently some girls, also) do. It was early in the evening, and I was walking Lucy back home.

Etta and Lucy were now living in a small house right on the north edge of town. The boys had kidded me about walking my "girlfriend" home, but by now I had gotten used to their good-natured ribbings.

Although I enjoyed being with Lucy more than just about anyone else, I was a long way from being at the stage of life where "girlfriends" were of any interest to me.

It was true—Lucy was a girl—and she was my friend; but she was more like one of the guys. At least that's what I told myself.

In the back of my mind, I was also figuring that there was a fair to middling chance that I might get invited to stay for dinner. Lucy's mom had done that on more than one occasion.

I was walking my bike because Lucy didn't have one—and I sure wasn't going to ride her double after all the Hoo-Haw's the guys had been giving me.

I was pushing it with one hand. My other hand held the baseball that Harley had given to me for Christmas.

I'd been working that baseball for almost four months now, and the grip in my right hand was getting stronger all the time. Harley had told me that a good pitcher had to have strong hands.

Although I had to really work at it for the first little while, now I barely even knew I was holding it.

As we approached Lucy's house, we could see a long, shiny black automobile parked on the street opposite the house. Standing outside the car, leaning against the driver's side front fender, was a man—a tall, slender man—with a thin, black moustache.

His black hair was slicked back like some of the guys in the movies had theirs, in those days. In fact, standing there, with his sports coat folded over his arm, he looked as though he had just stepped off an MGM lot. To say the least, he looked a little out of place.

Looking at that big, long, shiny black car, I just sort of naturally steered my bike in its direction. I had never in my life seen anything like it up close. I think I probably whistled. Lucy was following me, but I could see that she was a little hesitant.

As I got closer, the man looked down his nose at me and snapped, "Hey kid! Get away from the car—you put a scratch on it, you'll wish you hadn't!" He sort of hissed these last words at me.

That stopped me in my tracks. I'd never even considered that anyone would worry about a scratch on their car.

Most of the people around here drove cars that were filled with dings and dents and scratches—a few even missing fenders and bumpers—and so not a one of them fretted over a thing as trivial as that.

Even considering that, though, I could see why this man might be worried—I mean, it was the prettiest car I had ever seen.

I looked up at him and said, "Sorry mister—I didn't mean to…"

"Well then, see that you don't!" he snapped. I could tell that this was a man who had no love for children. His car, maybe… but not children.

The man turned to Lucy and smiled at her. His teeth were whiter than I had ever imagined teeth could be. It was a beautiful smile, but there was no warmth behind it at all.

In a voice as smooth and sweet as syrup, he said, "Hello Lucy, do you know who I am?"

With a look of pure dread on her face, showing that she did, indeed, know who this man was—but trying to convince herself that she might be wrong—she slowly moved her head from side to side.

"Sure, you do Lucy. I'm your father. I've come to take you home." He reached out for her, but Lucy drew back sharply.

In a voice that was no more than a whisper, Lucy said, "No, you're not." Then, with more force and conviction, she said, "You're not my father! My father is dead!"

"Is that what she told you?" The man shook his head and sighed, as though this both amazed him and made him very sad. "You were taken away from me, Lucy, and I've been looking for you—trying to find you—for a long time."

"But Etta told me…" she began.

"Etta told you?" he cut in. "Etta told you?!" His voice was rising. "You can't believe Etta! She wants to keep the money for herself. If she told you anything else, she lied about that too! That money belongs to me! He was my father!"

It was easy to see that this man was about as stable as the barn that young Johnny Muldoon had built last year. When the rains came this winter, they washed away whatever strength had been in the foundation it was sitting on. That whole barn had come down in one enormous pile of timbers, lumber, and shingles.

It didn't take much insight to recognize that the rain was eating away at this man's foundation as well. I feared that his sanity was on the verge of collapsing, just like Johnny's barn.

His eyes turned mean then, and he told Lucy to get into the car, or she would regret it. She should have run right then, but I could tell she wasn't going to.

She wasn't scared anymore. She was mad. Her jaw was set, and the fire was back in her eyes. She just stood there, shaking her head defiantly.

The man drew back as if to hit her, and when he did, I yelled something at him while trying to get him to stop. My bike was between me and him, though, and I knew I wouldn't get there soon enough.

Lucy knew it too, and she squeezed her shoulders together real tight, and closed her eyes—bracing for the blow that didn't come.

The man's hand froze in mid-air, and with a malicious smile, he reached over, grabbed my bike, and pulled it over to him. I came with the bike, and he just reached over and grabbed me hard by the arm.

"Maybe I'll hurt you instead!" he threatened. There was a look of menace in his eyes, and I could tell that it was no idle threat. This man would, indeed, hurt me—I knew this—and he'd enjoy doing it too.

He looked to be on the edge of whatever sanity he might have once possessed. He looked as though he could topple over that edge at any time.

I know I must have had a look of pure terror on my face, for that's what I was feeling right then. It was far from the brave man that young boys want to be seen as—especially in front of young girls.

But as Lucy turned to open the car door to get in, I shouted at her, "He's bluffing, Lucy! Don't you get in that car!" I knew that if she left with the man, I might never see her again. I wouldn't even know where to look for her.

Lucy stopped, turned around to face me, and said in a calm, controlled voice, "Don't worry Will, I'll be alright. Go back. I don't want you to get into hot water because of this."

As she said this, she winked at me. It wasn't a big wink, but I knew it meant something—but what? And then it hit me.

As they drove away in the evening's dusk, I jumped on my bike and pedaled away as fast as I could. Even though I was scared to death, I couldn't help smiling to myself a little. Way to go, Lucy—way to go! Now, I know where you're going!

The only "hot water" she and I knew about had to be the hot springs out at the old derelict hotel. I didn't know how she would do it, but I knew that somehow Lucy would get her captor out to the old Hope Springs hotel—and maybe even to the springs themselves.

That was a lot to expect from a little blonde-haired girl, but she wasn't just any little blonde-haired girl. The first thing I needed to do was to find some help. This was not something I could take care of all by myself.

Etta hadn't been at their house. I hadn't even bothered checking, because I knew that if she had been, she would have been outside checking on us before now.

This was a Saturday evening, so she was probably still down at the diner, helping Maggie. It was a little early for the weekly gathering of the farmers at the feed store, and so I figured Harley might be at the diner as well.

Harley and Etta were just stepping outside the diner's front door as I brought my bike to a sliding stop, yelling loud enough for everyone within four city blocks to hear.

"He took her!" I shouted. "He took her, Mr. Matthews! He took Lucy!"

I stopped long enough to gather my breath as Harley, Etta, and others gathered around to see what all the racket was about.

Harley put his big hand on my shoulder, as if to steady me. I guess I must have been shaking. He said, "Hold on, Will, just slow down a little. Take a couple of breaths and tell us what you're yelling about."

"He took Lucy, Mr. Matthews!" I tried to calm myself, but wasn't having much success.

Etta grabbed me by my shoulders and pulled me around so I was facing her.

"down Will. Who took Lucy?" Her eyes looked into mine, searchingly. The fear that caused her voice to rise was mirrored in the look of terror on her face.

"There was a man at your house when we got there," I began. "He was standing by a long, black car."

I heard someone in the crowd which had gathered yell out, "Hey! I saw that car!"

"What did the man look like, Will?" Etta asked me, still with her hands gripping my shoulders like vices. Her knuckles were turning white. I must have winced, for she suddenly let go. "I'm sorry, Will."

"He was tall—almost as tall as Mr. Matthews—and kinda thin. He had black hair—slicked back. You know, like some of them Hollywood actors. He had a thin little moustache, and...," I looked at Etta, and could tell that she knew the person I was describing.

"'And' what?" Harley asked.

"And he had these crazy eyes," I said, "but I don't think that's all that was crazy. Mr. Matthews, let's go get her back!" I'd worked myself up until I was crying, and I tried to stop but couldn't seem to make myself.

"Mr. Matthews," I snuffled out, "We just gotta get her back!"

Harley gripped my shoulder and said, in a voice that made me believe it was true, "We will... We will."

I dried my eyes on my sleeve and quit my crying—and then I remembered something else. I turned to Etta and said, "There's something else, Mrs. Prince—he said that he was Lucy's father."

Etta put her hand to her mouth, and Harley shifted his attention from me to her, with a question in his eyes—then he looked back at me. "We need to think this through. We don't even know which direction he took out of town."

He turned to the crowd of people which had gathered and asked, "Did anyone notice the car leaving town? Which direction it took?" Nobody answered him.

"Mr. Matthews," I said, "I know where they went."

People were still talking amongst themselves in excited voices. Harley raised himself to his full height and shouted over the crowd, "Quiet down, now! Young Will has something he needs to tell us."

He turned back to me then. "Alright Will, go ahead. Tell us what you know."

Even knowing that I'd be in trouble because I had taken Lucy out to the old hotel, and to the hot springs as well, I went ahead and told them Lucy's message.

"She was telling me she was going to try to lead him out there. I figure she was going to try to get away out there."

I heard somebody say, "That's a lot of figuring, young fellow. Just how do you suppose that she's going to get him to get off the highway and drive her way out there?"

"I don't know, mister," I replied, "but if anybody can do it, she can."

Harley knew that if I was right, then the sooner we got out to that old hotel, the better chance Lucy would have. If I was wrong, there wasn't a thing that he or any of the others could do to get her back tonight.

He turned to where Maggie was standing, with Frank's hand resting on her shoulder. There was worry and fear on both their faces.

"Frank," he began, "I'm going to need a car." He turned to the crowd and said, "I'm going to need someone to drive Will and me out to the hotel to look for Lucy out there."

He turned to Maggie. "Maggie, I want you to get hold of Homer Long and have him close the highway—north and south. If Will is wrong—or if Lucy isn't successful in drawing him out there—then they should be able to pick them up."

Bill Getty stepped forward, pushing his way through the crowd until he stood in front of Harley and me. "I'll drive you out there, Harley," he said.

"Thanks Bill." Then Harley turned to the crowd and said to them, "There's nothing more that can be done right now—you might as well go on back to what you were doing."

He turned back to Etta. "Etta, we're going to find her—believe me—we're going to get her back!"

"How will we do that?" Etta asked, her voice getting small as her fear grew. "How will we ever find her again? And how will we get her back?"

"I don't know yet," Harley replied, honestly.

Mr. Kimble was just bringing a beat-up old Ford pickup around, and Harley got up and walked to the passenger side door, with Etta walking close to his side.

He turned to her and said, "Don't worry, Etta. We'll bring her home safe."

She had tears on her face, but she held her head up high, and with a voice of quiet confidence simply said, "I know you will, Harley—I know."

Chapter
Twenty-Nine

It wasn't too difficult to see what had happened. In the failing light of the evening, Lucy had somehow convinced the man he had gone the wrong direction on the highway.

Later on, we learned he actually had turned the wrong way—with no urging on Lucy's part. It might have been that being a city boy, he had never before actually needed to use his sense of direction—or perhaps he just never had one.

Lucy must have worked hard, though, at getting him to take that old logging access road. By the time they got to the turnoff which led to the old hotel, the man was thoroughly confused and totally lost.

Seeing that the hotel was abandoned, and thinking that no one would ever think of looking for them there, he decided that this would be the perfect place to wait out the night. In the daylight, he could leave this miserable place and go home with his treasure.

The man had been too long around people who feared him—people who were all but paralyzed at the thought of his wrath—and so he was expecting the same thing from this little girl.

For a time, Lucy had been afraid—and still was, for that matter; but her paralysis had been short-lived. The terror of the situation had gripped her and held her tight, but it hadn't crippled her. Her mind was clear, and she was focused. That focus was only on *"how can I get away from this man?"*

She had been figuring it out in her mind, almost from the moment she had stepped inside the car. It would all depend on this man who called himself her father. She could lead him—but only if he would do what she thought he might.

What she had been hoping had come about when he had finally turned down the lane leading to the old hotel. This had been the last thing that she had needed to make it all work out.

She was pretty sure that she was faster and quicker than he was—and believed that she was perhaps a little smarter, too. These were the things which would give her an advantage.

It was a certainty that she had more sanity than the man. She wasn't too sure that being saner was going to help, or not. The trouble was, it's hard to know what a crazy person is going to do next.

She needed to be able to out-think the man—and in order for her to do that, she needed to know what he would do.

Even though there was a full moon that night, and in the open areas it was almost as light as the inside of most homes, there were shadows too, which would help to hide her in her escape.

She was looking for that to be to her advantage, as well. If she could keep to the shadows, she could get away unnoticed. But first, she needed to get away. She thought she had that figured out, too.

As the car slowed, approaching the hotel, Lucy suddenly threw the car door open and jumped out. The car wasn't going any faster than a fast walk, so it was a simple thing for an agile girl to land on her feet and start running.

The man dogged the brakes and jumped out of the car, but by then Lucy was racing through the front door of the hotel and into the darkness of the old hotel's lobby. By the time the man reached the front door, she had already shot out through the backdoor, unseen.

"*Now,*" she thought to herself, "*He will probably have to spend some time looking downstairs—at least—before he comes outside. While he's inside, looking for me, I'll be able to get away!*"

Thinking that she had bought herself a little time, she hid in the shadow of what had once been a grape arbor—so she could collect herself and catch her breath.

The man, however, was smarter than she had given him credit for. He quickly realized that if the girl had hidden in the hotel, then she was at least in a somewhat contained area which he could come back to, if a quick search of the outside yards proved fruitless—so he searched the grounds first.

As he stepped out through the back door of the hotel, Lucy looked up in surprise from her hiding place. This was something she had not expected.

She had thought that by the time the man had finished his search of the hotel, she would have been well on her way around the small mountain and across the pasture that would lead back to the highway—and from there on home.

Now, that way was out of the question, as the man was between her and her escape in that direction.

The only other way was to attempt to traverse the path which led to the springs. In the daylight, the pathway had seemed as wide and as easy to walk as the highway had been.

Now, with the trees lining its way, shading the path from the bright moonlight, it was a dark and foreboding way to go.

With no other choice left to her, Lucy waited until the man's back was turned, and then quietly left the dark shadows of the arbor and slipped out into the moonlight which fell between her and the pathway.

She reached the safety of the shadows once more before the man turned her way. As she slipped quietly toward the mineral springs, she inadvertently stepped on a fallen branch.

With the sound of the breaking branch, she stopped and held still in the shadows. Turning, she looked toward the man. As she did, she saw his head snap up. She could see the white of his teeth as the moonlight shone eerily on them. It caused a shudder to pass through her.

"I know where you are, Lucy," he said. "I'm coming to get you. Don't be afraid. I won't hurt you, Lucy. Don't you know how important you are to me?"

The man moved toward the pathway—walking slowly and deliberately—like an animal stalking its prey; knowing that its quarry doesn't have a chance to escape.

———

Even though she knew the trail was too narrow, and there was no place to hide on either side, Lucy couldn't help looking around, as a frantic animal might when being cornered by a predator.

Her fear was growing now—coming nearer to where she wouldn't be able to control it any longer.

She didn't have to be an expert to know the man who claimed to be her father was trying to play ball with a broken bat. The man was crazy! Clear thinking was what she needed right now. She needed to get hold of herself!

Lucy took a deep breath and forced herself to calm down. What would Will do? Will was practical. He could look at the situation and see the options available and then choose the best one. The problem was, there weren't any options.

The trail dead-ended at the hot springs, and the man was behind her on the trail. To her memory, there weren't any places which would offer any sanctuary between here and the end of the trail she was on. Will would probably tell her that her only choice was to just disappear.

Thanks, Will—why couldn't you come up with something better than…. Wait a minute! That's exactly what she would do. She would just disappear!

The man was coming up the trail at a slow, deliberate pace. Obviously, he wasn't concerned at all. And why should he be? She had no place to go.

About fifty yards before the trail reached the hot springs, it opened out onto a wide, flat granite rock. The mineral springs flowed out from this rock, several feet below the surface of the pool.

The pool itself was almost perfectly oval—and at its widest point was about eighteen feet across. It was here that Lucy disappeared. As the man came up the trail, he paused at this pool, and then walked away.

Lucy had waited until she could hear the man coming before she allowed herself to sink below the surface of the water.

She waited as long as she could—holding her breath until her lungs felt as if they would explode—and then rose to the surface.

With just her eyes and nose out of the water, she slowly looked up and down the trail as far as she could see from her vantage, and seeing nothing, was satisfied that her pursuer had moved on.

Slowly, and quietly, she climbed out of the water, dripping and shivering, and began to move back down the trail toward the old hotel.

Suddenly, blocking her path, the man loomed before her. She couldn't believe what she was seeing.

The man had tricked her again. The man hadn't gone on up the trail; he had merely waited in the shadows—between her and the hotel. He had correctly guessed that she was trying to disappear—and he had guessed how!

She couldn't help wondering if insane people were all as clever as this man.

There was no place to go, and so she turned and ran up the pathway toward the hot springs; continually casting about for something—anything—which she could seize upon to help her out of this horror.

Lucy looked back over her shoulder as she ran. She tripped, fell, and scrambled back onto her feet. She threw one more glance back at her pursuer before turning to run once more.

The man just seemed to be casually walking toward her—almost strolling up the path. He was actually enjoying this. He was playing with her just like Harley's cat, old Timothy, would play with the mice he caught.

That old cat would catch the mouse and bat it around a little, and then he would let it go. Not too far—just far enough so the mouse would start thinking that he was going to get away—and he did, for a while.

At the last second, though, the cat would pounce! Then the game would start all over again.

Lucy began to cry a little as she realized she was that mouse—and that eventually the cat would tire of playing the game, and then… She might as well give in.

Then Lucy remembered a time when she watched that old cat playing its devilish game with a defenseless mouse. That time, old Timothy let the mouse go, and then he pounced—as he had done a hundred times before—but this time the mouse was smarter.

Well, it may have been just coincidence, but old Timothy had pounced to the right, and the mouse had run to the left—and all the old tomcat came up were splinters as his paws dug into the porch floor.

Well! She thought to herself, if a mouse can do it, then so can I! Once again, she was ready to fight!

Chapter
Thirty

It wasn't difficult for us to see what had happened. When Bill pulled that Ford pickup to a stop out in front of the old hotel, we could plainly see the car sitting there with both doors flung wide open.

It was apparent he had stopped the car suddenly, with no concern about where he was parking. It appeared he was in a hurry. That could only mean one thing.

What that told us—and it sent an icy chill through each of us—was that Lucy had probably jumped out of the car and this deranged maniac was out there somewhere (or in the hotel) looking for her, becoming angrier by the minute.

If only she had waited, I thought, we would have come to save her. I prayed that if she had gotten away from him, she had somehow managed to stay away. I knew that Harley and Bill were thinking the same thing.

Harley was still in charge. "Bill, I want you to take your lantern and go into the hotel. Search it from top to bottom. I'd do it myself, but this leg of mine doesn't do too well climbing stairs. If you find anything, let out a yell and we'll come running."

"Where will you be?" Bill asked.

"Will and I are going up the trail to the springs. What she told Will seemed to have something to do with them," said Harley. "They aren't far, but I need Will to show me the way."

Bill had already lit the two lanterns we had brought from town, and taking one of them, turned toward the old hotel's front door. Harley picked up the other lantern, turned to me, and said, "Alright, Will—point us in the right direction."

After showing him where the trail to the springs began, Harley stopped me and said, "From here on, I want you behind me, Will. If things turn bad, I want you to turn around and run as fast as you can. Don't stop until you find Bill. Do you understand me?"

"Yes sir, Mr. Matthews!" I said. In my mind, though, I was thinking—if things turn bad, I'm not going anywhere. Harley would need my help in this—and Lucy was my girl!

"How far is it to the springs?" Harley asked.

"Not very far—a hundred yards maybe—maybe even a little further," I told him.

"The hot springs are maybe that much past that. This path we're on goes pretty straight for the first fifty, or so, yards, and then it begins a wide curve that straightens out just before you get to the mineral springs."

"From there to the hot springs, it's just a windy path," I explained, "that keeps going up until it reaches a rock cliff. That's where the spring is. That's the end of the trail."

We had just arrived at the mineral springs when Lucy's scream reached our ears. For a man with one leg, Harley was moving at an incredible rate of speed over the trail we were on.

Lucy's scream had seemed to lend wings to a man who had for years thought of himself as an incomplete and handicapped man. I was hard pressed to keep up with him.

As we climbed the last ten yards of trail, we could see Lucy struggling with a man—trying to get away from his grasp. I'll give this to her; she was a fighter!

She was kicking and clawing at him and using her elbows and knees in ways that were quite unladylike.

Even though I was scared to death at what was happening, I couldn't help being really proud of her!

She was fighting a losing battle, though. Time and strength were on her captor's side, and it was easy to see that in another minute or so, she would be completely exhausted.

By the time the man drew his attention away from Lucy and noticed our approach, we were within about fifty feet of them. He had worn the girl down, and could hold her firmly with his left hand.

With his right, he reached into his pocket and pulled out a revolver. "Get out of my way!" he snarled at us. "Leave us alone, and you won't get hurt!"

In a voice that was calm and even, Harley told him, "Let the girl go, mister. Let's talk about this, and see if we can't figure out how things got so out of hand that we're all up here on this trail in the middle of the night."

The man had those crazy eyes though, and he raised the gun—pointing it at Harley—and said, "I told you; get out of my way!"

Lucy yelled, "No!", as the man started to pull the trigger.

Harley had started to take a step toward them, and as the man fired the pistol, Lucy grabbed his arm and pulled it downward. The noise was deafening, and horror struck, I looked down to see Harley, lying on his back.

"Harley!" I cried. He turned over and pushed himself up on his knees. I could see then that the man's aim had been spoiled when Lucy pulled on his arm, and he had shattered Harley's wooden leg just below the knee.

There was no way that he was going to get up right away in that condition. That much was easy to see.

Lucy fought once more, temporarily giving the man all he could handle. Harley cast about for something which could help our cause, when his eye fell to my right hand—more to the point, to the baseball, which was still clutched in my right hand.

"Will!" Harley called to me. "Throw me your ball!"

I must have had a blank look on my face because he said more sharply than I had ever heard him speak, "The ball!! Your baseball, Will! Throw it to me!"

I looked down finally, noticing for the first time that I still held the ball, and was unconsciously gripping it—working it with my fingers—even during this whole trying evening. Quickly, I tossed it to Harley.

He caught it deftly in his big, bony right hand, and, from his position on the ground, threw a perfect fast ball—a strike that ricocheted off the man's forehead with such velocity that it must have traveled halfway back to where Harley was still on his knees.

I was already running toward them.

The man's eyes rolled back in his head and he took three steps backward, pulling Lucy with him. He shook his head, slowly from side to side, when his heel struck a small rock behind him—sending him reeling back to the edge, leaning back precariously over the water.

Just before he went over, I had reached them, and grabbing Lucy by her free hand, I held on as tightly as I could.

I held onto her with the same hand that had been gripping a baseball for all those months. My hand was stronger now than it ever had been—much stronger.

My grip was like iron. I knew it must have hurt her, but I continued to grip Lucy's hand hard; and I remember being sure of myself—at being able to hold on—of not letting go.

The three of us—the man leaning far over the water's edge, me on the bank, and Lucy—the tie that held the three of us together—were in suspended animation. For what seemed to be an eternity, we stayed like that.

At the last instant—as his eyes lost their insanity, and turned into pure terror—I pulled hard and yanked her free.

She buried her head in my shoulder and sobbed—and then covered her ears with her hands so as not to hear the screams that filled the night air as the man struggled in the scalding water below us. In a short time, though, the struggles and the screams were no more.

We met Bill Getty and Homer Long as we were coming back down the trail. The sheriff, and his hastily appointed deputies, had soon figured out that the kidnapper hadn't gone very far on the high-way, and so Homer had done a quick turnaround and come on out to the old hotel hoping that we'd had better luck.

When they arrived, they had found Bill just getting ready to follow us up the trail. Homer had left his two deputies down at the hotel, just in case Bill's search hadn't been thorough enough, and the kidnapper was still there, waiting to make his escape.

They'd no more than gotten good started up the trail when they heard a shot, and came running. We met them just short of the mineral springs—and Harley began to explain to Homer the way things had happened.

Bill and Homer both gave me approving glances when he got to the part about me pulling Lucy free. Lucy began to cry again, and Homer decided maybe we could get on back into town before he heard the rest.

First, though, Homer said, he had to recover the body of the man. Harley told him he might want to hurry on that because we'd left him in the water, and at that temperature there was likely not to be much left, other than the bones, if a person waited too long.

Homer and Bill went on up to see about dragging him out of the water, and by this time, the other two men had made it up this far, and went on past us, following after them, while we went back down the trail. It was pretty slow going, as Harley's wooden leg was no good, and he needed to lean on me for support.

It wasn't long before Bill got back, looking a little pale, and so we loaded into the pickup truck and headed back into town. Bill wouldn't talk about what he had seen up there—and when Bill Getty found something he didn't want to talk about, then it must have been a gruesome sight.

We pulled up in front of the diner a few minutes later. When we all got out, there was a crowd of people—all asking different questions, all at once, to where you couldn't understand anything that they were saying.

You could understand their faces, though. When we had pulled up, Etta's face was strained, wrought with the anxiety of not knowing—so scared that she didn't want to know, and yet so hopeful that she had to find out.

When the doors to that old rig opened, and we piled out—and she caught sight of Lucy—her face broke into a look of pure delight.

That's when everybody started in asking questions, and Harley—leaning against the rusted-out fender on the front of that pickup, so he'd not fall—raised his hands above his head as he raised his voice to the people.

"Alright now folks, settle down. As you can see, we got Lucy back—and she's safe and sound. More than that, we can't say until after we've had a chance to speak with the sheriff. Let's all go on about our business and let this family have a little peace—Lord knows, they could use it."

It took a little time, but the crowd finally dispersed, leaving just us few who had been a part of it all. We went into the diner and sat down to wait for the Sheriff.

Homer Long and his temporary deputies came back into town a little later with the body. They took it to the sheriff's office and laid it on the cot in the small barred up room Homer used on the rare occasions he would have an overnight guest.

The coroner would have to be called to come in from the county seat, so Homer went ahead and made the call, and then left the office and came on over to the diner.

"Harley, I'd like to see you and Etta, and those two kids in a little while," he said after he'd come inside. "We need to talk over a few things."

"Down at your office?" asked Harley.

"No, I've got the body over there—you might as well just come on up to the house. I'll have Edna put on a pot of coffee. She'd enjoy the company."

He said it as though he was inviting us over for an afternoon meal after church. But Homer was like that—never got too excited without there being some reason for it.

"Would you like to stay for a cup right now, Homer?" asked Maggie. She was another who didn't get ruffled much without good cause.

"No, thanks, Maggie. I better get back down to the office. I left it open for the coroner, and I think I just saw a couple of kids heading that way," he said with a grin.

"I'd probably better go back and see if I can herd some calves back to their mamas. Why don't you give me an hour or so before you come?"

I heard later on that he'd snuck up on Lyle and Del as they were just peeling back the blanket which the sheriff had used to cover the body.

They had never looked at a dead person before. This being the first—and them being a bit on the nervous side of things right then—when the sheriff came up behind them, and spoke all of a sudden, it scared them so bad that each one said later on that the other had wet himself.

Neither would admit to it, and I guess that only Homer could have said for sure. Since he never would tell, I can only guess they must have both been right.

Chapter
Thirty-One

A couple of hours later that evening, Harley, Etta, Lucy, and I walked on over to Homer's place. Frank had fixed the strap on Harley's leg—at least temporarily.

Frank was getting pretty good at fixing things, working at the garage. It probably didn't hurt that he was spending most of his free time around Maggie. It appeared she had a knack for fixing things as well.

Etta was nervous looking as we went along—sort of like she was scared of what was about to happen. She put her arm through the crook of Harley's, with her other hand resting on his forearm.

Just before we turned off of the street and onto the short path that led up to the Long's house, she stopped suddenly and turned to Harley.

"Harley, I've got something that I need to tell you—something that needs to be explained before we go inside."

Harley could tell that there was something that had been bothering her, but had figured that it was just the effects of what they had gone through earlier in the day.

He frowned and said to her, "Alright Etta, but is it something that can wait until later? I mean, it's getting late, and the sheriff is needing to see us."

She bit her lip and sighed—and then said, "I suppose it is something that he needs to hear too. I was hoping to just leave it back there, but I guess it doesn't always work out the way we want, does it?"

She turned then and walked over to where Lucy and I were already standing on the porch of the house. Harley shook his head in confusion and followed.

Edna Long wore a look of concern on her face as she ushered us inside and said, "Come along into the kitchen, now. Homer's waiting in there for you. Just grab a chair and sit down at the table."

There was a plate with some cookies on the table, and she poured Lucy and I both a glass of milk—then took the coffeepot off the stove and poured the adults a cup, each. "I'll leave you to your business, now."

Homer had been writing in an old notebook, and now looked up at us, with a pair of glasses perched far out toward the end of his nose. I'd never known he even wore the things. They made him seem more business-like—as if he were a banker getting ready to settle some accounts.

Then he grinned at us, and reached out to shake Harley's hand, saying, "Thanks for coming, Harley." He nodded, and said "Etta", and then looked at Lucy and me. "Are you two alright? Can you talk about what happened out there?"

Lucy and I looked at each other—then back at Homer. With mouths full of cookie, we both said, "Yes sir!"

We spent the next half hour detailing the events that had oc-curred, and surprisingly, we pretty much told the same story—which seems to be a rarity in police investigations, I'm told. Homer turned to Harley then and began the same line of questions.

Harley, of course, could only tell what had happened from when I came riding my bike, screaming, "He took her!" Through all of this, Homer had been jotting things down in his notebook.

Having the details of his report in order, he looked at Harley and Etta and said, "There's one thing that is puzzling about all of this."

He shifted his gaze to Etta. "From what I can gather here, the man identified himself as Lucy's father."

Homer had laid his pencil down and had leaned forward, his forearms on the table, with the fingertips of one hand gently tapping those of his other.

"What about that Etta? It seems to me like you probably know more about this than what you've told us up to now. I'd like to hear everything. I'm not accusing you of anything—I'm just asking."

Etta had been quiet during the sheriff's inquiries, but she still appeared nervous. She swallowed and said, "I suppose it's time that you know the truth—all of it." Etta looked at Harley, their eyes upon one another.

She sighed heavily, and then reached out and took Lucy's small hand in her own, and began to speak. "Do you know who Prince Chesterson is?" she asked.

Even as the words crossed her lips, she knew it was foolish thing to ask. Everyone knew about Prince Chesterson. Chesterson was a household name, almost the same as Getty, or Rockefeller, or Lindberg.

Prince Chesterson had been given a name that most people would have had trouble living up to. Chesterson, however, was not only capable of doing just that, but seemed to thrive on the kind of pressure which caused lesser men to turn aside in failure.

He had been in on the discoveries of some of the major oil properties in Oklahoma in the early part of the century; and with his fortune securely planted in Oklahoma, Chesterson took his holdings and moved them to Los Angeles.

In the early days of the moving picture industry, he found himself on the ground floor of a money-making business once again. It was there, Prince Chesterson built his second fortune.

It had been rumored that he had been at the groundbreaking of a new venture out in the desert in a little town called Las Vegas. If there was money to be made, Chesterson worked his way into it somehow, sometime, and some way.

The only thing he had ever failed at was his son, Royal Chesterson. Royal had been born to high expectations. As high as his father had reached to lay hold of all he possessed, Royal stooped down and rubbed a stain on the carpet of his father's legacy.

Royal Chesterson had been a boil on the backside of his father since he had been old enough to take the car out on his own. That his father owned a movie studio only exacerbated the problem.

Wherever there were good-looking women to be found, Royal Chesterson would be there as well. More than one hopeful starlet-in-waiting had lost more than her pride while listening to the promises of the studio owner's son.

Finally, the father cut the ties that bound father and son. In this case, those ties were in the form of an unending line of credit that the son had taken for granted.

Although he dealt severely with his son, Chesterson also dealt fairly—giving Royal an allowance—large enough to live on, but nothing which would impress the people he'd grown accustomed to.

Some time ago Prince Chesterson had died. He had amassed a fortune in his lifetime—two actually—and there was much discussion, and speculation, as to where that fortune might finally wind up.

Royal, of course, laid claim to it—as he was the only living relative—his own mother having passed on some years before.

However, when the will was read, it named a child as the sole beneficiary. Royal, at some point in his life of abandon and recklessness, had fathered a child with one of these poor, hopeful young women.

The child, though, had disappeared. According to Prince Chesterson's will, the child had one year to come and collect the inheritance. If it had not been collected in that years' time, the entire amount would be given to an unnamed charity.

We knew all of this. It was in all the newspapers, as well as the newsreels. It had been an interesting topic of conversation for a little while—even here in Hope Springs. But it didn't really affect any of us here, and so we soon forgot about it and moved on to other more important things.

Harley was doing some fast figuring. Old Prince Chesterson had been dead and gone for about nine months now. Etta and Lucy had arrived in town about a week after Chesterson's granddaughter had gone missing. It didn't seem possible, but...

"Are you trying to tell me that Lucy is old Chesterson's granddaughter?" he asked her slowly, as the idea was settling in. Etta was nodding, so he guessed he was on the right track.

He continued, "And that you and Royal Chesterson....?" He couldn't even finish the thought.

Her eyes got wide with horror at that. "No! Lord no, Harley," she exclaimed. "Don't you know me any better than that by now?"

"I thought I did," he replied. "I thought I knew a lot of things that I guess I don't."

"Not me," she explained, "my sister, Ellen." Then she lowered her head, and it was easy to see that this was a memory she did not like to recall.

"Ellen was my older sister," she continued. "She came out to California, thinking that she would become a star. She had these big dreams—just like a lot of girls have had, I suppose. I came out later on—after she had quit writing to me—to find out what had happened to her.

"I found her, finally. She hadn't become a star. She hadn't become much of anything—except a mother, who was working two jobs to get by—trying to raise a little baby on her own."

She paused, as the shadow of a smile briefly crossed her face—thinking of how determined her sister had been—and how proud she was of her child.

"She told me what had happened—how excited she had been when the son of the studio owner had singled her out—of the promises he'd made; and how she had believed every word.

"Of course, he was only telling her whatever she wanted to hear. They were all lies. In time, she found out the truth. After she told him she was expecting their child, he dropped her—told his 'people' that he wouldn't be 'available' to 'that woman' from that point on."

She bit her lip, and an edge of bitterness came into her voice as she continued.

"Because of that, she had no other options. She didn't let anybody back home know about any of this, of course—she was too proud, I guess. Instead, she worked as hard as she could to support herself and the baby on her own.

"Somehow the baby's grandfather learned about it and offered to help. But Ellen's pride would never have allowed that—and so he stepped back and allowed her to raise her child the way she wanted.

"I suppose he knew Lucy's father too well to ever want him to have any contact with his grandchild. He was Prince Chesterson. The baby's father is his son, Royal Chesterson."

She paused for a moment, and then continued, "As the years passed, Lucy's grandfather would send gifts; nothing too extravagant—on birthdays and Christmas'; always with a brief note to my sister, letting her know that if she ever needed anything, he would be there to help her and the baby."

She gave Lucy's hand a squeeze, and when I looked at Lucy, there were tears running down her cheeks.

"Ellen died last year," she continued. "She'd been sick for a long time, but she hadn't let on to any of us how bad it really was until it was too late to do anything for her. I doubt we could have done anything, anyway.

"She was bedridden for the last few weeks. Not long before she died, she called me into her room and placed Lucy in my care. She also contacted the child's grandfather and had him come to her. She told him what she had decided concerning his grandchild.

"The old man wanted to take her in, and take care of her himself, but he consented to Ellen's request. I think he saw how well my sister had done raising her—saw that she was loved—and saw that there was nothing he could give her she didn't already have."

She raised her eyes and looked at Harley again. "He told her, though, that he had made Lucy his sole beneficiary. He told her that although he knew she didn't want his money right now, there might come a time—later on—when we would change our minds.

"To make a long story a little shorter, after he died—and the will was read—Royal found out that his father had left all that he had (and that was considerable) to Lucy.

"However, if Lucy didn't collect her inheritance in the space of one year, it was to be divided up among a number of charities."

Although this was an inquiry—and it was the sheriff who had asked—Etta had been facing Harley as she spoke, as though it was only the two of them in the room. Harley had remained quiet during all of this, allowing Etta to lay it all out.

Finally, when it looked as if she was finished, the sheriff said, "I guess I don't understand all of this Etta. When you showed up here in town, you were broke. I mean, you had nothing! But what you just told me is that you and Lucy can lay hold of millions of dollars—anytime you want it! Don't you want it, Etta? Surely seems like you could use it."

Etta shook her head. She turned back to Homer now. "It's not that Lucy and I were against accepting the inheritance, Sheriff—it's what that would have caused to happen that I feared. The only way that Royal Chesterson was going to ever get his hands on it was if he were to get his hands on Lucy. There's not enough money in the world that's worth that!"

Harley nodded his head as he began to fully see the consequences. "So, you and Lucy left town—and the inheritance—behind," he said. "You made the choice of giving Lucy love and a home over giving her riches."

He reached over and put his large hand over her small one, and gave it a little pat. "Etta Prince, I'm awfully proud to know someone like you."

A thought came into his mind just then. "Etta Prince isn't your real name, is it?"

"No," she admitted, "only Etta." She gave him a sheepish glance. "My real name is Etta Johnson. It was a gesture of respect for Lucy's grandfather, I suppose. In his own way, he really was a good man."

Then a startled look came across her face. "Do you think that's how they found us? Oh, Harley! I'd hate to think that I was the one who led that man here."

"I don't know, Etta," said Harley. "I doubt it. It doesn't matter now, anyway. What's important is that we found Lucy—and we got her back. You don't have to worry about it anymore."

———————————

There was, of course, an official inquiry that had to be held. After all, a man had died. Harley and Etta went down to the courthouse at the county seat to testify before a grand jury.

Lucy and I went also, but we didn't have to say anything. Homer, deciding to tell the grand jury only the pertinent facts of the case, as was generally his way, left out a few things which were better not said.

Homer had been happy to write a report concerning a deranged stranger who had abducted a child and, in the process, had lost his life in a terrible mishap.

In the official report, Homer listed this man as a John Doe. Homer handled any future queries from outside authorities in such a way as to leave no doubt that the man who had lost his life was no one important—just a crazy man who had died in the commission of a crime.

When it came right down to it, no one really knew for certain the man was Royal Chesterson.

Only Lucy and I had gotten a good look at the man. Harley had seen him—but at a distance, and that in the moonlight. By the time they had pulled him out of the water, a positive identification would have been extremely difficult.

The disappearance of Royal Chesterson was pretty big news for a short time, and there was a lot of debating as to what might have happened to him, but in the end all the concerned authorities were more than happy to have him gone; and they certainly would not spend much time or money looking for him.

It was generally accepted that some of those whom he owed money to—mostly gambling debts—had probably collected their payment.

If not that, then it could have been that one of the women he had seduced was a girlfriend, or a wife, or a sister or daughter of someone who was powerful enough to remove the problem.

No matter what had happened, the authorities looked at it as being more of a solution to a problem than the problem itself.

The only one who suffered because of his disappearance was a certain Douglas Blackman, who wondered why his lawyer never showed up. He had a lot he could have told the authorities had he ever been given the opportunity.

It turns out, though, a man like Mr. Blackman makes a lot of enemies inside prison.

Chapter
Thirty-Two

Not long after the excitement of Lucy's kidnapping and rescue, Granddaddy received word that Momma had passed away. I guess I had never really believed she was going to be healthy again—not enough, at least, so she could come back home and we could be a family; but it hit me pretty hard, anyway.

It hit Granddaddy even harder. I didn't know then what I know now; that losing a parent doesn't even begin to compare to the loss of a child. Momma had been Granddaddy's only girl—only child, for that matter.

Although he knew I was still there, and that I still needed guidance more now than ever before—even as suspect as my Granddaddy's guidance might have been—Granddaddy just couldn't seem to pull himself up to where he could be the one to give it.

He had always struggled with the bottle. Well, if the truth were told, the only bottle struggling he had ever endured came when he was too unsteady to pull the cork.

I guess what I mean is that in his own way, Granddaddy really tried. He just couldn't seem to make it happen. After Momma passed, Granddaddy didn't try anymore and just seemed to slip further and further away from me.

By early summer, Granddaddy Morgan was in the grave as well. This left me in a precarious situation. The county had looked the other way when I had been left to fend for myself before, because it knew there was an adult relative who was at least somewhere in the picture. Now there was not.

The county had more than enough orphans to cope with, though, and so it encouraged local authorities to settle the issue. If they couldn't—or wouldn't—then the county would have to step in, and that meant a trip to the county run orphanage.

After Granddaddy's funeral, Harley and I went off by ourselves so we could talk. I was pretty sure I knew what he had on his mind—and so I wasn't surprised when he said, "Etta and I have been talking it over. We plan on getting married sometime this summer."

Well, that wasn't news. The surprise would have been if they hadn't planned on it. Everyone had been expecting this for months. I told him how happy I was for him and for Etta as well.

"That isn't what I wanted to talk to you about, Will," he continued. "Etta and I would like for you to come live with us. You're already like part of the family. What do you say, Will?"

Now, if Harley had asked me that same question last year at this time, I'd have thought I'd died and gone to heaven. My Lord, he was my hero, after all. Now, though, I just shook my head and said, "I don't think that would be a very good idea, Harley."

"Why not, Will?" he asked, sounding both surprised and a little disappointed. Then he nodded his head, already knowing the answer. "Lucy?" he asked.

I nodded my head now. "I don't think I want to be Lucy's brother, Harley. I just don't think it would work out very well."

"Yeah, Etta and I talked about that too." He looked down at me and said, "You're a little young to be having such serious thoughts, aren't you, Will?"

"Probably. A guy can't help the way he feels, can he, Harley?"

Harley seemed to be thinking about his own feelings toward Etta. "No, Will—I guess a guy can't."

Then he turned his attention back to me, and said, "What are you going to do then? You can't just go on living on your own. The county won't abide it forever."

"I don't know—but I'm sure hoping that something turns up."

Immediately following that day, offers began rolling in. There were so many people who were willing to take me in that I was touched.

It causes a lump in my throat to this day when I think of the kindness of the people in that small community—how they would share what little they had with an orphan boy who needed someone to help him.

Most of the offers came from people who were honestly trying to help—though there were a few that came from people like Tinker Bellum—people who had thought to get a farm hand for room and board.

It took me a while, but I finally came to see that although there were many people who were willing to take in an orphaned boy, there were not many who really wanted to.

Paul and Katherine Anders had only been blessed with one child, Paul Jr., whom they had lost to sickness several years before.

Losing their son had left a hole in the lives of each of them—a hole which neither had been able to fill.

Each felt that they had been denied the opportunity to give to a child all the love they had intended to give to their son.

They knew love needs to be expressed—not just in feelings—but in the living of life. Their feelings for their son had never lessened—and never would; but those feelings were bound to the past—to a boy who would never be more than eight years old.

What they saw in me, though, was an opportunity to give the love and the care they had been denied when their son had died. They wanted to be given that opportunity again. They wanted me to be a part of their family.

In the end, I suppose, it really wasn't that hard to choose after all.

Epilogue

The young reporter closed his notebook, shook his head, and looked at me skeptically. "I don't know, mister—it sounds a little far-fetched to me.

"Do you really expect me to believe some story about a decades old unsolved missing person case, where the missing person is none other than old Prince Chesterson's son, Royal? Right here in Hope Springs, Oregon?

"And who would believe that the law would cover it up—or that the rightful heir to the Chesterson fortune would just walk away from it?"

I just looked at him and shrugged. I suppose it must have sounded a bit ludicrous—but that's a reporter's job, isn't it? Sifting through what sounds ludicrous on the surface and finding the truth?

He was shaking his head and I could tell that he was a little upset that he'd wasted so much time on what he figured was just a whole lot of hooey, concocted by some guy trying to have a little fun with him.

"You had me going there for a while, old timer." It seemed the respect that was in his voice earlier had departed with his patience in tow.

"But when you started telling about a boy and some one-legged ex-ballplayer fighting off a crazed kidnapper—and that kidnapper being Royal Chesterson—well, that's just too much."

I just shrugged my shoulders again. He'd already made up his mind, and there was really no point in trying to change it. After all, the story was what it was. It appeared that my first impression had been correct. A reporter! Huh!

I left my bench then and walked on over to the old grocery store on the other side of the street to visit with Bill Getty for a minute or two. Everybody still called it Girvan's Groceries, even though Tom Girvan had been dead and gone since the early sixties.

Bill had been running the place ever since—he and Alice, that is. Alice held the purse strings to the business, and took care of the more mundane aspects of running a store, while Bill took care of the day-to-day operations.

Bill was always a lot better suited to meeting the public than his wife ever would be. If it involved talking, Bill was your man.

Bill did eventually settle into the life of a store owner in the way Tom had always hoped he would—becoming a respectable member of the business community.

We were all a little taken aback when he suddenly decided to join his family one Sunday morning for services over at the Methodist Church.

I understand he is now a deacon there—although, when I came through the front door of the store, Bill was standing at the counter, staring out through the front plate-glass window with a wistful look on his face. I could swear he was looking at the tavern across the street.

Bill and Harley have been friends for a lot of years; though I can still recall Harley saying—when Bill and Alice married—that he sure hated to think of Bill Getty reproducing.

Harley might have been right after all, as one of Bill and Alice's boys became a lawyer—the other a politician. Even Bill shakes his head at that.

Homer Long is still living in town, long since retired from lawman's work. Hovering close to ninety years old, Homer isn't as sharp as he once was. He has a difficult time remembering what day of the week it is—but ask him anything about his days of sheriffing, and his mind is like a straight razor freshly stropped, quick and sharp.

Edna passed away a couple of years ago, and poor health doesn't allow him to get out of the house much anymore, but the kids look in on him regularly, and make sure that he doesn't want for anything. Each has grown up thinking of Homer as if he were their real father, the same as I did Daddy Paul and Mama Kate. He's "good people".

I'd heard that there was a man from the city who had been coming by talking to him about the "old days"—trying to capture the essence of a time almost lost to a generation of moon walks and color TVs. I hope he does—it's slipping through our fingers just like a fistful of sand.

After his mother was convicted of murder, Jamie Felton disappeared. Although Homer was pretty sure that Jamie had aided his mother in the burying of the bodies, he didn't have any indication that he had helped her with the murders. There wasn't any evidence to support such a theory, even if it had been correct—which Homer doubted.

I doubt Homer spent much time or money looking for the boy. Knowing Homer, he probably figured that although it was unfortunate, being simple-minded wasn't against the law. At least not in his part of the county. If it were, he'd need a bigger jail house.

Tinker's farm became the property of the county. It seemed that Tinker had taken a rather lackadaisical attitude toward paying his property taxes.

An auction was held to dispose of the farm, with the idea of paying the back taxes and mortgage that was due.

I never knew how it became arranged, but at the auction there were only four people who showed up—and it had been well advertised. I have my suspicions that Homer Long had something to do with it.

There was the auctioneer, the county assessor, Homer, and Dave Tompkins.

It was sold to Dave, for the beginning bid of one hundred dollars over the amount left on the loan at the bank—which didn't amount to much over three hundred dollars. The county tax assessor threw a fit, saying that he couldn't be expected to properly assess people's properties if people just gave them away for next to nothing.

Homer just shrugged his shoulders when he was accused of everything from intimidating potential buyers, to wanting the piece of property for himself. The auctioneer—who had wisely chosen to auction this particular piece for wages instead of a percentage—just smiled and got back into his car, waved, and drove away.

Dave then deeded it over to Alvie Baker. I guess that everyone just figured that Alvie was born to be a farmer, and had it not been for Charlie's bad luck to be on the downhill side of a bull, Alvie would have one day had himself a mighty good farm.

Of course, Alvie was a few years away from being old enough to take on a place like that by himself, so Dave, and Paul, and others also, helped to run it for a few years until he was old enough.

I can't say as I've ever seen Alvie be the picture of happiness, but in the years since, he has been the picture of competence and satisfaction.

One of the best decisions that Maggie ever made was to ask Mr. Kimble to stay on and work at the filling station.

It was obvious to all that Frank Kimble was no mechanic—but that wasn't the reason Maggie let him stay. He needed help—and Maggie Davis wasn't the type of person who could ignore someone in need.

But, even with all her wisdom, I suspect that she never realized that she was a person who had needs as well. Or, maybe she did, and she was wise enough to see in Frank Kimble the answer to the things that her life lacked.

Whatever the case might be, during the long months that she quietly helped him put his demons to rest, he became a part of her life.

She had helped so many others find the answers to their particular problems—being happy to move on and focus on the next one that came along. With Frank Kimble, Maggie became the answer to what he needed—at least part of it.

Maggie was taken completely by surprise. Her life had been filled with running the diner and trying to orchestrate the lives of all the others around her.

In both pursuits, she had been successful. But, as Momma Kate had once said concerning Harley, "there are other things which are needed".

Maggie found she couldn't just "move on" from Frank Kimble. She didn't want to.

Frank had turned out to be more than just another project—and so, although Francis Kimble was a very private person, and Maggie Davis was the epitome of openness, less than a year after Mr. Kimble had walked into Maggie's Diner to purchase a bus ticket to some unknown destination, Maggie and Frank became husband and wife.

———————————

The newly married Edith Tompkins had decided that it would be best if she resigned her position as school administrator, as she now had more pressing duties to attend to.

Seeing to the happiness of Dave was at the top of that list. There really seemed to be only one sensible choice as to who should replace her—that being Francis Kimble.

As I have said, Mr. Kimble was no mechanic—but he was a wonderful educator. Now that he had gotten his problems straightened out, no one could see any reason not to rehire him.

Although he was competent in his new position as administrator, it was easy to see that his heart belonged in the classroom, and so, at the end of the next school year, Mr. Kimble went back to teaching.

During his year as the administrator, Mr. Kimble was instrumental in the hiring of Harley as a custodian at the school. This allowed Harley a more normal schedule than his job as a night watch at the sawmill—which was no doubt more conducive to his new life as a family man.

Mr. Kimble also hired Harley to be the coach of the High School baseball team—a position he held for the next thirty years.

During those years, he coached several teams to district titles, league titles—and three different teams to state championships.

Though I never did master the intricacies of a curve ball, I was on the first of those championship teams—in 1942.

Lyle Fletcher, though, was given a scholarship, and played college ball for a while. He put college on hold for a time so he could "do something a little more important than just playing games".

It didn't sound much like Lyle, and I was awfully proud of him when he made that decision. I was in the process of joining the army at about the same time.

He was part of the first wave that hit the beaches in Normandy and never made it back home. I think of him often, and still miss him all these years later.

As I look back at it now, I suppose Harley never achieved any real degree of greatness—except that which might have been granted him by a skinny little twelve-year-old boy.

That's all right, though—because that's all the greatness that anyone ever really gains—what is seen through the eyes of others.

We walked back to the house early in the afternoon, as I knew that the afternoon meal would be getting put on the table soon—and also seeing that if we stayed any longer, the grandkids would soon have their dinner spoiled by cotton candy and soda pop. I knew who would answer for that.

After dinner, I'd be going up to the cemetery to visit with some folks who've been laid up there in the years since I was a boy in this town.

Maggie and Frank Kimble are up there—side by side together—as they had been since the day Frank walked into Maggie's diner to buy a ticket on the next bus out of town.

Dave and Edith Tompkins are there also; as well as Tom Girvan, Jim Clancy, Foss Tilman, Edna Long, and many, many more. It seems like my entire childhood will be buried up on that hill before too many more years have passed.

Mama is there too. Several years ago, when I had the opportunity, I had Mama taken from where they had laid her in the cemetery at the State Sanatorium, and brought to Hope Springs so that I might lay her up on the hill that overlooks the town.

She's next to her father, Granddaddy Morgan—and though I don't suppose that it makes much difference in the long run, it makes me feel good to know that they are finally able to spend some time together.

I know he grieved terribly over not being able to be there with her in her last days. She's close by now.

Daddy Paul and Momma Kate are there as well—the best set of folks that a boy could have hoped for. I laid them to rest on the other side of Granddaddy Morgan.

Without my knowledge at the time, but with my gratitude ever since, Daddy Paul had paid to have Granddaddy buried in such a way as to be a part of the Anders family plot. Because of this, they are laid between Granddaddy and their son, Paul Jr.

Daddy Paul had taught me everything he knew about farming—and that was considerable; and I know that he and Momma Kate had planned on me continuing to run the farm after they were gone, but I wasn't born to be a farmer.

Daddy Paul finally had to accept that I wasn't going to stay on, and so, not long before they passed away, they put the farm on the market and sold it.

After the war, I left for a while so I could pursue my education. I wanted more for my family than the opportunities which Hope Springs would be able to afford. Daddy Paul was as proud as a peacock when I received my degree in agriculture.

Momma Kate told me how he took the notice which was in the paper to the Saturday evening gathering so he could show it to the old timers who had known me "back when he used to deliver the paper" and "now—just look right here!—my boy is in the paper!"

I'd gone to Salem with my degree, and over thirty years later I had worked my way up through the ranks, and was in consideration for the post of Secretary of Agriculture in the new administration in Washington—taking for granted that it would be a new administration.

I wasn't going to take it, though. The move to D.C. wouldn't be good for the family—and I'd learned a long time ago that a person who loves his family is willing to make sacrifices for them.

When I returned from my visit to the cemetery, Harley was sitting there in his old rocker on the front porch with my two grandsons sitting on the porch steps—listening intently to what he was saying.

As I got within earshot, I realized they must have asked him how he had lost his leg and he was telling them the story. My granddaughter had already heard this one before, and was in the kitchen helping.

"... and so, kids, what happened was all my fault. You see, boys, that's the danger of strong drink. It causes a person to do things he never would do otherwise."

He looked up at me, winked, and said, "And so now you know the true story about how—and why—I have a wooden leg."

About that time Etta came out onto the porch, with Lucy behind her.

"Harley Matthews!" Etta scolded, "You quit telling such horrid stories to the children. It'll give them nightmares!"

The boys looked up at me and said, "Papa, is Great-Grand-daddy telling us a story—or is he telling us the truth?" You see, they knew their "Papa" wouldn't lie to them.

"Do you really want to know the truth about how Great-Grand-daddy lost his leg?" They both nodded their heads vigorously.

"Well," I began, "your great-granddaddy was a professional baseball player—just like the ones you see on T.V. One night he was pitching, and the score was all tied up in the bottom of the ninth. There was a runner on third base, and his catcher let a pitch get past him.

"The runner charged for home, and it was up to your great-granddaddy to cover home plate. He blocked the plate with his body, and when the runner hit him, the leg snapped—!"

I made a loud snapping sound by clapping my hands together. Everybody jumped—even Harley. Even he'd been paying attention.

I waited, and then my younger grandson finally asked, "Did he tag him out, Papa?"

I couldn't help myself. "Of course, he tagged him out! What kind of ballplayer do you think your great-granddaddy was?"

Lucy reached over and gave me a little slap on the shoulder to let me know I ought not to be deviling the boy.

His older brother—who probably had wanted to ask the same question himself—snickered at it, and gave his brother an elbow, saying, "Sheesh! What an idiot!"

Then they both looked at me sideways, as though they were about half wondering if they might have just been taken in. "Is that really the truth, Papa?"

Only hours before, a young reporter had questioned the veracity of what I'd been telling him; and now, my own grandsons were looking at me like I had just told them a big fib.

Perhaps I needed to brush up on my storytelling a little. But the little scallywags had seemed to see right through what I had told them. The reporter? He could learn some lessons from them.

Now, ordinarily I'm a person who sticks to the facts. I hold truth and honesty as things that should be held in high esteem by everyone. This world would be a much better place if more people thought so, too.

But I had also learned a long time ago that although truth and honesty are wondrous things, this world needs its heroes as well—and truth and heroes don't always walk hand in hand.

Those boys would learn about truthfulness soon enough. Their lessons in honesty and integrity? Those lessons would be taught in their appropriate times. Right now, let them have their heroes.

So, I smiled at them, and said, "Yes boys, that's really the truth.... at least that's what I was told a long, long time ago."

That night I thought about the day that had passed and the people I had seen—as well as of my little walk down "memory lane" earlier. Of Harley and Etta, and all the old friends I had known in my growing-up years. Many of whom I had gone to visit earlier at the cemetery, on the little wooded hill that overlooked the town.

It had been a long time ago, and yet it had been just yesterday. As aggravated as I had been at that young reporter, I had to admit he had helped to bring my childhood years back into focus more clearly than I had seen them in a long time.

I remember hearing Maggie Davis say, so many times, as she looked around at the work she had done—and the people she had helped— "It's been a good day; a very good day".

She was a wise woman. This had been a good day. Those had been such good years!

And Granddaddy Morgan—for all his faults—had been right, as well. We are, each one of us, on the cusp of greatness. Some of those people in my growing-up years seemed to shy away from any form of greatness at all.

Some of them, in fact, had turned to lives as far from greatness as the east is from the west. People like Tinker Bellum—and his wife, Myra. Douglas Blackman comes to mind also, as does Royal Chesterson, of course.

But some stepped across from ordinary to extraordinary; even if only in the life of a young boy. Wasn't I the lucky one?

Oh, and the "girl"? Well, that's the one part of everything I said to that reporter that wasn't true. Turns out she was no trouble at all.

The End